THE MAIDEN

AND

THE SERPENT

Book Three

The Scroll Saga

This book is dedicated to my daughters among the seventy-two; to my maidens of virtue among the one hundred and twenty; and not only to them, but also to their daughters for generations without end.

Prelude

The dragon's features glinted in the light of the fire, revealing a sinister grin upon its face and a hint of anger and rage within its eyes. All was still. The crackles of the flames echoed upon the walls of the cavern. A woman was seated across from the dragon upon a rock that had been carved to form a chair, or as she thought it to be, a throne.

"Well?" she said impatiently after a moment of silence. "Are we in agreement?"

"Of course," the dragon said with a smile. "I will give you the beauty, wealth, and power, and you will win for my master the minds of the ignorant."

The woman smiled. "They will all follow the Great Dragon, some of them willingly, but most of them without even realizing it. They will follow him to their own peril."

The dragon's tail moved slightly at these words.

"You serve our master, even though you know that he desires the downfall of your race," the dragon declared. "Why?"

"For two reasons," she said with a look of disgust upon her face. "First, for my own exaltation. But mainly, because I hate Him of whom we do not mention. I want to see Him rejected by the world."

"And you think you've found a way?" the dragon asked.

"Our father discovered it, long ago, in the beginning," the woman replied. "But only now has it come full circle. The women are the key, for they are the life-givers; they are the makers of mighty men. We will capture their hearts, and in doing so, their men will become weak, and the hearts of their younglings will also fall away. Within fifty years, the last of them will die, with no children to follow in their steps."

The dragon laughed.

"Yes," it agreed. "We will wipe the remnant off of the face of this land."

"And what about the prophecy?" the woman asked. "They say the girl survived the great fire. If that is correct, then she is destined to undo all that we have accomplished."

"If she indeed did survive, then you must find her," the dragon commanded.

"And should I destroy her?" she asked.

"Oh no," the dragon replied with a look of pure evil. "Don't crush her; you must instead turn her. She must become the very opposite of what the prophecy declares."

"Of course," the woman answered with a smile. "We will make her reject the Scroll. She will seem, to the world, strong and beautiful and in control. And in appearing so, all future generations will follow her example."

Chapter 1

Many will scoff at the story I am about to tell you. They will label it with words that sound sophisticated in an attempt to destroy that which they abhor. Few there are today who understand. Few have ears to hear and eyes to see. And yet, perhaps, the Great King will use my story to help remove the scales from your eyes. I offer you only the truth. It isn't sugarcoated or changed to be more attractive. If you find it to be sweet, then it is a sign that the Great King is calling you. If you find it bitter, then I would advise you to petition Him to change your heart. For His mercy is immeasurable, and He honors the repentant. It is never too late to change, as you will soon learn through my humble testimony. For I was rescued out of the darkness more than once, though I was never worthy of it. My story begins on a night when Providence reduced all that I knew to ashes.

The night was still and brisk. I lay in my bed, my heart filled with a mixture of emotion. I was still holding back the terror of what I had witnessed that day, being lured into the forest by a woman's voice, watching a black dragon devour two helpless men and then run away in utter horror and fear. I tried to forget it. It was the most terrifying thing that ever happened to me. I instead tried to focus on the face of my dearest friend, Caleb, and his promise to me that in the morning we would go together to the Castle and receive training on how to fight dragons. He was only one year older than I, and yet he was in my eyes such a brave young man. Most other nine-year-old boys that I knew didn't think about killing dragons but were rather focused on things that were childish and dull. But not Caleb. He wanted to serve the Great King, and that is why I saw him as my best friend in all the world. Even at such a young age, something in me wanted to be highly involved in the process of seeing Caleb become a great man of the Scroll.

Such thoughts brought peace to my soul. I reminded myself over and over that dragons will not come out of the forest, and that I was safe, as long as I didn't enter the forest again. I then heard the deep breathing of my friend, Bree, who was asleep on the other side of the room. She was my next door neighbor, and had been entrusted to us by her parents that evening, as they were going on an errand and needed my family to watch her for a few days.

I was unable to sleep, for my mind was still tossed back and forth between excitement, fear, and the uncertainty of what tomorrow would bring. Would I really learn how to wield the bow? Would I really learn how to kill dragons? The thought of facing a dragon like the one I had seen that day brought terror to my heart. How could a small arrow kill such a giant foe? Surely, I was just fooling myself. Surely, I was setting myself up for disappointment. No, I said to myself. It has to be true. The Great King has to be real. Many people I knew thought He was real, though it also seemed like more and more people were beginning to doubt. I kept thinking of the dragon, and every time I did my heart was likewise filled with doubt and dread as I remembered those two men being helplessly swallowed, suddenly robbed of all life and hope.

I tried to think of something else, but it was a useless endeavor. The yellow eyes, the deceitful voice, they just kept appearing in my mind. Fear was beginning to overtake me. How I wished that Caleb was with me! His presence always brought me joy and hope. I sensed a darkness coming upon me, and though a voice within me said not to fear, I felt powerless against it. I sat up in my bed and took a deep breath. The full moon was shining outside; its white light entered into a small portion of my room. The light of the moon always comforted me, for I had heard that it was written in the Scroll that the moon was 'the faithful witness in the sky.'

I slowly walked over to peer outside, but as I did, I thought I saw something that made my heart seem to stop within me. I thought I saw something pass in front of my window. It passed quickly, and I only caught a brief glimpse of it before it disappeared. It looked like something reptilian, like a set of spikes which stemmed off the scaly spine of some creature. I took a step away and froze, unable to move. I knew that I should close the wooden shutters, dive into my bed, and hide myself under my quilt, but I couldn't. I had to see if it was real. I knew that dragons couldn't exit the forest, at least, that's what I had always been told. I slowly advanced to the window and peeked my head outside, looking right and left. Nothing. Just the bright blue moon illuminating all it touched. The neighbor's house was only a few yards away, and all was quiet in the village.

I then looked down at the ground. Something was there, in the dirt. It looked like prints of some kind, but I couldn't make them out. Surely my eyes were playing tricks on me! They couldn't be dragon prints, could they? My heart still sensed the fear, but my curiosity was also at work.

I slowly and cautiously crept upon the sill, my lungs breathing in the crisp night air. And then I gently landed on the ground outside my window. I looked quickly about me. Nothing. I then looked down on the ground. What I saw made me think I was dreaming, and I reached out my hand to feel them. Dragon prints. How could they be here outside of the forest? I began to shake violently, and what I did next I cannot explain. I began to follow them, barely able to step because of the violent shaking of my body.

There was another glow ahead reflecting off of the walls of the surrounding homes, but it wasn't white like the moon. It was red. I then turned the corner and saw the sight and heard the screams all at once. Fire. Many houses were ablaze. It was as if it had all happened within the last few moments. I turned on my heels toward my home, but as I rounded the corner, I saw that which I feared: it was a dragon, lying in wait directly outside my window.

It didn't look like any dragon I had ever heard of. It was long and slender, like a snake, and yet it had four thin, spikey legs coming from its body. It was about fifteen feet long and stood three feet off of the ground. Somehow, I knew deep within me that this creature was the source of all the fear I had felt within my room. It was smiling, and from its jagged teeth only one word emerged: "Lily."

I turned and ran as fast as I could, away from the dragon and away from the fire, into the darkness of night. Whether smoke or clouds I couldn't say, but something was now blocking the moonlight. I didn't look behind me, but I could feel a kind of darkness pursuing. I could now hear more cries and screams coming from the village, as if the entire town was now awake. I thought of my parents and Bree. I wanted so badly to be back with them. Why had I left the safety of my home? I then realized that I was approaching the forest.

I felt trapped! I couldn't bring myself to turn around—I was too afraid—but neither could I continue to run. I was out of breath, cold, and exhausted. I finally stopped only a few yards away from the forest. I found the strength to turn and look behind me. I saw nothing save the village, now a few hundred yards away, seemingly all ablaze with fire. Were my parents safe? What about Caleb?

I then decided to run straight to the village and not stop until I was around other people. I took only one step before I was lifted from the ground by a force stronger than I could have imagined. I instantly knew what had happened. I was in the claws of a giant dragon. Fear I had never known took hold of me, and I quickly fell from all consciousness.

6

Chapter 2

It took time for me to decipher what was real and what was fiction, for I was drifting in and out of consciousness, my dreams being just as dark and terrible as my reality. I could feel myself being carried; the cold grip of scales pressed against me. A constant deep gurgling sound was in the recesses of my mind, for I was being held against the chest of my captor. I awoke in nearly pitch darkness, the only light coming from some distant portal, for I was in a cave of sorts.

I was unaware of how much time had passed since I was taken. My stomach was empty, and my throat was parched. I could feel that my ankle was chained, and I soon realized that I wasn't alone, for two deep voices of dragons were very near to me.

"Are you sure you have the right girl?" said the first.

"Of course," said the second, seeming to take offense. "I was given her description by Gadreel. It wasn't hard to find her."

"And the boy?" the other asked.

"No doubt dead from the fire."

My heart sank within me, and I tried not to cry out or change my breathing, for I assumed they thought I was still asleep.

"And so what will we do with this one?"

"That is up to Gadreel, though I think I could guess."

"Kill her?" asked the other.

"Of course not! She's too frightened for that. Her fear alone will bring years of pleasure to us all. We do not want her to die—at least not yet. We want her to suffer. We want her to suffer to such a degree, and to fall into such despair, that she becomes something she never intended, and thus loathes herself. We will ruin her. We will make her spit upon the Scroll and curse the One in whom she claims to believe. She will love us instead and yet hate us at the same time. She will eventually find life to be nothing but a never-ending downward spiral of depression and hate."

"Ha!" said the other. "I love it."

"You have much to learn," said the first. "You must remember that it is not merely death that our Master desires for these humans. He wants them, most of all, to blaspheme the one we do not name. He wants them to be a testimony of His inadequacy and failure. The more they blaspheme the Scroll, the more people realize the truth: that we are the greater and that one day we will be victorious."

"But is it true?" the lesser asked. "Is it true that we will defeat Him one day?"

I then heard the first dragon hiss, and it made my blood freeze. "How dare you!" it said with raised voice. "You must never question our Master! His words are true! If I was to tell one of our chieftains, you would be skinned alive!" The lesser dragon whimpered in fear as it begged for mercy.

"You foolish snake!" the first said. "I will spare you this once, but never question the wisdom of our Master again. His wisdom is supreme. That's how the battle began, long ago. The one we do not name created all things and made them with a certain level of intelligence. His greatest creation, no doubt, was our master.

"But then, to His downfall and shame, He made men and gave them dominion over this planet. How foolish. To put the dust of the ground in charge of all things. That is when our master knew that things must be different. He knew that for the cosmos to be run rightly, he would have to elevate himself above the Creator. And that is what he is doing, but he has only just begun. His greatest device, his most brilliant strategy, he is saving for last. Oh, how I hope I will be there to see it! The Great King, ah, curse His name, will finally receive what is coming to Him. Then we will rule, no longer confined to the forest, no longer hindered from what our eyes and lust desire. On that day, the Scroll will be broken, and all the hopes written therein will be dashed to the ground."

At these words I couldn't hold back any longer. A small cry, faint as it was, echoed in the dark cavern. The dragons then became perfectly quiet.

"Well, well," the first said. "Let us have some light."

A sudden spark lit the cavern, at first causing my eyes to hurt. They soon adjusted and I could faintly make out a ceiling about thirty feet above. Three walls of the cavern I couldn't see, but only the one nearest me, to which I was chained. I dared not look upon the dragons but kept my gaze down at the ground.

"Look at me," the first dragon said gently.

I trembled violently and couldn't bring myself to do so.

"Look at me now," it repeated. "Don't worry. It will get easier to do as time goes on."

I slowly lifted my eyes and beheld the two creatures, the first much larger than the other. They were red dragons. I couldn't stop shaking and quickly closed my eyes and began to weep.

"I love that sound," the first one said. "Crying is so entertaining. Welcome to your new reality, child. You thought that you were loved by the Great King. Ha! He has abandoned you! He is, indeed, not the benevolent father you thought Him to be. You will never again see the light of the sun or the moon. Your days will be desperate and lonely, for even if the Great King did love you, He could never reach you here. We are too powerful." I looked around in desperation.

"No one is coming for you," the lesser said. "You are here, and here you will stay. You will live here, and you will die here. You will never again see the blue sky or the leaves of the trees. You will never see another living soul or animal—only us."

"Agreed," said the first. "There was a time that warriors of the Castle were a threat to us, but those days have long passed. There are no heroes today. Their swords are all dull, and their bows are mere decorations rather than tools."

"The warriors of the Castle used to be a threat?" the lesser dragon asked the first. "I didn't know that."

"That's because you're still a fool," the first said. "The warriors of the Castle were indeed a threat, long ago."

"What happened?" the lesser asked.

"We convinced them that the Scroll wasn't truth," the greater answered with joy in its voice. "We convinced them that they could be warriors for the Great King, while at the same time following the principles of the world."

"Ha," laughed the lesser. "What fools they are!"

"Yes indeed," agreed the first. "And so, our path for victory is set before us. The beauty of it is that they really think they are still fighting. They think their religious activity actually accomplishes something. They have Castles, swords, shields, bows, and arrows, and yet they don't know how to fight. Ha! We convinced them to focus upon increasing their numbers at all cost and on keeping everyone happy, instead of training up the remnant. And, therefore, they have forfeited any hope of succeeding."

"But there still is a remnant, isn't there?" asked the lesser. "Aren't they out there somewhere, still training according to the Scroll?"

The other dragon paused for a moment, its wicked breath echoing in the chamber.

"They are," it said bitterly. "Though they are few. They are, indeed, our last enemy on this earth. Many of the warriors of the Castles are our allies without even knowing it. But the remnant, they unfortunately still know how to fight. And what is worse, they train up their children. We convinced the Castles to stop doing that decades ago. But the remnant still trains up their nasty children according to the Scroll."

"What about the bearded man," asked the lesser dragon, "the man from Ravenhill? Is he a threat to us?"

"Ha!" answered the first. "He is an old fool. He talks big, but his sword is slow and rusty. Not only that, but…"

Suddenly something changed, for the dragons ceased their speaking abruptly and looked at each other. They seemed to be inhaling deeply, as if they were smelling something.

"Do you smell that?" asked the lesser, but its companion never answered. For at that very moment a sound like a cleaver cutting through wild game was heard, and the dragon's head fell lifeless to the ground.

Chapter 3

The image of the dragon's head falling to the cavern floor below caused me to go into shock. The last thing I beheld as my vision left me was a hooded figure leaping into the air as the remaining dragon, filled with a blood-chilling rage, spewed fire from its gullet.

My dreams were lucid, and yet also random and ever-changing. I saw the dragon's eyes looking at me. Then fire was everywhere. I heard my parents yelling from our burning cottage. Caleb was also calling my name. Then I was seized by a dragon. Fear. Hopelessness. Doom. These were the emotions swirling through my thoughts. I almost felt void of life itself and wondered if I was dead. My last thoughts were of the Great King. *Don't abandon me*, I prayed. *Please be real. Please save me.*

When I awoke, I found myself in a simple cottage, which contained only one room. My bed was small, as if made for me, and another larger bed was across the room, with only a small table and chairs in between. A small stone chimney rested upon the wall, and the only door of the room was open, allowing a cool breeze to circulate through the dwelling and the bright rays of the sun to lighten the room.

For a moment I was very disorientated. What had happened? Where was I? I then remembered the dragons, and my heart clenched within my chest. I recalled the robed figure, though I couldn't remember if that part was real, or only a figment of my imagination. I wanted to get up but found myself sapped of all strength, and I laid my head again upon the soft pillow. I breathed deeply, trying to find peace within all the uncertainty which surrounded my thoughts.

I heard what sounded like another person breathing, and looking to the corner, I beheld a figure, hunched over in a chair that had escaped my earlier notice. It was an old woman, seemingly more aged than any I had ever known. She was veiled in a hood and was smiling at me. Despite her kind countenance, I found myself terrified at the uncertainty of the moment. She seemed to notice my apprehension at the knowledge of her presence.

"Do not be afraid, little girl," she said softly, her voice hoarse and aged, yet sweet to the ear. "You are in a safe place."

My first thought was of deception. Was this an illusion of the dragons, trying to win my trust so they could torment me more thoroughly?

"Who are you?" I asked with trembling lips. "Where am I?"

"You are in a small home on the edge of your village," she replied. "My name is Martha, and I am here to make sure you receive anything you might need. I have food and drink here. You must be hungry considering all that you've been through."

I was indeed famished. I felt a pain in my stomach I had never before experienced. I then remembered the dragons' care of me and shuddered again. I felt that I was on the edge of emotion and, depending on what happened next, would either smile and relax or burst into tears and panic.

The woman again seemed to sense my inner turmoil, and slowly rising from her seat, she took some food out of a basket and began preparing a meal.

"I have bread and fruit," she said. "Some girls picked these berries for you this morning."

Watching her arrange the meal brought my mind back from the darkness of the dragon's lair to the pleasant things of the world. I began to feel peace in my soul, but not enough to yet leave my bed.

"Perhaps this would be best eaten where you are," she said, slowly bringing me the dish along with a cup of cool water. She then sat upon the edge of my bed and offered me the food and water which I now gladly accepted. She remained there, looking upon me with fondness as a grandmother would look upon her progeny.

"What is your name?" she asked.

"My name is Lily."

"Ah," she said, "such a beautiful name. A delicate flower."

"Martha," I said to her, my mind returning to my life as I knew it. "Where are my parents?"

Her expression changed, and I saw pain in her eyes. She softly took my hands in hers. "The fire burnt most of the village," she said slowly. "Your parents are no more."

I don't remember for how long I wept, allowing the stranger to hold me, but I do remember that during that time, a bond of heavenly measure was formed. It was as if that time was a ceremony, or an initiation, of a relationship between us.

"And the girl, Bree?" I asked eventually.

"Also gone," she said gently. "I am sorry."

My attention suddenly turned to my dearest friend, who through the grief and pain of that moment I had temporarily forgotten.

"Caleb?!" I said passionately. "What of Caleb?! Do you know of whom I speak?"

"I don't know anyone of that name," she replied, "but there are people here who will be able to help you. Don't fear my child. We are all followers of the

Great King, and His presence is here with us. He will keep you safe and bring you peace in the midst of such heartache."

"Why did this all happen?" I asked, tears still full in my eyes and upon my cheeks. "Why did the dragons want me?"

"This is a mystery that we are also trying to solve," she said. "Maybe it was all just coincidence. Or maybe they had a strategic reason to seek you out. Regardless of the answer, you are safe now."

A few moments later, a man entered the room. He was older with white hair and a long white beard. His eyes and face had the look of wisdom, courage, and gentleness mixed together. He offered a tender smile.

"Hello young one," he said kindly.

"Her name is Lily," Martha commented.

I hesitated. His gaze remained, steadfast and kind, and I felt more confident that I was no longer in harm's way.

"Did you save me?" I asked. "From the dragons?"

"I did," he said with a look of sober gentleness. "I am very sorry you had to experience their captivity. According to my honor, and according to the power of the Great King, you will never feel their claws again."

Having heard both Martha and the man mention the Great King, all remaining trepidation and uneasiness left my soul, and I suddenly felt that I was completely protected.

"Who are you?" I asked.

"My name is Samuel," he replied. "I am a captain amongst these people."

Chapter 4

"These people?" I said. "You mean a Castle?"

"Well," he said, seemingly choosing his words carefully. "We are the Castle of the Great King, but we don't meet in the Castle you are accustomed to seeing. We believe in the Great King and in the Scroll. We do life together, train together, and hunt dragons together."

"All of you hunt dragons?" I asked.

"Most of us do," he said with a smile. "And those who don't are training to do so. I am a friend to you. You need not fear anything here." I sat up in my bed, comforted by his words.

"She has already learned of her parents' fate," Martha informed Samuel, "and of the girl who was with her. She now asks the whereabouts of a boy named Caleb."

"He is still alive," said Samuel. "Or at least, I believe he is. He escaped the fire, but no one knows of his whereabouts. I thought, when I came to your rescue, that you were he. I was both disappointed and pleased when I saw it was you instead of him; disappointed that he remains missing, but pleased that such a dear creation of the Great King was found."

"But where is he?" I asked aloud, losing myself, as tears returned to my eyes. "We must find him!"

"We will," he said gently, putting his hand upon my shoulder. "I have sent scouts in every direction, and I too will join them soon. But first, I need to ask you some questions."

I waited in anticipation, and he continued.

"Do you have anyone to go to, any next of kin? Or perhaps a friend of your family?"

"No," I said after a short pause. "There is no one."

"We are trying to find a home for you, child," he said. "We must be diligent in this matter. For now, you must rest. Tomorrow is King's Day, and all of the community will gather. I must prepare for our assembly."

"Samuel," Martha said. "This girl is a believer in the Great King, and she wants to learn how to follow Him."

Samuel looked at Martha and then returned his gaze to me and smiled. "How heavenly," he said. "If your strength allows it on the morrow, I hope you will join us. In the meantime, I will continue to seek out the best way to help you."

The sun was now setting. Tiredness overtook me again. Martha came back to my bedside and sat next to me. We spoke into the night, mostly about the Great King.

I awoke the next morning well rested and strengthened. The cottage was empty, the only light being from a smoldering log within the fireplace. I stood up and walked to the window. The day was just beginning to break. There were some remains of the last night's dinner upon the table, which made for a good breakfast. I wrapped a shawl around myself, which Martha had supplied the night before, and walked out into the cool morning air.

The day had enough light now for me to observe my surroundings. The cottage rested on the edge of my village, upon a gentle rise in the hillside. I could see the township in the distance and could make out the black char of the homes destroyed by the fire. I paused for a moment, thinking of my parents and the fact that their remains were likely ashes. A pain rose to my heart. I closed my eyes and took a deep breath.

I then noticed, about fifty yards away from me in the direction of the forest, four men. They were standing in a circle with swords drawn. They didn't seem to be in combat, but were likely friends. One of them looked my way and waved at me. I then recognized that it was Samuel. I slowly made my way to where they were. It was intimidating, but I felt I could trust Samuel.

"Good morning," he said with a smile. "You look like you slept well. These are my friends: Benjamin, Stephen, and Jonah. The three men bowed. Benjamin looked much like Samuel, older and bearded. Stephen was a middle-aged man, and as I was looking at him, a young child came to his side. Jonah, however, was younger, likely twenty years of age. Samuel invited me to sit upon a nearby stump. The four of them seemed to be talking about sword fighting, or more specifically, fighting against dragons. After another half hour, others began to arrive. One of them was Martha, who seemed to take such a kind interest in me. She was such a dear woman. Samuel then approached me.

"Lily," he said. "It will still be another hour or so until we begin today's meeting. We ensured that all of the victims of the fire have been buried, and we located the tombstones of your parents. I can't make you go, but if you think it would be a good idea, I really think you should, if you're ready for that."

I looked down at the ground for a moment. "Will Martha be able to come with me?" I asked.

Samuel smiled, "Of course."

Martha took my hand, and together we made our way to the village. The main street of the village, which only a few days before was filled with laughter and ordinary activity, now seemed as empty and hopeless as the grave. Martha led me to the village cemetery, and there we found my parents' graves. I stood there weeping as Martha silently and patiently stood beside me holding my hand.

We then made our way to my home. Nothing but ashes. More tears. As I continued to look upon the pile of ashes, slightly stirred by the morning breeze, I realized that the life I once knew was finished. I would no longer be the same. I felt so alone at that moment, and yet, not alone. I had lost one family, but I hoped with all my heart that I had gained another. Martha and Samuel were all I had left, though I still held on to the hope and prayer that Caleb would soon walk up beside me and smile. I kept looking around me at different people who were going about their morning, but Caleb wasn't among them.

"Are you ready to return to the fellowship?" Martha finally asked. I was ready, and we made our way together. We had stayed longer than I anticipated, and much of the meeting had already taken place. There were archery targets full of arrows, as well as the evidence of swordplay and training. Everyone who was gathered, around fifty people, were now seated in a half-circle, and the man I had met earlier, named Benjamin, was addressing them from within the middle. He was reading from a scroll. As the words hit my ear, they seemed to penetrate my soul.

Martha took notice and whispered in my ear, "Captain Benjamin is reading from the Scroll of the Great King. They are the very words of the One we follow."

I knew of the Scroll but had never seen one, and I marveled at the reality that the Great King had written something we could actually take up and read. Captain Benjamin continued: "Sorrow may come in the evening, but joy will awaken the morning. The Great King is with us. Therefore, we will not fear. We will not be dismayed. Even if we are pounded to dust, we will rise from the ashes."

He then lowered the Scroll and addressed us. "There is legend of a bird that is a picture of this reality we find in the Scroll. Far to the South, in distant deserts, they speak of the phoenix. This bird, it is said, after 500 years of life will spread its wings in full light of the sun and ignite into flame. It will burn to ashes, and yet, within those ashes, a young phoenix rises."

He paused and seemed to be looking deep within our souls. "Our trials and suffering are hard. They hurt and often burn us down to what feels like ashes. We never remain in the ashes, however, but instead rise. We rise renewed and strong. Why? Not because of anything good in ourselves but because the Great King dwells within us. So, take heart. Be of good cheer. The Great King is with us. He is sovereign. He is good. All who believe in Him and follow Him will always rise."

The words of the Scroll and the teaching of Captain Benjamin pierced my soul. I had been reduced, so I felt, down to nothing. I had just come from seeing all that I once was, all that I had, and all that I knew to be true, burnt into a pile of ash. The wounds of my parent's death were still so fresh, as was my terror of the dragons and my agony over Caleb's disappearance. But I then realized, as best I could, that I had passed through loss, fire, and darkness, and had come out the other side a different person. It was as if the Great King had chosen me to be His. He had called me to a life different from the populace. He had reduced me to ashes and was now raising me up as a beautiful bird of fire.

As this realization was taking place, I noticed that Samuel's eyes were upon me. It was as if he could see within me and was perceiving what was happening. He smiled kindly and turned aside his gaze.

The fellowship then prayed a prayer that each seemed to know by memory, and then a feast began. As I looked at the people, I observed many things all at once. They were more alive than other people. There was a love and devotion that was so obvious and present that it made me all the more desirous for what they had. The girls were wrapped in modesty and beauty. The men were strong and noble. Martha took me by the arm.

"Come with me," she said. "Let's go to the cottage and visit with Captain Samuel."

As we entered the comfortable dwelling, I noticed some food upon the table.

"Sit and eat," Martha said. I did so, very grateful for the food. At length Samuel entered.

"What do you think of what you see here?" he asked.

"It's beautiful," I said. "It's like nothing I've ever imagined."

"It is only the beginning," he said. "I see, or think I see, the Great King at work within you."

"He is," I said honestly and unashamedly. "I feel Him calling me to follow Him."

"And so you shall," Samuel replied, "and I will be with you and teach you."

He looked kindly upon me with a face of complete sincerity. I felt that he was hinting that he wanted me to stay with him, or perhaps with Martha. I didn't know if they intended for me to stay there for a short while or permanently, as a guest or as family. A part of me felt that it was too soon for such commitments. It had only been the second day since I learned of my parent's death, and yet, even amidst such pain and confusion, something within me was clear. It was crystal clear. The Great King was calling me to follow Him, and this man standing before me was my new father. My heart seemed to be knitted to his. I suddenly felt the deepest longing imaginable that he would adopt me, and that I would be part of the community that he helped lead. I realized that without him, I would likely have nothing and no one to help me. I looked at him with eyes of anticipation and dread of what might or might not happen.

"Lily," he said slowly. "I have a question of great importance to ask of you, but I want to make sure you are comfortable and will answer honestly." He paused with serious hesitation. "Will you allow me to be your father, to protect you and provide for you, and to love you as my own daughter?"

I fell into his arms and sobbed; my arms wrapped around his neck.

"Yes," I said with joy and sadness mixed together. "Thank you." And I did not hear any reply, though I guessed it was because the man was unable to speak.

After another moment Samuel and Martha led me back to the feast that was still taking place.

"Listen please," he said, getting everyone's attention. "This is the girl I have been telling you about and for whom you have all been diligently praying. She has suffered much and has also been entrusted with much, for it is clear that the hand of the Great King is upon her. She was, as you all know, recently in the clutches of the enemy. Why they desired her, I know not. She has lost her parents and everything she knew. Her old life is now gone, and a new chapter is dawning."

He then turned his attention to me. "Lily, your name is beautiful. But I believe it is time that you receive a new name. The dragons have sought you out. And though you are safe here, in my home, upon the edge of the village, we should still take necessary precautions."

"What do you mean?" I asked.

"You now have a new life," he said. "And with a new life, comes a new name."

"What will you call me?" I asked nervously.

"If it is acceptable to you, you will now be called Elizabeth," he said gently.

"Elizabeth," I repeated, and to my astonishment, the name brought peace and joy to my heart. I suddenly knew that I was no longer Lily. Lily had burnt in the flames of the fire. Elizabeth would rise from the ashes and conquer. I smiled at my new father and took a deep breath.

"My name is Elizabeth."

Everyone cheered and circled tightly around me.

"We are your family now," Martha declared. "We are your brothers, sisters, mothers, and fathers. You are now one of us."

"This may take some getting used to," Samuel said. "Please don't hold anything back from me. As your father, I want to make you as comfortable and at home as possible."

In that moment something happened to me. I felt a peace like I never had before. I knew despite all that had happened, the Great King was with me and He loved me. Everyone prayed over me and the celebration continued. Many people introduced themselves to me, but I was in such an emotional state that I could hardly keep track of them all. Two people, however, made a strong impression on me—a young couple named Nathan and Leah. Nathan was tall and strong, with a large sword upon his back. Leah was plain in her appearance, yet was so radiant and full of life that I fell in love with her at once and enjoyed talking with her so much.

"We are so excited for you to be here with us," Leah said. "My husband and I were just married a week ago today."

"That is so wonderful!" I exclaimed, for I hadn't known many people who were newly married.

Leah and I spoke about her wedding, a topic which fascinated me. Nathan was nineteen years old, Leah seventeen. She was from a distant village and had met Nathan during a wedding ceremony of a friend, three years earlier.

"I have no doubt that we will become dear friends," Leah said. Her love and kindness to me was as medicine to my soul.

She then introduced me to Nathan's younger sister, Ruth, who was fifteen years old. She joined our conversation and I found her to be absolutely wonderful. She was the young lady that I wanted to become. Our time of fellowship was cut short as my father called for silence.

"My people!" he said, raising his voice for all to hear. "The day is still young, and yet, my daughter and I must retire, for we leave at dawn upon a quest for which we ask your prayers."

"Where are you going?" Jonah asked.

"We are going hunting," Samuel replied.

"Hunting?" Jonah questioned. "So soon? She has not yet been trained."

"We are not hunting dragons," Samuel replied, "but a person. Pray that we are successful, for the enemy is, I believe, also searching."

I took my new father by the hand. "Who are we going to look for?" I asked hopefully.

He looked down upon me with kind affection. "Caleb," he replied. "We are going to find him before the enemy does."

Chapter 5

A surge of excitement and hope shot through my veins at the name of my dearest friend. I embraced my new father and after the fellowship prayed for us, we quickly returned to our cabin and made ready for our departure. I was already awake before the sun rose. From the depth of the melted candle upon our table I guessed that the dawn was nearing.

"Already awake?" Samuel asked, sitting in the corner, rocking slowly with his head rested back upon the chair and his eyes closed. "I was just praying for the success of our journey."

"Do you think we will find him?" I asked.

"I don't know," he replied doubtfully. "But if we do, you will likely have a brother. Ultimately, it is in the hands of the Great King, and in that fact we can take much comfort and hope."

We ate a hurried breakfast, hooked our wagon to my father's horse, and began to leave. Jonah then approached us.

"I wanted to offer my services, Captain Samuel," he said.

"You are without a doubt the fastest of all our scouts," my father replied. "But I feel that this is a journey for me and my daughter alone. I charge you in our absence to help the captains in any need they may have. Farewell."

We journeyed away from Ravenhill. I had never before left the village, and to say that the months which followed were extraordinary would be an understatement. We went as far as the Great Mountains to the West, and to the bright oceans to the East. In nearly every village, we stayed with followers of the Great King. They were people who always reminded me of the fellowship of Ravenhill, which welcomed me with open arms. We also searched the Castles, for our hope was that Caleb would have gone to a Castle for help.

During this time, Samuel taught me much about the Great King. Continually, as we got up, walked along the road, and sat down, this was the topic of our conversation. Samuel spoke of the Scroll, which the Great King had given to us. He did not have one with him, yet he knew nearly all of it by heart, and he told me the great histories of our people. Soon the creeds of our people were upon my lips. Soon the story of our heritage was in my heart.

We traveled for nearly one year, always hopeful that the next village would give us that which we sought, and each time we were disappointed. Finally, after many months and miles, we returned back to Ravenhill. My heart was downcast. I felt that despite all of the tragedy that had befallen me, if only I could have Caleb back that all would be well.

We came upon the ridge that revealed Ravenhill just as the sun was rising. "I just wish I knew," I said to Samuel. "I just wish I knew whether or not he is still alive."

"As do I," he said solemnly. "But as I have told you before, whether living or dead, he is in the hands of the Great King."

We returned to our tiny cottage in which Martha had been living during our absence. She and a young girl, about my age, were sitting upon the porch.

"Ah!" Martha said with joy. "You have returned!" She embraced me with tears of joy. "I prayed for you every day," she replied, "and the Great King has answered my prayers." She then looked at the wagon thoughtfully. "Did you find the boy?"

"No," my father answered. "We learned nothing of him, either good or bad."

"Then I will continue to lift him up to the Great King," Martha said. She then took notice of the young girl who was with her.

"Elizabeth, this is Hannah," she said, introducing the girl. "Her family has been with our fellowship a few years now, and she has been a great helper to me in my work as of late. Besides helping me with some of my chores, she also sells produce in the village market."

Hannah smiled and bowed, and I did the same. She was a cute girl with pitch black hair, blue eyes, and rosy lips.

"An excellent introduction to be made for sure," my father said. "Why don't you girls take a walk and get to know each other. After being away for so long, I'm sure Elizabeth would like to stretch her legs upon her childhood grasslands." I gladly accepted the suggestion and Hannah and I headed out onto the prairie together.

"How old are you?" she asked me.

"I am ten years of age," I said. "You?"

"I am also ten," she replied.

"We are both so young," I said with a smile. "What do you want to do when you are grown?"

"Be a wife and mother, of course," she replied. "I want to serve my husband and raise many wonderful children. But most of all, I want to follow the Scroll. I want to please the Great King."

Hannah and I spoke for many hours as we walked or sat under shade trees and picked wildflowers. She was such a kind girl, and I was so thankful for her friendship. Most of all, however, I was thankful that she wanted the same things in life that I did and that her heart was consumed with love for the Great King.

Hannah and I were instant friends and were nearly inseparable. We filled our days with laughter and work, for we helped Martha and eventually took on responsibility at the marketplace.

Occasionally we would spend time with her parents. They were kind and I enjoyed speaking with them, though I sensed that Hannah didn't regard them the same way I regarded my father. They seemed distant to her, like she was either ashamed of them or didn't feel loved. When I would ask her about it, she would always change the subject.

During the next three years, we grew as close as sisters, meeting early in the morning and spending most of our days together. During that time, Nathan and Leah had a son whom they named Levi. I spent much of my time with them as well, watching baby Levi grow and helping Leah with household chores. My father also taught me how to shoot the bow. I wasn't a very good shot, but as time went on, I improved. Martha was also with me often, encouraging me and teaching me. She was as a grandmother to me.

On the morning of my thirteenth birthday, Hannah came to me early in the day with a wonderful idea. "Would you like to have lunch with my family?" she asked excitedly. "I'm sure your father wouldn't mind. We could ask my parents, and then go and get permission from your father if need be."

"That sounds wonderful," I said joyfully.

"Alright," she said thoughtfully, as if formulating a plan. "Follow me. I'm going to ask my mother to make her special raisin cakes for us all."

We walked up to the shed that rested along the corner of Hannah's garden.

"You wait here," she said. "I will ask my parents and then let you know what they say."

We both peaked around the corner. Her father was on his knees, tending the garden while her mother sat upon the porch crocheting.

"I'll be right back," she said. She then approached her parents.

"Hello, Mother and Father," Hannah said.

"Hello, Hannah," her mother said without looking up from her work. "Did you get your chores finished today?"

"Yes ma'am," she answered. "I finished them earlier."

As they were speaking, I couldn't help but peak around the corner.

"Today is Elizabeth's thirteenth birthday," she said.

"That's wonderful my dear," her mother replied without much change in emotion as she kept her eyes fixed upon her work.

"I was wondering if she could join us for lunch?" Hannah asked.

Her father looked up from his gardening. "Of course!" he said cheerfully. This brought a smile to my face, though it was quickly removed.

"I'm afraid not," Hannah's mother said almost simultaneously with her husband's words. The husband looked back at the wife with a confused expression. "Our lunch today is a bit scarce I'm afraid," the wife said.

"There's always room for one more," the husband said wishfully to his bride.

The wife gave her husband a look which sent a chill down my spine. It was a look I hadn't seen at all during my three and half years living amongst the fellowship of believers. The only way I could describe the look was as challenging. It was as if Hannah's mother was dueling with her husband. He had an intention, and she challenged him to a duel of wills. The challenge wasn't accepted, however, for Hannah's father returned to his work with a deep sigh.

"No guests today, sweetheart," he said to his daughter. "Soon though I'm sure."

Hannah turned away from her parents and rejoined me. Her disappointment was very evident, and so I tried to make up for it by mentioning how wonderful her garden looked. We then said farewell and I made my way back to the cottage.

As I returned home, I was pleased to find Martha there, singing as she rocked upon the porch, preparing some potatoes. Nathan and Leah were also there, inside the cottage, speaking with my father. I sensed the conversation might be sensitive and so I joined Martha upon the porch.

"Have you been enjoying your time with Hannah?" she asked excitedly.

"I have indeed," I replied. "Although," I continued, my spirit troubled within me, "I am a bit confused by her parents." I looked for the right words to continue my thoughts, but none came. Martha seemed to perceive my thoughts.

"Hannah is a wonderful young girl with much potential," she said. "The Great King is gracious in that He takes the children to greater heights than the parents. Hannah's parents are good people, that is to say, they believe in the Great King and are trying to follow Him, but the more you embrace the philosophies of the world when you are young, the more difficult it can sometimes be to drive them away. And yet," she continued with a smile, "our Great King is a multigenerational King. And so our hopes rest upon you and Hannah and others within our fellowship. You all have great potential."

Martha's words encouraged me, yet I still couldn't shake the awkward and cold attitude in the exchange with Hannah's parents. It was as if another spirit was present, something very opposed to the Great King. I asked her about the expressions I had seen upon the faces of Hannah's parents: the look of challenge by her mother and the look of surrender by her father.

"Very often," she explained, "when a husband is challenged by his wife, he will relinquish the authority that is rightfully his. For the husband, it isn't worth fighting for, seeing as he would be battling against the very bride for whom he was given the authority, to love and lead and nourish and protect. You must, my dear Elizabeth, make every effort to rid your heart of this negative and worldly attitude of wanting control. You must believe in the power of a yielding and honoring wife."

"I will," I said earnestly. "I want to have a marriage like Nathan and Leah, not like those of the world."

"Well that is, indeed, a good couple to watch and follow," Martha said with a chuckle. "They are so blessed, for they willingly embrace their roles as defined in the Scroll. Their parents did such a wonderful job training them up and exemplifying for them the culture of the Kingdom."

I took a deep breath and formed a smile. I was still discouraged by what I had seen with Hannah's parents, but at the same time I was thankful for the example of Nathan and Leah, as well as others from our fellowship.

"I love seeing couples who are in love and have joy even in hard times and who honor the Great King," I said reflectively. "It makes me so happy."

"Well," Martha said kindly. "In that case I think I know what to give you for your birthday."

"You remembered!" I said joyfully.

"Of course," she replied thoughtfully. "And now I will show you that which you enjoy the most: a couple that is in love." I looked around us, thinking that a man and woman were approaching. "I'm not talking about out there," she said with a grin. She then pulled me closer to herself. "Close your eyes, my child, and you will see. Trust me. Close your eyes, and learn the mind of the enemy and the cure of the Great King."

I didn't understand what was happening, but I obeyed. In the presence of that peaceful afternoon, I closed my eyes and lay my head upon Martha's shoulder. At first, it seemed like the sound of the gentle breeze was getting farther away, as if I was fading. I remained still. I then saw an image in my mind, a story unfolding as if it was a dream. It was far away but quickly came so near that I was suddenly inside of it, watching it unfold.

There was a young couple who seemed to be in love. The man was handsome, bold and strong. The woman was young and beautiful, with red hair like me, long and wavy. They were sitting together in the shade of an oak tree out on the prairie and seemed to be recently married. Watching them hold each other and whisper words of love made my heart leap with joy. It was so beautiful. They looked at each other the way I longed for my future husband to look at me. It seemed too good to be true, yet something told me that it was true, that it was real. These two lovers were one in mind, soul, and body.

They then opened up their basket and began laying out a pleasant meal of berries, bread, and cheese. They prayed together, calling upon the Great King to bless them. They looked at each other with passion in their eyes and spoke of their deepest dreams and longings. And then the vision faded from my mind and I opened my eyes. I was back upon the cottage porch, just as I had been before.

"Did you enjoy what you saw?" Martha asked kindly.

"I did," I replied. "What was that? How did that happen?"

"It is my ability," she explained. "I can share the stories of others. True stories that give us insight into our own lives."

"That's amazing!" I said. "And how did that story end? Has it ended? Has it even begun?"

"You will find out in time," she replied. "Don't worry."

My father then exited the house with Nathan and Leah.

"There's my girl!" he said excitedly. "Today you turn thirteen. That's a special number. You are no longer a little girl, but are now transitioning into womanhood. I've been speaking to Nathan and Leah, who, as you know, have always taken a liking to you. They have come to me with a special request that I think is perfect timing with how the Great King is growing you."

He then turned to Nathan, as if to give him an opportunity to speak.

"Well," Nathan began with a smile, as Leah was snuggled up beside him, "how would you, Elizabeth, like to join us on an adventure?"

Chapter 6

I was so surprised and curious at Nathan's question that all I could do was remain still with a big smile upon my face.

"We are traveling to my bride's childhood village," he explained. "It is far away, upon the outskirts of the large city of Anthropolis. All of her family is still there, as is my sister Ruth, who has been there since early winter. We are going there for a few months to visit and minister, and we were wondering if you would do us the honor of joining us."

I quickly looked to my father, my eyes begging for permission to go.

"It's up to you, my child," he said kindly.

"Yes," I replied with delight. "Thank you!"

"We leave tomorrow morning," Leah said, also excited. "You won't need much, only some essentials. We will be here to pick you up at…" She paused, and then turned to her husband.

"When will we set out?" she asked.

"I would think around sunrise," he replied.

"We will be here at sunrise," she said with a smile. "Until then, rest well my sister."

I had never felt so excited. I loved my daily routine and way of life, but the thought of being continually with Leah and Nathan was something I would never have imagined possible. I was also thrilled at the notion of seeing Ruth and spending time with her.

I quickly went and told Hannah of the new plans. She was happy for me but also sad that I would be away. My father gave me a small list of items to pick up from the marketplace, and I quickly set off to purchase them. The market was in its usually state of busyness. The common smells of the market, mixed together with the hay and dust of the road, were as familiar to me as my cottage. As I purchased a bundle of dates, I noticed that some of them weren't as fresh as others that were available, and I asked for a different bag. The vendor was not very kind in his response.

"I don't have time for picky girls," he said. "You're dressed like a princess. Why don't you act like one?"

"Shut your mouth you foolish man!" a woman said from behind me.

I turned to look at her. She was young, about Leah's age, and was extremely beautiful. She glared at the man. My heart began beating heavily, and I tried to leave.

"No, you stay right here," the woman commanded. "You asked this man for better dates and he's going to give them to you."

"Oh, am I?" he said defiantly.

The expression on the woman's face suddenly changed. Her expression of anger and malice was soon replaced with something unexpected. She smiled at the man and with her hand shifted her long blonde hair from one side to the other.

"Surely, my handsome man," she said seductively. "Surely, you won't let this little lady down? Surely, you will show her how kind a real man can be?"

34

The look in her eyes was unlike anything I had witnessed before. It resembled, in a way, what I had seen in Leah's eyes when she looked at Nathan, but it was also different, and I sensed it wasn't pleasing to the Great King. The man's expression and attitude changed instantly.

"Well," he said smiling at the woman. "Of course this little lady can have different dates. I will even throw them in for free, especially with such a pretty lady like you asking." He then gently handed me a new bag filled with luscious dates.

"Why thank you so much," the woman said as she led me away through the marketplace.

"Did you see that man?" she asked smiling. "Did you see how I was able to toss him back and forth as if he was under my very control? Ha! What a fool." Her expression then changed to one of terror. "Never succumb to obeying men," she said. "They are beneath you, both in intellect and appearance. You are the superior creation. Do you understand?"

I nodded.

"Very good," she said stretching to her full height and relaxing a bit. I was again overwhelmed at her beauty. "I am passing through this town," she continued. "It is a long journey, but I will be back someday and will look you up. What is your name?"

"Elizabeth," I stammered.

"That's a beautiful name," she replied. "It is a strong name. Farewell Elizabeth. Remember: Men are the problem, and we are the cure."

She then turned and walked away. I watched her for some time, her hair blowing in the wind. Her last statement had puzzled me exceedingly. I didn't really understand what she meant, but the image of her beauty, and the feeling of worth and attention I felt when I was around her, burnt into my mind.

I then hurried home and spent the remainder of the day with my father, sad to be departed from him, but happy for the adventure that lay ahead.

Early the next morning I found Nathan and Leah, along with their son Levi, waiting outside my cottage in a horse drawn carriage.

"How long will it take us to get there?" I asked curiously.

"Hopefully no longer than four weeks," Nathan replied. "Though we have plenty of provisions for the trip."

I said farewell to my father, a bit shaken by the sudden reality that I would be away from him for the first time in nearly five years.

"Don't be afraid," he said smiling. "I will miss you dreadfully, but this is a good opportunity for you. Be a servant. Be a learner. And above all, never forget that the Great King is with you."

We said a prayer and departed. The carriage was of average size with a nice cover to shade us from the midday sun. As we trekked across the prairies, I spent most of my time in the bed of the carriage with Leah and Levi. Occasionally, I would sit on the front bench seat with Nathan, who took the time to teach me how to manage the reins. In the evenings we could all fit fairly comfortably in the wagon to sleep. I found it such a delight to be continually around Nathan, Leah, and Levi. The way they treated each other, and the joy that was experienced between them, was like a pleasant aroma that never grew dull.

One sunrise, as we traveled along in the cool mist of the morning, Leah broke the peaceful silence. "You and your father have traveled much of this nation," Leah said. "Did you ever go to Anthropolis?"

"Never," I replied. "It was in the opposite direction of where we believed Caleb could have journeyed, and my father told me it is a dangerous place. That's confusing to me because I've heard it is a magnificent city, the second largest in the realm. I would have thought that the larger the city, the safer it would be, seeing as there are so many people to work together and help each other."

"You would think so," Leah replied with a smile, "but it is, unfortunately, almost always the opposite. The more populated, the more dangerous, both physically and spiritually."

"But that's so odd," I commented. "Do you know why that is?"

"I don't know why, to be honest," she said. "It has always baffled me as to why big cities are more prone to progress down the path of darkness than a rural village is. Nathan, do you know why?"

"Not entirely," he said modestly. "Though what I typically observe in cities is that the family isn't together as much as they should be. People leave the home often and bad company is abundant; so character is corrupted. In rural living, the shepherding father has an easier time raising his family. In the city, there is much competition, and it seems to pull all members of the family away from each other. But what you spoke, my dear, is certain. All populated cities, for whatever reason, seem to embrace the latest philosophies to a far greater degree than rural communities. It reminds me of the Great Tower that men built in the ancient world. They seemed to desire to stay together, all in one place, with giant citadels reaching to the heavens, and it turned out to be their downfall and judgment. It also reminds me of our father, Abram, and his nephew. They chose where to dwell. The one who went to the countryside was blessed, while the one who went to the city found destruction. I can't bring myself to say that living in a city is wrong; only that it is dangerous."

"I believe you are correct, my love," Leah said, after which she turned her attention back to me. "My community dwelt upon the edge of the city," she explained, "much like our community in Ravenhill, but over the years since my childhood, the city grew at such a pace that soon our community was swallowed up by it."

"And that was harmful?" I asked.

"It was indeed," she said. "The Scroll tells us that bad company corrupts good character. This is not only true regarding individual relationships, but is also true regarding culture and environment. My husband speaks the truth: large cities are dangerous. People who are immersed in them are often led astray, not always, but often. And so, for our village, it posed a serious problem."

"So what are your people going to do?" I asked.

"One of two things, I believe: either relocate or strengthen themselves and train to resist the darkness. But they must do something. The influence and tension of the city culture is building. This is one of the many reasons for our journey, to help them figure out what to do."

"It is a difficult decision," Nathan commented. "A part of me thinks that they should infiltrate the city; that they should take dominion of what they can for the glory of the Great King. But their numbers are nothing compared to the city. And so, another part of me thinks they should come out from such a wicked city and go to another city that is more their size. Both choices have advantages and disadvantages. I pray the Great King gives them wisdom."

I remained quiet in thought. Leah looked at me and smiled. "You mentioned your friend Caleb earlier," she said. "He sounds like he was a faithful companion of yours."

I returned her smile as best I could. "He was the best," I replied.

Our traveling continued. Every evening, Nathan would make a fire, and Leah would prepare our meals. She was an amazing cook and taught me many skills of the trade. Levi was now eighteen months old and was such a joy. His bright expression always brought us laughter.

Eventually, on the thirty-third day of our travels, we began to see the glows of Anthropolis on the horizon. Little villages and homesteads began to stretch across the landscape. On the following morning we came over a gentle hill, and there I beheld the vast city of Anthropolis. It was unlike anything I had ever seen before. My jaw dropped, and my eyes remained open. Large keeps and citadels rose into the air. The city seemed endless.

"Don't look so amazed," Nathan said laughing. "The Great King made us all in His image, capable of doing amazing things. If mankind can make such things in their fallen nature, just imagine what we can accomplish when we follow the Great King! The unfortunate reality of Anthropolis, however, is that it tends to bring about the glory of man instead of the glory of the Creator."

"How much farther until we arrive at your community?" I asked Leah.

"Not long now," she said with a smile of anticipation. "We are almost there."

There were by now people everywhere, bustling about with the activity of daily commerce. The prairie gave way to housing and workshops. We made our way down a narrow lane. To the South I beheld the forest looming high in the air.

"That forest looks so different," I said.

"It is a different landscape here," Leah commented. "There are trees and animals here foreign to our home in Ravenhill."

"What about the dragons?" I asked curiously. "Are they the same as in Ravenhill?"

"They are very similar," Leah replied. We then came to a patch of tiny homes that seemed distinct from all others. "We are here!" Leah exclaimed, taking Levi and descending from the wagon.

I initially noticed that there was no one about. Everywhere outside the edges of the small community people were active and lively, but inside the cluster of homes no one could be seen. Leah looked about curiously. Nathan also descended from the carriage, taking it all in.

"Do you think they all went to town?" he said. "Or hunting perhaps?"

Leah then went to a home and opened the door. "Mother?" she said as she walked in. She then exited with a look of concern on her face.

"Is no one at home?" Nathan asked.

"The house is empty," she replied, "empty of people and of furniture."

"As if they moved?" he asked.

"I don't think so," she replied. "As if it was ransacked."

"Ransacked?" he replied. He then entered another home and found it in the same condition. Within ten minutes, all twenty homes had been searched and found in the same condition. All seemed to be plundered, torn apart as if they were at the mercy of looters and thieves.

"What happened here?" Nathan said aloud.

Leah put her hand to her mouth, and tears formed in her eyes. I stood in shock, a lump forming in my throat. Levi began to whimper a bit, sensing his mother's pain.

"Are you one of them?" an unknown voice called out to us.

We all turned to see a young man. He seemed to be about my age, twelve or thirteen. He had a look of wonder mixed with concern upon his face.

"Are we one of whom?" Nathan asked calmly.

"One of the people they ran off," the boy replied.

Nathan quickly glanced at Leah, and I thought I perceived in his eyes a look of wrath, sympathy, and fear all wrapped into one.

"Tell me, young man," Nathan said gently, "what happened here?"

"A group came and ran these people away," he said.

"What group came?" Nathan asked.

"The mobs," the young man answered. "The mobs of Anthropolis."

"Why did they chase the people away?" Nathan asked.

"Because of their intolerance," he said. "The people here weren't willing to change, to agree, to see the truth."

"Where did they chase them off to?" Nathan asked.

"Well," the stranger said, choosing his words carefully. "Well, they didn't want to drive them off. Some of them wanted to arrest them all. Others were calling for their heads." At these words Leah gasped.

"But in the end," he continued, "the people here ran to the one place where no one would follow them."

"Where's that?" Nathan asked. The stranger pointed to the South.

"The forest," he said. "They all ran straight into the forest. I've never seen anything like it, you know, with the dragons and all. Much of the mob followed them into the forest, but quickly returned, fearful of dragons."

Nathan took a deep breath and seemed to gather his thoughts.

"How long ago did this happen?" Nathan asked.

"About three days ago," he replied. "After they left, people wanted to burn down their homes, but they were afraid that the fire might spread, so they just took everything out of them. There was a big celebration that night, with all of them gone out of the city."

"And did you celebrate?" Nathan asked.

"Oh, no sir," the young man replied. "Not me. I belong to one of the Castles here in Anthropolis. Some Castle-goers did celebrate, I'm sad to say. Some of them were even part of the mob. But not me. I liked the people here. I didn't really know them, but they always seemed nice. My papa tells me that it was wrong what happened here. My captain also thinks it was wrong."

Nathan remained silent for a time, still in thought. He extended his arm to Leah, who then came to his side and put her head into his chest and wept.

"Three days in the forest," he said to her. "I believe they can hold their own, but eventually they will run out of provisions."

"Titus and Timothy are with them," Leah said, trying to find comfort and strength. "With their leadership they will be safe. I'm guessing they led them out of the forest to a safe place."

"Titus and Timothy?" the stranger repeated. "I know who they are. They were caught by the mob, taken to the prisons. We still don't know what's going to happen to them. Many are talking about it. I fear that it will be their heads before too long."

Leah gasped again and her weeping continued. "Titus and Timothy arrested," she said. "This has turned from bad to worse!"

Nathan paused once again, trying to assess the situation.

41

"We are faced with a dilemma then," he said. "We have a fellowship that needs help, two captains who are likewise in trouble, and a dear girl and our son who are in our charge."

Leah wiped the tears from her eyes in an effort to be strong. "I'm with you in whatever you decide," she said resolutely.

Nathan looked about. "Do you have any advice?" he asked his bride.

"Only to consider the Scroll," she said.

"True," he said. "Give me a moment." He then walked about, looking at the forest, looking at me and then looking at the ground. "I need to find someone I can trust," he said at last. "A captain of the Castle I suppose. I must have a message sent to Samuel informing him of what we are going to do."

"And what is that, my love?" Leah asked.

"We are going to find your people," he said.

Chapter 7

"They are likely in need of help and encouragement," Nathan explained. "They are made up of mainly women and children. We will search for them and find them before the enemy does."

"Oh, I love you so much," Leah said with a deep breath. "We must hurry then."

"Young man," Nathan said. "What is your name?"

"Micah," he replied.

"Micah, you said you knew a captain who wasn't against us. Is he near?"

"Very near," Micah replied. "The Castle is close to here."

"Good. Please go get him, and bring him here if you can. The sooner the better. No time can be wasted."

The young man turned and ran. Within only a few minutes he was back. "I found him walking in the market just over there," Micah said excitedly.

A man then approached us. He was young, likely about Nathan's age, and was dressed like a warrior of the Great King, though his raiment seemed to be a bit more extravagant than what I was used to.

"I hear you folks need some help," he said.

"Yes, thank you. My name is Nathan. We are going into the forest to find our friends and were wondering if you could somehow send a message to Ravenhill."

"Ravenhill?" the man said with surprise. "Well, that's interesting, for I am to be transferring there within the month to take over the leadership of the Castle."

Nathan then took a more careful look at the man. "You are young," Nathan said.

"Yes," the man replied, seeming to take no offense. "I just graduated from the Great Castle here in Anthropolis, and the Castle of Ravenhill sought me out."

"Is there any way we can get a message to them quickly?"

"I would think so," the young captain replied. "I believe that some of our warriors are heading there in the next day or two. I could send a message along with them."

"That's right," Micah confirmed. "My father is leaving with them. He has work to do amongst the Castle-goers of Ravenhill."

Nathan quickly took parchment and a pen from his supplies and began to write. As he did so he read aloud what he was writing so that Leah and I would understand what was happening. The letter read as follows:

> To Samuel, leader of the community of the Great King at the northwestern edge of Ravenhill, greetings:
>
> 'It is the thirty-fourth day since we left you. We have arrived at Anthropolis and have found Leah's community abandoned. We have been informed that they were driven into the forest by mobs of Anthropolis who sought to imprison or execute them. Both Titus and Timothy were captured and are currently either imprisoned or dead.

Seeing as the fellowship is in grave danger, I have decided to seek Leah's community with all speed and urgency. I have no time or opportunity to entrust my son or your daughter to someone I can trust, and so I have decided to take them with Leah and me, come what may. I ask that you send Jonah at all speed to seek out our fate. May the Great King show us favor.

    With all love.
    Nathan

He then handed the letter to the young Captain.

"I trust this message into your care," Nathan said. "Please do not fail me."

The man took the letter with a sense of confusion. "You aren't really going to go in the forest, are you?" he asked.

Nathan's eyebrows arose in curiosity. "What is your name?" he asked the captain.

"David," the man replied.

"Well, David. Why should it surprise you that we are going into the forest? We are warriors of the Great King. The forest is where we thrive in battle. You just graduated from the Great Castle. Surely you are a dragon slayer."

David took a deep breath. "Well," he said. "I have killed some of the dragons that the Great Castle breeds for our training, but I'm not sure if…"

"Oh, don't be fooled, sir," the boy said to Nathan as he cut David short. "Captain David is the best warrior in the land. I wager that he has killed hundreds of dragons! You should take him with you."

At this a look of concern came upon David's face. "I can't go," David said defensively. "I need to deliver this message."

"It can be delivered by my father," Micah said. "I will give it to him before he leaves. Please go, Captain David. Then you can bring me back a dragon's claw and tell me all about the adventure. I don't know anyone who has done that."

"We would love to have your help," Nathan said. "It's up to you."

David hesitated and took a deep breath.

"Please," Micah insisted. "I want to tell everyone the news of you going into the forest. Just think of what they would say!"

"Well," David said. "I suppose I can travel with you folks for half an hour or so, as long as you stick to the stone path."

"The stone path?" Nathan asked.

"Yes," Leah explained. "There's an ancient stone path that leads into the forest. It is from the days before the sin of our first parents."

"That is ancient indeed," Nathan said. "Is it wide enough for our horse and wagon?"

"I think so," she said. "It is overgrown in some areas but has greatly stood the test of time."

"Excellent," Nathan said. "That will be to our advantage. Everyone, get in."

Nathan then took the letter from David and handed it to Micah. "You must not fail me," he said. "Get this to your father."

"I will sir."

Nathan then removed the cover off of the wagon. "I fear it may hinder our movement," he explained. "And I want you to have complete view of our flank."

"A wonderful precaution," his wife complimented.

We then got into the carriage, Leah, Levi, and me in the back, while Nathan and David sat in the front. Within ten minutes we were entering the forest upon the stone trail. The trees loomed high above us on each side. We traveled at a medium pace, quickly, yet carefully.

"So," Nathan said to David, "tell me about your training in the Great Castle. What did you learn?"

"Oh, many things," replied David as cheerfully as he could be in the present situation. "I have been trained in the ways of the Scroll, with a particular emphasis

on the latest findings of modern scholarship. I have also been instructed on military formations, blacksmithing, and the identifications of dragons."

"That is wonderful," Nathan said. "And tell me about your studies of the Scroll itself. What do the latest findings of modern scholarship reveal?"

"It is most remarkable that you should ask," David replied. "I was just talking to another captain earlier today about a fascinating proposition that the Great Castles are now presenting regarding the beginning of the Scroll."

"The beginning of the Scroll?" Nathan inquired. "You mean the account of Creation, the temptation of our first parents, and the rescuing of our people from Mizraim?"

"Exactly," David answered. "As you know, it has traditionally been taught that Mosheh wrote down that first part of the Scroll under the inspiration of the Great King."

"True, true," replied Nathan, and I could tell that he was already filled with a curious concern as he gripped the reins, his ears attentive to every syllable.

"Well this new insight claims that the traditional claim is false," David said.

"False?" Nathan repeated. "If Mosheh didn't write the first account of the Scroll, then who did?"

"It was actually assembled thousands of years later while our people were in exile in the land of Babel."

"Interesting," Nathan said attentively. "And what do they call this teaching?"

"It is titled the Documentary Hypothesis," David answered.

"Documentary Hypothesis," Nathan repeated with a hint of disgust. "You have given a fanciful idea a fancy name. If you could be so kind as to inform me, why do they think this? What evidence has come to them that we have been missing of all these centuries?"

"Well," David said, "part of it, I believe, is just common sense. After all, Mosheh wasn't there in the beginning to witness things like Creation. How would he have had such an accurate account? And also the simple reality that the stories themselves are so exaggerated. It seems to be self-evident that there were many centuries of oral tradition between the actual events and when they were written down. That is usually how stories go from being reasonable and relevant to over-embellished and farfetched."

My heart shuddered, for I could see Nathan's deep concern over this teaching.

"My brother," Nathan said softly and soberly. "Listen to my words, and pray that the Great King has mercy upon your understanding. There is no story in the Scroll that is exaggerated. Nothing has been embellished. The Great King Himself said that Mosheh wrote it. How can you deny His words? The Scroll is history. The Scroll is without error. Your tutors are trying to convince you that the Scroll is wrong and modern thinking is correct. You must pray that the Great King will open your eyes. For with the abandonment of the Scroll comes the utter loss of any hope of following the Great King."

As Nathan spoke I beheld both fear and doubt grip the heart of David. He was like a reed, swaying to and fro with the differing perspectives of the Great Castle and Nathan. He took a deep breath. "I know that is how you and others who are more traditional think," he said, trying to add an air of respect. "But…" His words stopped.

"But these men are the experts," Nathan finished.

"Yes," David said hesitantly.

"Well," Nathan said, now a bit more relaxed. "You must do what you think is best. After all, you are going to be leading a large army on behalf of the Great King. You are going to be calling the shots. You are the one who will answer for the state of the army and whether or not it is in alignment with the Scroll. And so, you had better begin now in choosing for yourself whom you will believe and what you will do."

As they continued to talk, I noticed Leah gaze into the forest. It was a serious look, and she continued to turn her head from one side of the forest to the other.

"What's wrong?" I asked her in a whisper.

"They have already found us," she said. "It is as if they were waiting for us."

"Who?" I asked.

"Dragons," she replied.

"Dragons?" Nathan overheard. "But we are barely within the forest."

He pulled the wagon to a stop and hopped out, his sword drawn.

"Umm," David said with a nervous tremble in his voice. "Shouldn't we run?"

"Not at all," Nathan replied humbly yet with a bit of humor in his voice. "Dragons rarely travel in groups and are usually alone. They don't like to share glory. There should only be one or two of them. We will stand and fight."

"There are more than two of them," Leah said with a calm urgency. "I've counted five."

"Five!" Nathan said with surprise. "Are you sure?"

"I think so," she said. "I saw them beginning to encircle us. I can't see them now, but I fear they will charge any second now."

Chapter 8

Leah then looked to her husband. "What should we do?" she asked.

Nathan looked about for a few seconds and then jumped back in the wagon and grabbed the reins. "David," he said. "Be ready to take the reins if need be." He then raised his voice. "Ladies! Ready your bows!"

He then slapped the reigns upon the horse, and we took off at full speed. No sooner did we advance, then did three red dragons spring out from behind us and begin their pursuit.

"I don't know what to do!" I shouted. My heart was racing, and I felt helpless.

"Shoot them!" Leah shouted in reply. "Aim for their eyes!"

The dragons seemed to be running as fast as they could, a swiftness that caused them to slowly gain on us. Low lying tree branches whipped about us as we sped down the path. We released our arrows. Leah quickly shot the nearest one in the front of its knees, slowing it down. I watched three of my arrows strike the second dragon, though they didn't penetrate.

"Their hides are thick!" Leah shouted above the rumble of the pursuit.

"I need arrows ahead!" Nathan shouted. "Now!"

We turned around to see two dragons charging from ahead of us.

Leah nocked two arrows and let them fly. One arrow pierced the throat of one of the dragons, causing it to fall to one side. The other dragon lowered its head as one would a battering ram. Nathan pulled the wagon to the far-left edge of the road, while slashing his sword upon the beast. David shouted aloud. The dragon cried out in pain as Nathan's sword sliced through its forehead.

At the same time the sudden jerk in the steering caused our wagon to come up on two wheels. I grabbed Levi with one arm and the side of the wagon with the other. The wagon landed with a loud clang upon the hard, stone path and continued on. As I reoriented myself, I looked behind us to notice a dragon's mouth opened and only three feet away from me. I cried out in horror. Soon Nathan was in the back of the wagon swinging his sword feverishly. David had been given the reins and was doing his best to keep us from stopping. Leah took down another dragon. Now only two remained. They inhaled deeply to blast us with their fire.

"All behind me!" shouted Nathan as he kneeled with his shield between himself and the dragons. We all obeyed and soon a cloud of fire encircled us. David cried out in pain. The wagon jolted from side to side. The left wheel then crumbled, and half of the wagon began to drag upon the stone path. The dragons had now stopped their pursuit.

"Pull back on the reins!" Nathan ordered.

David hesitantly brought the wagon to a stop. He was singed and bruised, but not seriously injured.

"What do we do now?" he asked, fear piercing through every fiber of his being.

"We prepare for another attack," Nathan answered soberly. "Is everyone alright?"

"We are, my love," Leah said as she situated Levi upon her back. She then looked at me. "Stay close to me," she said. "You did well in the wagon. I saw many of your shots strike the enemy. You showed bravery for your first encounter."

Nathan quickly detached the wagon from the horse and with David's help tipped the wagon up on its side to form a barricade. My heart was filled with both fear and comfort. The dragons terrified me, but I was so thankful to be with Nathan and Leah.

"Alright," Nathan said calmly. "The dragons are no doubt hunting us. David, do you have any advice to offer? Where is the enemy? Which one of us will they attack first? What should we do?"

David's expression said more than any words possibly could. He had no idea what to do.

"Let me help you," Nathan offered. "The enemy will always be down wind, for the love of the stronger scent. And they nearly always attack the one most plagued by fear. That means they are coming for you, my brother, and are behind you. Can't you hear them inhaling? If you don't dive behind that tree you will soon perish."

The words of Nathan were so calm and straightforward, that I wondered whether or not he was jesting. Fortunately, David saw the look in Nathan's eyes and instantly obeyed. No sooner did he dive behind the tree that Nathan mentioned than did a strong blast of fire consume the spot where he had just stood. A dragon then came amongst us and was met with Nathan's shield and sword as well as Leah's bow. It was soon lying dead upon the ground.

David picked himself up from the ground and put his back directly upon the tree trunk.

"Don't give in to fear!" Nathan commanded, knowing the struggle in David's heart. "I did not bring you out here to mock you, my brother, but to give you a hope and courage for the future! Stand at my side. Hurry! The last dragon is nearly upon us! Don't give in to fear, David. This opportunity will soon pass. Come now!"

To my astonishment and joy, David came to Nathan's side as Leah and I remained behind them, our bows drawn and ready. The two men stood side by side with swords drawn, and though fear was attempting to enter my heart, the presence of Nathan and Leah kept it from me.

"I see it," David said trembling. "It is coming."

"Turn and face it," Nathan ordered. I looked between the two men and beheld the eyes of the dragon, crouched upon the edge of the thicket.

"This dragon is much stronger than the creature we just defeated," Nathan said soberly. "It is aged and experienced. We must stay together. It will take all of us to beat it."

"I don't know what to do," David said. "What should I do?"

"You do what the Scroll says to do," Nathan said gently. "You stand."

"And you stand strong," Leah added. "Strong and without fear."

Nathan let out a pleasant laugh. "Ha! My bride is my backbone. With her by my side, I can live and die without fear. I then heard another voice. It was the dragon's, and it filled my heart with dark memories.

"What fools you are!" the dragon said, its eyes seeming to pierce within our souls. "Two men, one of whom is filled with fear, an overzealous bride, and a young girl. Her blood will be sweet. None of you will leave here alive. Oh, and what is this? A young child upon your back? He will serve as my slave."

"Its language is that of lies," Nathan said. "Do not pay any heed. If we stand together as one, we will not fail, for the Great King is with us."

With these words the dragon burst forth with both claw and fire mixed together. David was violently cast to the ground as Nathan struck back with righteous fury, causing the beast to retreat for a moment. Nathan then reformed our line, placing Leah to his right and me to his left. David was still upon the ground and slow to rise. The dragon returned, this time attempting to bring its full weight upon Nathan in order to pin him to the ground. Leah and I released our arrows as Nathan dodged and countered, cutting into the dragon though also receiving a claw to his side, which hurled him into a nearby tree. He rose with a groan and called upon the Great King for aid. The dragon was also injured but seemed just as determined as Nathan.

"I will kill you," the dragon hissed with hatred in its voice as it pulled our arrows from its hide. "You will surely perish. And your people will soon follow suit."

"If you kill me," Nathan replied amongst labored breathing, "then it will be according to the will of He who is sovereign over all. But it will not likely be so."

The dragon let out a shout that seemed to make the earth tremble. Its tail swung around with such speed and power that it knocked down a young oak in the process. Nathan commanded us to fall back and fire as he leapt over the tail. The arrow of Leah caught the dragon in its neck, causing it to stumble back. It seemed to see its end in sight and in desperation decided to devour David.

The young novice captain was barely upon his knees and was still trying to recover. His wind had been knocked out of him and all he could do was utter, "Oh Great King, help me."

The dragon then came down upon him, its jagged teeth ready to chomp upon him as a viper does to a rat it has trapped.

Chapter 9

For a moment all hope for David left me, and my heart broke for this young man who, under the pressure of a young boy, had chosen to join us. But something happened that I didn't expect. Somehow David moved across the ground. It was not of his own doing, for he was powerless to do anything. And yet, as fast as a cheetah, his body slid across the surface of the ground far away from the dragon, as if a rope had been attached to him. The dragon struck the surface of the ground and rose again looking about, seemingly as shocked and confused as I was.

Its confusion was soon removed as it felt a blade sink into its back. The dragon shouted in pain and spun around to reveal Nathan, standing in all boldness and fearlessness. The dragon swung down upon Nathan who easily dodged the attack and countered. Again, the dragon tried to attack, and again it cried out in pain. Leah released more arrows, causing the beast to fall to its side. I then beheld Nathan sink his sword deep within the chest of the dragon, and the ground trembled as the dragon was dashed upon it, lifeless and headless.

"Goodness!" David cried, as he slowly rose to his feet. "That was too close!"

"Too close indeed," Nathan said, catching his breath. "And yet, it wasn't close at all really, for the Great King is sovereign. And seeing it was His will for you to survive, you weren't close at all to death. Death, indeed, was as far from you as the East is from the West."

David continued to look upon the dead dragon in both fear and wonder.

"You stand amazed at what you see," Nathan observed. "You do so because of what you've been taught. You see, this is why your beliefs about the Scroll are so important. If your Documentary Hypothesis is correct, and if the stories of the Scroll are mere fables, then they have no true inspiration for us at all. But if they are real, which indeed they are, then the same power and valor which moved in those men and women of old is also available to us. We can overcome just as they did. I beg you, my friend, don't reduce the Scroll to something void of power. It is the true, perfect, account of our people. The same Great King and the same Spirit of Truth are also present and available to us."

"But wait," David said, seemingly not hearing Nathan's words. "The dragon was going to swallow me. I moved. How? How did that happen?"

"It was my husband's ability that saved you, sir," Leah said respectfully.

"Ability?" David said. "That was an ability?"

"Of course," Nathan replied. "You certainly know of abilities, don't you?"

"Well, yes," David answered, still trying to breathe normally. "I just didn't know they took this form." David took a good look at Nathan and then at the dragon. "You are so young," he observed. "How were you able to do this?"

"I trained," Nathan replied humbly, "and have been training since I was young."

His answer didn't seem to satisfy David, so he continued.

"It is a different training than you received, David. I received training in slaying dragons, while you received training in the managing of the modern Castle. I hope that this experience has accomplished a few things for you, my brother. First, encouragement, for you stood strong beside your brethren and before a very mighty dragon. You did not give in to the fear that was battling within your heart. For this, you should rightly be commended, and so I say to you, well done.

"But I also hope that this experience has exposed to you the reality that there is much training needed that cannot be found at the Great Castles. And so, you are stepping into a grave situation. For you are entering into a position of leadership that, according to the Scroll, is very sobering in responsibility. You are in essence saying to the flock, *'I will lead you down the correct path. Trust me.'* And, therefore, you will one day have to answer unto the Great King Himself for how you shepherded His people. It is a noble ambition you seek, and yet, if you are not prepared, you will likely bring judgment upon your own head. So, I say to you, wait. Receive proper training, as the Scroll commands."

David stood in deep thought. And I surmised that what he had just experienced was unlike anything else in his life up to that moment. "How long?" he asked. "In your opinion, how long would it take for me to be ready to truly lead people?"

"In my opinion," Nathan answered in deep consideration, "about three years to become a proficient warrior, perhaps less if the Great King sees fit to bless you thus. And regarding the wisdom you would need to lead the people well, maybe a few years more."

David looked dejected. "That is too long," he said, though he said it very quietly, almost as if no one was supposed to hear him.

Nathan remained quiet.

"I think I should return to Anthropolis," David said respectfully, "if it is possible."

"Of course," Nathan replied. "The road from here back to the beginning is no doubt free from dragons, and we only traveled for twenty minutes or so. I guess you will make it back within an hour. But still, you will be alone. Are you sure you don't want to travel with us?"

"I can't," David said after a few seconds of thought. "Forgive me, but I can't."

"There's nothing to forgive," Nathan said. "By the will of the Great King, we will one day visit within the glades of Ravenhill. Farewell, my brother."

Then David bowed, turned, and slowly made his way down the road.

"I believe I have erred," Nathan said quietly.

"How do you mean?" Leah inquired.

"It is usually not wise to overwhelm brethren with such experiences as the one we just had. It can, at times, do more harm than good."

"May the Great King use it as He sees fit," Leah prayed.

"Amen," Nathan replied.

***

Our carriage was now useless. One wheel had been destroyed in the battle, and we could no longer use it. I was beyond exhausted and was soon upon the horse with Leah and Levi as Nathan quietly led us down the path while guiding the mount.

"What are your thoughts about David?" I asked. "Do you think he will lead the Castle well?"

"In some ways, perhaps," Nathan answered, and I could see that there was pain in his heart. "Though it is unlikely that he will lead others deep into the ways of the Great King unless something changes. For one cannot lead others down a path that he himself hasn't traveled. He is our brother, and he is greatly deceived. We must pray for him as the Great King brings him to remembrance. And we must learn from his circumstances, that we might better prepare the next generation for success."

An hour before sundown we came upon Leah's people. They had found a clearing in the forest, which they had been hastily reinforcing. In only a few days they had hewn many trees and made a barrier as best they could. Guards were stationed continually around the perimeter. They were in danger of dragon attacks within the forest and of mob attacks from without. Leah and Nathan were quickly recognized, and everyone came to greet them, encouraged at the presence of the couple. Leah dismounted the horse and ran to embrace her mother and younger siblings, and Nathan was reunited with his sister Ruth.

The people were currently resolved to hold their position until a plan could be formulated. Their provisions were in short supply, however, and they knew they must soon make a decision. Their number was around sixty, and in addition to Titus and Timothy being taken, they had also lost three of their men to the wrath and violence of the mobs. The three men had been severely injured and died shortly after entering the forest. One of them was Leah's uncle. I stood with her as she looked down upon his grave and wept.

The following morning, I was awakened by Leah. The cool morning mist was filling the forest and the small community was beginning to stir.

"Come," she said.

"What are we going to do?" I asked.

"We are going to train," she replied. "This is real training. You are of age now, and you are within a battlefield. It is high time for you to fully embrace the bow."

Archery targets had been erected by Ruth, who was awaiting us.

"Good morning, Elizabeth," she said. "I am excited about what this day has in store for us."

I liked Ruth. She was young and beautiful, and yet, much like Leah, had a sense of such maturity and honor about her. Leah held up the bow in her hand.

"Before you hold the bow," she said, "you must believe that it is your calling. Your aim will only be as accurate as your faith. What you believe will determine your direction."

I gripped the bow in my hand and looked at it closely. I then repeated her words aloud. "I must believe."

"This bow was made for a purpose," she continued. "It isn't a club that one can swing aimlessly. Its purpose is to propel the arrow. You were made by your Creator with a purpose in His mind. You must embrace that purpose." She then paused to allow me time to contemplate her words.

"But what is my purpose?" I asked curiously.

"Excellent question," she replied. "Let us consult the Scroll. Here it is," she said, unrolling it only a little. "In the beginning, the Great King made man in His image, according to His perfect plan. He made him male, and his helper, female. For this reason, a woman will cling to her man, and the Great King will make them one." As she read, she motioned with her finger so that I could follow along.

"A man without a woman," Leah explained, "is much like an arrow without a bow. The arrow is beautiful and powerful but can accomplish very little. Your purpose is to one day propel your husband forward to the goal the Great King has for him. You are the bow; he is the arrow. Keep that in mind every time you wield the bow. It is a symbol of who you are. Together, with your husband, you both will accomplish much for the Great King. Your submission will be your strength, for the more you bend, the straighter and truer your husband will fly toward his mark."

As she spoke these words she bent her bow. "If the bow doesn't bend, will the arrow shoot far?'

"No, ma'am," I replied.

"Exactly," she confirmed. "Look at these words." I then joined her gaze again to the Scroll: "Wives, yield to your husbands. Just as you yield your life to the Great King, so you must likewise yield to your husband."

"You must learn to bend your will," Leah emphasized. "Without bending your will, your husband will go nowhere at all. And, therefore, neither will you."

"But it is not only the will of your husband that matters," Ruth said. "Ultimately, you are bending your will to that of the Great King. And not only are you to bend it, but to mold it. You must allow your will to be renewed to the point

that what you desire and what the Great King desires are one and the same. As this happens, you will be the backbone of your husband."

"But what happens if I don't marry?" I asked sincerely.

Ruth put her hand on my shoulder. "Then the Great King Himself will be your arrow and you will serve Him in mighty and wonderful ways. You can be a mighty vessel to further His kingdom whether or not you marry."

"Make yourself ready," Leah said. "Take the bow, aim, and shoot."

I followed her leading. The target was about fifteen yards away. I let the arrow fly, and to my joy it landed close to the bull's eye.

"Your aim is good," Leah said, "but you lack power. Dragon hide is more difficult to penetrate than straw and grass, as you discovered yesterday.

"The bowstring is sometimes hard to pull back," I said.

"You may find this hard to believe," she added, "but it is you that makes it difficult. Remember what I told you? You must be willing to bend. You must be willing to be led, and not only that, but to yield your life to the Great King. This must not be merely accepted; it must be embraced. Think on that. Surrender your will and try again."

I nocked another arrow and repeated the process, this time thinking well on her words. *I must be willing to yield. I must embrace my calling.* The string seemed to come back a bit easier. The arrow was let loose, and it stuck, just on the edge of the bull's eye.

"Well done!" both ladies exclaimed cheerfully.

"You have much to learn," Ruth said, "and with each principle of the Scroll you embrace, your shot will improve markedly."

She then nocked her own arrow and quickly pulled it back and released it. The arrow not only hit the bull's-eye, but it stuck far deeper than my own.

"There is a sharpness and strength of your weapon that you can't yet imagine," Leah added. "But we will show you the way." And with these words she too nocked an arrow and let it fly, but it seemed to disappear, for the arrow wasn't seen on the target.

"What happened?" I asked in astonishment. "Where's the arrow?"

"Go and look closely," she said.

I ran to the target and looked, and there, close to Ruth's arrow, was a tiny hole filled with darkness. I felt within with my finger and perceived the end of Leah's arrow. It had sunk so deep within the target that it couldn't be seen.

"How did you do that?" I exclaimed with wonder in my voice.

"You will do even better," Leah said.

At that moment two things happened. First, I looked to the sky with overwhelming gratitude. I knew that I had gained something that I never had before, and the opportunity I had always dreamed of was now before me. I knew that I would never be the same again and that I had been put, by the Great King it seemed, into an amazing situation.

Second, as I looked down from the sky, I glanced over at the nearby forest line and blockade. There my eyes met with something that immediately drenched all my jubilation and replaced it with immeasurable fear. My knees buckled and my voice let out a shrill scream that filled the countryside. Two large dragons were crouched upon the edge of the tree line, their yellow eyes fixed upon me, their teeth clenched in evil aggression.

Chapter 10

Not even one second after my cry, I could hear the quivers of Leah and Ruth being emptied. I didn't see their arrows fly, for my body was upon the ground and my head was buried under my arms. An alarm was sounded, and soon the dragons were gone. I then felt both ladies' hands upon me, trying to comfort me.

"It's alright," Leah said, causing me to look up, my eyes red with tears. "The creatures are gone."

"Don't worry," Ruth added as she comforted me. "We are well guarded here. We won't let them touch you."

"Forgive my response," I said as I wiped the tears from my eyes. "Seeing them look at me brought back a terror within me that I didn't know existed. The night of the Great Fire, that same night, a dragon tempted me from my window and spoke my name. He looked at me with the same hideous glare."

Ruth looked at Leah with a curious stare. "How did a dragon come to your window?" she asked. "They can't leave the forest."

"It was a serpent," Leah said.

"What's a serpent?" I asked, still trying to calm down. "My father had tried to explain this to me when I was young, but the pain and fear was still too real at that time, and so we've never finished the conversation."

"A serpent is much like an illusion," Leah explained. "They can't even touch you really, except when you allow them to do so. But ultimately, they can't physically hurt you as long as you're walking in truth."

"They can't hurt me?" I asked, quite shocked by what I was hearing. "You mean to say that the dragon that I saw outside of my window on the night of the fire wasn't a real threat?"

"That's correct," Leah testified. "They are only as dangerous as you allow them to be. Their threats are empty, for their power is based upon what you believe concerning the lies of the enemy. They prey upon your fear. On the night of the fire, if you would have stood face-to-face with that creature, declaring truth and peace amidst its empty threats, it would have shrunken until it vanished. They always appear as long snake-like creatures, each with four skinny legs."

"But if they are able go anywhere," I said, thinking aloud, "then why aren't the villages full of these serpents?"

"In a way they are," Leah said. "Lies and deceit plague the people. But you must understand this, dear Elizabeth. The enemy, ultimately, doesn't desire to be seen. The most effective enemy is the one whose opponent doesn't know of its existence."

"Then why me?" I asked. "Why did it reveal itself to me? How did it know my name?"

"I don't know," Leah said sympathetically. "But I do know that your father and the elders have been trying to figure out this mystery ever since you came to us. There is something special about you, Elizabeth. We are blessed to have you with us."

I found my situation to be both a blessing and curse: a blessing in the sense that the Great King had given me such a wonderful family and calling, and yet a curse in that I was wanted by the enemy. It was flattering to know I was somehow special but a terror to be hunted.

There was a council planned for that morning and everyone attended. I didn't know the names of the men who spoke except for Nathan.

"We must make a move soon," one man said. "We have seed we could sow here, and this opening is now large enough to grow food, and there are deer and other animals, but how can we live in peace within the realm of the dragons? We must make our way back towards the prairie and find another city for our people."

"But what of Titus and Timothy?" another asked. "We can't just abandon them."

"Their destiny is in the hands of the Great King," spoke another. "We must tend to our families now. If we go back to seek Titus and Timothy, we will likely join their fate."

Many other men spoke up and shared their thoughts. Nothing could be agreed upon. Finally, Nathan spoke.

"I am not of this gathering," he said. "And so, I have waited to speak. But now I bring to you the best counsel I have. It is this: You don't know what to do. I don't know what to do. But the Great King knows. Come, my brethren. Let us join together in prayer to the Father of us all."

Everyone agreed with Nathan's wisdom, and coming together, we all cried out together to the Great King. For nearly twenty minutes our prayers continued to be raised to heaven. Suddenly, Ruth gasped. Everyone stopped and pulled both sword and bow, as if expecting a sudden attack.

"Look!" she said, and she suddenly grabbed my hand and Leah's hand. My eyes were opened, and I saw what I guessed were angels. They looked as warriors of light, and they were setting up some kind of fortification around our encampment.

"What's happening?" I asked in fear.

"It's Ruth's ability," Leah said with awe in her voice. "She can see the invisible realm."

Others who were able to put their hands upon Ruth also gasped at what they likewise beheld. The warriors of light continued to build.

"It is the same battlements that they put upon the outside of the forests," Ruth said with joy. "And look! They are putting them down the stone path as well! We are safe from the dragons and have safe passage in and out of the forest!"

"The Great King has heard us!" Nathan shouted, and everyone erupted in praise and thanksgiving. "The Great King has given you a haven of protection in the midst of your enemies!" he continued.

"That is what we will call this place," a man said. "It is the Haven."

"The Great King be praised," Leah said with tears of joy. "My people are safe. Now we can help them build their homes and plant their gardens."

"Not all of us will help them build," Nathan said. "Not yet at least."

"What do you mean?" Leah asked.

"Titus and Timothy," he replied. "We cannot abandon them to the will of the mob. We must find them and procure their freedom."

Chapter 11

"It's too dangerous," Leah said. "Only a few days ago the mobs tried to kill our people."

"It should be alright," Nathan replied. "I am unknown in this city and shouldn't stand out. We must do something as our brothers are innocent men. They deserve a fair trial, for that would certainly secure their release."

"I should come with you then," Leah said, "for I know the city."

"I feel it is too risky for you to come, my dear," he said. "Don't worry. I will be able to find my way."

Leah closed her eyes and took a deep breath. "I know you will," she said, "but please be careful." And she kissed him.

The following morning Nathan departed on his horse. I spent most of my time helping Leah's family build their new home. The area that had been initially cleared by the community was about two acres. Yet Ruth was able to see the entire area that had been given to them by the Great King, and it numbered around thirty acres. With the help of Ruth, the men began clearing a border which would define the Haven. After only two days the Haven was beginning to take shape. Families had worked together in choosing parcels, and gardens were beginning to be planted.

As the sun was setting that evening, Nathan arrived back with urgent news. "There is hope for our brethren," he announced. "A billboard was installed within the courtyard before the chief citadel of the city. It said that there would be a trial tomorrow evening and that all elders from our community that wanted to speak on behalf of the accused could come and freely speak. The mobs are no longer active. The people have calmed, and I overheard many say that what happened to our people was a grievous event."

Nathan and four others volunteered to go in the morning. We gathered around them and prayed for their protection. By the time I awoke in the morning, the men had already departed. That afternoon, during baby Levi's nap, Leah and Ruth invited me to walk with them down the forest road.

"So there really are barriers set up on both sides of the road?" Leah asked as we walked together.

"Absolutely," Ruth testified. "It is amazing to behold."

"So," Leah said as she looked at Ruth with a smile, "you have been amongst this group for nearly six months, my sister. Do tell me, are there any young men catching your eye?"

Ruth smiled in return. "There are some," she confessed, "but none that I believe are a complete match. A particular benefit of my ability is that I can see people how no one else can. There is a particular light that I desire in a man; a light of courage, of hope in the Great King, of confidence in the Scroll. I long to see it."

"Does Nathan have that light in him?" Leah asked curiously.

Ruth laughed. "You already know the answer to that, my sister."

Leah then stopped and looked around. "We've walked quite a way."

"Yes," Ruth said. "I think we are only a mile from the beginning of the forest road."

I then noticed something down the road in the direction of the city. The other ladies joined my gaze.

"It's a man," Leah said.

"Is he an enemy?" I asked.

"He can't be," Ruth testified, "for I see the light of the Great King shining within him."

It was Micah, the young boy we had met a few days before. As soon as he noticed Leah and me, he began to run towards us, continually looking to his right and his left, as if he was on the lookout for dragons. We assured him he was safe and allowed him a brief moment to catch his breath.

"I had to find you," he said, his face filled with panic. "Why are your men in the city?"

"For the trial that is this evening," Ruth replied calmly.

"There is no trial," he said.

"No trial?" Leah repeated. "It was announced that Titus and Timothy were to be on trial."

"The men are to be executed at dawn," Micah declared. "There was never going to be a trial."

"But what of my husband?" Leah asked with fear in her eyes. "Have they found him?"

"They found all of them," Micah said sadly. "They all wandered right into the courtyard earlier today. They will all swing upon the gallows at dawn."

Leah and Ruth let out a cry, and I turned from them and covered my face.

"We must go back and tell the others," Ruth said. "We must get help."

Leah was, from either shock or some other emotion, as still as a statue. After a moment she spoke.

"Who would we tell? Most of the fighting men have been captured, and I'm not going to risk another husband and father to be lost. I am going into the city."

"You?" Ruth said. "Alone? What will you do?"

"Save my husband," Leah replied with resolution.

"But how?" Ruth persisted. "You can't appeal to this court. They are obviously a bloodthirsty mob. And what of Levi?"

The name of her son pricked Leah's emotionless state and she took a few deep breaths as she looked down at the ground in deep thought. "He will understand in time," she said, "even if the worst should happen."

"You cannot fight the entire city militia on your own," Ruth said. "And what of the Scroll? It says to submit to the governing authorities."

Leah replied without hesitation or pause. "It also says that the governing authorities are commanded by the Great King to commend the good and punish the bad. These men are not serving the Great King. They have broken covenant with Him, and with the people, and so I no longer see them as a lawful authority."

Ruth turned about and looked into the forest, deep in thought, as she wiped tears from her eyes. "I'm going with you," she finally said. "He's my brother, and you are my sister. If this is the end of you two, then I'm going to go with you through the golden gates of the Celestial City."

"So be it," Leah said soberly. "Elizabeth, you must return now and tell my mother what we are doing and warn her of the danger. No one else is to go. By the authority of my husband I command it. The rest of the group must stay in hiding and continue to build up the Haven."

I hesitated and remained silent. During the conversation of Ruth and Leah, my heart was also stirring within me. Leah looked at me and was able to read my eyes.

"You aren't going," she said in a strict tone. "It is absolutely forbidden. Go back now and tell my family."

"But," I began. "But you and Nathan are like family to me. I must go with you."

"Absolutely not," she replied. "You are too young. You must stay here with the people. If the worst should happen to Nathan and me, you will eventually be restored to your father. That is my final word, Elizabeth. I love you. There is no time to spare. The sun will be setting soon, and then the dawn will come."

I wept as I watched them walk away. I realized that I didn't even get to hug them goodbye. Finally, after a few minutes of weeping, I turned and walked back towards the Haven. Every step I took felt wrong and difficult. Everything within me seemed to be pulling me toward Anthropolis. What if I could help Leah and Ruth? What if I was able to save Nathan? I wouldn't be in any real danger. After all, no one in the city knew me at all. To them I would just be young girl. I hesitated. I then heard a voice that broke my thoughts. It was Mark, a young man of fifteen years of age from the fellowship.

"There you are," he said kindly. "I was sent by Leah's mother to inquire of how you all are doing."

I just stood there, speechless and looking at him, for such a length of time that he became quite uncomfortable. A battle was raging within me. Two forces were fighting. One knew it should submit to Leah's orders. The other was motivated by love and sacrifice. Finally, I spoke.

"Mark. Listen carefully. You must go to the fellowship and tell them that something has happened. Ruth, Leah, and I have been called upon an errand to the city. The men are in danger. Everyone is in danger. But none of you must come. Everyone must stay at the Haven and pray. Please tell the few men left to stay and to survive and to provide leadership and protection for the women and children. Do you understand?"

"I do," he said soberly.

"Remember," I said, with tears in my eyes, "no one else is to go to the city until one of us returns. Stay hidden and quiet and safe. Do you understand?"

He nodded. I turned and hurried back towards the city. By the time I reached the beginning of the forest road, it was dark, and torch light filled the busy and crowded streets. I put my quiver under my cloak and tried to conceal my bow as much as possible. I was soon lost in the busy streets of Anthropolis, with no knowledge at all as to where I needed to go or what I needed to do.

I then perceived an uncomfortable sensation. Evil. It was as if my surroundings were saturated by it. It was everywhere. I sensed all the impurities that the Scroll forbid. Such things I was aware of in the dark corners of Ravenhill, but in Anthropolis it was as if everything was unashamedly in the open. I began to feel very alone and wished that I was back in the Haven, or better yet, in my cottage with my father in Ravenhill.

After another hour I could tell that I was getting closer to the center of the city, for the buildings were larger and the streets more crowded. I suddenly came upon the sign that Nathan had mentioned. It seemed to have the words about the trial marked out, and written atop those words it read, *Execution of all Intolerant Extremists at Dawn*. Adjacent to the sign was an enormous citadel with a gated courtyard attached to it. The building was adorned in such a way that made it look like one of the chief buildings of the city. I noticed two guards at the entrance, who no one seemed to pass without permission. Within the courtyard itself I could perceive a tiny fire, with a few figures sitting around it, and a wooden door which was cracked open and led into the citadel itself. A few of the windows of the building were slightly lit; otherwise, all was dark. It was now late, a few hours before midnight I guessed, and the streets were beginning to be less crowded.

I was without a plan and without a friend. I looked about. No sign of Ruth and Leah. They might have been captured already, or worse. My heart was pounding. I felt that I must break through the citadel stronghold at all cost. An idea then entered my mind: I would just walk in, right past the guards, without a second's hesitation. If they stopped me, they stopped me. I didn't second guess myself, I just did it.

I walked straight into the courtyard with a confident look upon my face. I expected someone to stop me at once. No one did. I turned, not knowing where to go, and made my way to an open door I had discovered. I was waiting for someone to shout at me or come after me. Nothing happened. Did they not see me? Or did they think nothing of me? I didn't know.

I approached the door, but couldn't muster enough courage to go in. I simply sat down upon a pile of large bricks, about chair height, and reassessed the situation. I could faintly see the backs of the guards as they stood outside the entrance of the courtyard. They were unmoved. The few people around the dimly lit fire also remained still, someone making a comment every now again. To my amazement none of them seemed to take notice of me. I was just about to go into the wooden door when it opened further. A woman stepped out and looked right at me. My heart stood still within my chest!

"There you are," she snapped at me. She was older and unpleasant to look at because of the scowl upon her face. "You're late!" she hissed. "The mistress is waiting. Hurry up and get inside!"

I quickly sprang to my feet and followed her inside, up the stairs, and into a room that I perceived to be a kitchen. She told me to wait there, and then she left. I obeyed, and though I was tempted to look about for Nathan, I remained still. After a few moments another woman entered who was not at all like the first. She was young and had beautiful features, with short, black hair. She was dressed in clothes that were provocative, and yet had a royal air to them.

"Make seven bowls of food," she said. "Actually, no point to do that. Make five. Don't waste time glaring at me peasant girl. Get to work!"

I turned and looked at the counter. There was a pot of stew. I quickly found wooden bowls, then spoons. There was a tray. As I readied the meals, the woman sipped what I guessed to be red wine from an exquisite chalice as she looked out of the window which overlooked part of the city.

"So many people," she said quietly to herself. "So many people just waiting for something or someone to follow." She took another sip of wine and continued.

"So many people who don't know that they are slaves." She then smiled. "They will all serve me when the time comes."

After one minute all five bowls were ready, and I was carrying them, as carefully as I could, as I followed the woman. We went up another flight of steps. It was hard to see, for the only light I could see was coming from the woman's large candle she carried, in addition to the occasional torch upon the wall. We then passed two shrouded guards, who stood before a locked oaken door. The woman took out a set of keys and opened the door. She beckoned the guards to follow her, and together, the four of us went into the dimly lit room. There I beheld seven men, one of whom I knew to be Nathan. I hung my head a bit as to not make eye contact, though our eyes did meet, and he seemed to have no reaction.

"Give them food," the woman said, "though only five of them."

She then pointed to two men I had never before seen.

"Do not serve them," she said, "they will not need it. They will be lying in their own blood in only five minutes from now."

Chapter 12

I tried not to tremble as I set the bowls just outside of the cell, but within reach of the prisoners.

"Go ahead and beg," she mocked the two men whose cruel fates she had announced. "Go ahead and beg for your lives. It won't do you much good, though perhaps I will extend your executions a few hours if I find your plea to be sincere."

"You misunderstand us, madam," one of the men said. "We are not at all worried about your threats of the noose or the guillotine. Our hearts and minds are at complete rest."

"Oh, you foolish men!" the woman exclaimed. "You think you are so noble and so heroic! Nothing could be further from the truth. You are scoundrels and villains and oppressors of women. You reduce your women to mere servants and breed them without any concern for their wellbeing. Don't you know who I am? I am Jezebel! I will soon be governor of this city, and when I am, I will fully dispose of the rest of your men and liberate your women and children."

The other man smiled. "With all respect, Ms. Jezebel, you can't do anything to anyone unless the Great King allows it, and so, we aren't afraid of you. Indeed, we pity you and pray for you."

His words so angered Jezebel that she walked in a few slow circles, gripping her fist and trying to calm herself.

"We would gladly die for our women and children," the man continued. "We would gladly sacrifice our lives for theirs in whatever situation that required such action. We don't oppress our women, we exalt them."

"You foolish man," Jezebel said with a smile. "You don't get it, do you? It is the very idea you now try to exalt that makes you worthy of death. You think that women are more fragile and that they need to be treated in a special way and that they need your protection and leadership. Heresy! We don't need anything from you. We aren't any different than you. If anything, we are stronger, smarter, nobler, and more righteous. You think you are noble in treating women differently. It is your downfall. For by doing so you enslave them without their knowledge."

"By treating them special we bring the Great King glory and give our women true fulfillment," the man retorted.

"Silence!" she shouted in a rage. "I will hear no more of your blasphemy! There isn't a woman in this great and glorious city who would agree with such nonsense. They've been truly educated. Guards! I order you to pierce both of these men, Timothy and Titus. Kill them!"

I froze, not sure what to do. I looked at Nathan. He grinned slightly to me, as if to say that he knew this was the end and that he had committed his life to the will of the Great King. The two guards lifted high their spears. Titus and Timothy stood straight and unmoving, as pillars of masculinity without fear or malice in their hearts. They were truly at peace.

Then something happened. The guards didn't throw their spears, but remained as still as statues.

"What are you waiting for?" Jezebel said. "Hurry up!"

One of the guards suddenly spun in a full circle, resting its spear just under Jezebel's throat. Then the guard spoke, and I instantly recognized her voice.

"I do think that I should tell you, my dear Jezebel, that there still are women in this city who would disagree with you. I for one, do not at all feel enslaved when my husband treats me with deference and honor. In fact, I feel very blessed to be made by my Creator to be the more fragile gender and to be honored with the gift of submission to my husband."

Jezebel's eyes were open wide with wrath and her face was stiff with bitterness as the blade rested under her chin. "How dare you!" she said. "Who are you? How did you get in here?"

"Who am I?" Leah said. "I am my husband's helpmeet, created to serve him and fulfill his vision. And as far as our *breeding* as you call it, I was created with the purpose of bearing children, and I plan, if the Great King wills it, to bear many."

Jezebel could hardly contain herself. She was just about to burst forth and try her best to defeat Leah when Ruth, who was disguised as the other guard, quickly put her spear up to Jezebel's side, taking away any temptation to resist.

"Give us the keys," she said to Jezebel.

"What are you going to do?" Jezebel asked, trembling with rage.

"We are going to put you in the cell," Ruth replied.

"Impossible," Jezebel replied. "I would rather die than be found by my associates alone in a prison."

"Well," Ruth said calmly. "That just won't do. We aren't going to kill you, Jezebel. That wouldn't be the right thing to do. We will pray for you, that the Great King will grant you repentance."

"Never!" Jezebel declared.

"You have no idea what you're actually doing," Ruth said, "but we are running out of time. I'm not going to address your errors now, perhaps another time. But one thing I will say is this. You cowardly lured my brother away from his family with the intention of killing him. Such behavior is unacceptable."

"You can be sure…" Jezebel began, but she didn't finish, for she was soon lying unconscious upon the floor, thanks to a swift swing to the back of her head from Ruth's spear.

"Thank you, sister" Nathan said with a smile. "I think she was in need of a brief repose."

Leah quickly retrieved the keys and freed the men. She and Nathan embraced. She then turned to me with a smile. "You and I are going to have a serious talk when this all is finished," she said.

The men quickly found three ropes in a supply closet, tied them together, and lowered us out of a rear window, then over a wall, back through the shadows of the town and into the forest. It was an hour before sunrise when we reached the Haven, and I soon fell fast asleep from exhaustion.

I arose the following morning to find the entire community weeping together as they poured out their hearts to the Great King. Their tears were a mixture of both joy and concern: joy that the seven men had been rescued, and concern at how hostile and hateful the leadership of Anthropolis had become. Titus soon lifted his voice for all to hear.

"Listen to me, my brothers and sisters. My parents, who were likewise part of this fellowship in decades past, experienced a good relationship between our community and the people of Anthropolis. Even though most of Anthropolis didn't believe in the Great King, or rather, didn't follow Him, they still lived according to a worldview that was in agreement with the Scroll. They valued honesty, hard work, love, and friendship. They believed in gender roles, the family, and morality. But things have changed. As the culture of Anthropolis has turned away from the principles of the Scroll, so have its people become hostile to us.

We must remember the words of our King: *If they hate me, they will also hate you.* And also He says, *They hate the light, and don't want the light to shine on them.* By the grace of the Great King, we are the light that they hate. Do not let it trouble you. It is the Great King they reject, and to Him they will have to give an account on the Day of Judgment. We must pray for them, love them when the opportunity presents itself, but also protect our families and way of life. Being hidden here, for the time being, will require us to band together all the more closely and rely on each other. This is good. For now, seeing as the Great King has hemmed in this Haven for us, we will remain here for the time being. The day may soon come when we will be led to again infiltrate the society and culture of Anthropolis, but until that day, let us work hard, love one another, and experience the blessings of the Great King."

We then broke bread together and gave thanks to the Great King. One of the men rescued from the hands of Jezebel and the mobs of Anthropolis was Barnabas. He was betrothed to Rachel, a young maiden of seventeen years who was there with us. I watched them closely, and enjoyed seeing their interactions and overhearing their conversations. The way they treated each other left me with questions that I took to Leah.

"I have been watching Barnabas and Rachel," I said to Leah.

"I've noticed," she said with a smile.

"I never knew you or Nathan before you were wed, and so, I've always wondered what you were like. Were you much like Barnabas and Rachel?"

"Oh yes," Leah replied. "They are a wonderful example of what betrothal according to the Scroll should look like."

"Rachel seems like a wonderful woman," I said.

"She is," Leah agreed. "We are blessed to have them both. I believe that Barnabas will one day help lead this fellowship. He is a true follower of the Great King, and Rachel is a perfect match. Together they will accomplish much for the Creator, and their children will accomplish even more."

"How can you be so sure?" I asked sincerely.

"Well," Leah said with a laugh. "I can't know for sure. Only the Great King knows. But I hope so. And my hope is in alignment with His Scroll. He desires the children to accomplish more than the parents. He desires for the parents' ceiling to be the children's floor, to pick up where they left off. Barnabas and Rachel understand this. Their parents brought them far; by the grace of the Great King Barnabas and Rachel will take their own children even farther. Barnabas knows that his role as husband and father is paramount above all else, such as commerce or even his role within the fellowship. And Rachel, well, she is one of the most Scroll-like women I have ever met, which is amazing for one so young. She doesn't desire to make a name for herself, either in the Castle or in the market. She doesn't desire the selfish life that more and more women seem to run after. With all of her heart, her desire in life is three-fold. First, to be a woman of the Scroll, that is to say, to be in covenant with the Great King. Second, to be a wife of noble character, who fully embraces her role as the one the Great King created to fulfill and complete her husband's vision. And third, to raise children who are devoted to the Great King. She wants to raise strong sons, men of courage and honor, and she wants to raise feminine daughters who are filled with the gentle and quiet strength of the Most High."

The words that Leah spoke made sense to me, and I found them to be beautiful. I was learning from these people the power of family. I found myself hungry for as much knowledge as possible.

"Leah?" I said.

"Yes, my sister?"

"I noticed that Barnabas and Rachel don't touch each other the way that most other couples do who are planning to marry. Why is that?"

"What a wonderful question," Leah replied cheerfully, "for it is straight from the heart of the Great King. Barnabas and Rachel don't behave the way most people do because they believe something that most people don't."

"What's that?" I asked.

"They believe that all physical affection should wait until they are married, such as holding hands, kissing each other, putting their arms around each other and being alone. They are saving all of it until they are married because they believe that purity matters. You see, Elizabeth, the Great King gives everyone a heart that is beautiful and special. It is a heart that is to be reserved, first and foremost, for the Great King, and secondly, for a person's spouse. Barnabas and Rachel have made the most important decision already: to give their heart to the Great King. Many people don't even do that, and sadly, they also neglect the sanctity of their heart. They enter into marital activity prematurely, and so they spoil that special part of their heart, mind, and body that was to be reserved. Barnabas and Rachel understand the importance of their bodies and souls, and so, out of respect for each other and for the Great King, they choose to remain pure. This is also why they have never linked. There is only one heart they want to link to, and they are waiting patiently, with self-control and holy discipline."

"Did you ever link?" I asked curiously.

"Not at all," she said with a smile. "I will confess, however, that there were times when I was tempted to. That is to say, there were times when I was greatly attracted to certain young men and thought about how wonderful it would have been to have their affection. But thankfully my parents had rightly convinced me of the traps associated with linking. I never succumbed to the temptation. Truth be told, there really never was a temptation, only a longing for that which I anticipated."

She then took my hand in hers and continued. "Elizabeth, you must understand that your heart is a precious jewel. It is a jewel that is meant to be given to only two people: the Great King and your future husband. I know you wish to marry one day."

"I do," I replied, and I thought of Caleb.

"Never give away your heart to anyone else," she said. "Wait for that special man, just as Rachel is waiting for Barnabas. Never succumb to the empty ideas of linking. The more of your heart and mind and body that you save, the more special it will all be when you and your husband come together as one."

Leah's words were so beautiful to me. Even at my age, I wanted what she was describing. I wanted to be like Rachel, pure and in love. And I wanted a man like Barnabas, noble and courageous. I wanted my husband and me to be exactly like they were.

"This is why," Leah continued to explain with pleasure in her voice, "we dress the way we do. As I was saying before, there is a special part of your heart reserved for your husband. Likewise, much of your body is meant to be viewed by him alone. When ladies grow accustomed to boys seeing much of their skin, or even the clothed shapes of their bodies, it makes them overly ready to likewise share the special part of their hearts. You see, the body and soul are connected. If you open the viewing of your body to anyone, it will condition you to likewise reveal your soul to anyone.

"We also respect our men and know that how we dress can set them up for failure or success in temptations of the mind. Ultimately, they are responsible for their thoughts and actions, but we do not want to give any cause for them to stumble. This is why our ladies cover themselves. They understand that what they allow in the physical will carry over to the emotional and spiritual.

"Other girls, unfortunately, don't see this. They bare much of their bodies to the view of whoever is about, not knowing that they are slowly desensitizing themselves to the purity that they craved in their childhood. The parents are also often taken off guard. They protect their child's heart, but not their discretion. They underestimate the power of modesty. The lie that ladies believe is that true beauty is found in the admiration of others. The truth is that true beauty is found in the discretion and propriety that the Great King commands. You must continue down this path. If you do, you will not be disappointed in the end."

I was so inspired and moved by Leah's words. "I will follow the discretion and propriety of the Great King," I said joyfully. "Nothing will ever change my mind."

* * *

For the following eight weeks, we built homes and tended gardens. Soon a beautiful village was established and thriving. Our first harvest soon came, and the men of the Haven declared that a great thanksgiving celebration was to be held. I loved little else more than thanksgiving celebrations. They were so enjoyable and uplifting to my soul.

Preparations were being made and Leah, Nathan, and Ruth took me hunting with them for venison and boar for the celebration. We were tracking the wild game when I came upon tracks I didn't recognize.

"These are odd," I said softly. "They almost look like lion tracks, though there is an extra toe, and the paw is enlarged.

Ruth came to my side. "I've never seen these before," she said. "They are fresh, not yet an hour old."

Nathan then looked at the tracks. "I don't believe it," he said with an uneasy voice. "Quick!" he continued quietly. "Make a circle. Stay perfectly still."

"What is it?" Leah asked.

"Hell hounds," he replied.

Chapter 13

I saw a look of panic in Leah's eyes that I had never before seen. She quickly fell into formation and drew me close to her side. "Should we not head back to the Haven?" she whispered.

"We must wait for a moment," Nathan replied, also in a whisper. "If they are near, they already know we are here and will wait for us to lower our guard. Do you think this is a good plan?"

"I do," she replied, trying to soften her breathing.

"They breathe fire," Nathan gently informed us. "It is much hotter than dragon's fire. Be on your guard."

I had never heard of a hell hound before, though my imagination quickly drew a sketch of what one might look like. Suddenly I saw two of them sprinting towards us from the forest slope before me, and I realized just how lacking my imagination had been. They were like a mix between a lion and a wolf with hard shiny scales instead of fur. They were very large, around four feet at the shoulder, and their skin was blood red with strips of very dark purple and black throughout. They growled ferociously and had white foam coming from their mouths. I could almost feel how deeply they wanted to tear us apart.

Leah, Ruth, and I quickly crouched behind Nathan and shot our arrows. Leah and Ruth's arrows pierced the first hound, though he kept charging at us with great power. Nathan met the beast with his sword and shield, and we were soon scattered about on the forest floor. I pushed myself off the ground and beheld the first hound dead with a slash in its neck from Nathan's blade and two arrows protruding its hide.

I heard a yell for help and turned my head quickly to find that the second hound had Ruth cornered against a cluster of trees. Her bow had been flung far from her, and she was therefore without a way to defend herself. Leah was lying unconscious upon the ground, and Nathan was slowly rising to his feet. The hound inhaled deeply. Ruth yelled in horror at the prospect of being burnt alive. I tried to notch an arrow but knew I would be too late. The stream of bluish and yellow flame left the hound's mouth. I gasped in horror. But just as the fire came at Ruth, something else happened.

An invisible shield of sorts, though I could not tell what it was, suddenly appeared in front of Ruth, and it seemed to be deflecting the bright fire streaming toward her. The fire was so hot I could feel its heat even from where I stood. Ruth cried out in pain, for even though she was not consumed by the fire, it was still near enough to burn her. The fire continued, for the hound had inhaled deeply.

I then heard another voice. It was the voice of a man, also shouting in pain, but filled with anger and bravery. The fire finally ceased, and I beheld Jonah, the scout of Ravenhill, standing strong and true between the hound and Ruth. By way of his ability, which allows him to move as fast as a cheetah, he had come between the beast and Ruth just in time.

Jonah then charged at the hound full of adrenaline, fury, and skill. The beast was no match for the speed Jonah possessed and soon lay dead upon the ground.

No one was greatly injured, and we joined together to give the Great King praise for His goodness and protection. Ruth thanked Jonah for his courage. They had grown up together in the community at Ravenhill but now were no longer children. They were now warriors of the Great King.

"I take it that Captain Samuel received my letter?" Nathan inquired.

"He did," Jonah said. "He sent me at once."

"Your timing is from the Great King," Nathan said, shaking the hand of his lifelong friend. "You saved my sister, and for that I am ever in your debt."

"It was my pleasure," Jonah said in all humility and honor. "But I also come with news. The same aggression that Scroll-followers are experiencing here in Anthropolis is also being felt in Ravenhill. It isn't as aggressive, but Samuel feels that the seeds are being sown, seeds of blasphemy and man's reason above the authority of the Great King. There are strangers roaming the marketplace of Ravenhill, and they seem to bring destructive philosophies with them. Captain Samuel is asking that we all return to Ravenhill very soon."

Nathan looked at his wife, and I read from his expression that this news brought pain to his heart, for he knew it meant that her time with her family in the Haven would likely be cut short. She seemed to understand his mind.

"Do not fret," she said, putting her arm around him. "Our people in Ravenhill need us. I follow you, my husband."

"We will celebrate with our brothers and sisters in the Haven tomorrow," Nathan decided. "On the following day, we depart for Ravenhill."

"I am with you," Leah said with a smile. "Let us praise the Great King for His goodness to us."

The following day was such a joy and blessing to me. We feasted, danced, sang, and prayed. But the highlight of it all was the marriage that took place. In light of his rescue, Barnabas and Rachel decided that they didn't want another day to pass without being husband and wife. Rachel was a lifelong friend of Leah and came to her for marital advice.

"Your three greatest weapons," Leah explained to her in my presence, "are love, forgiveness, and thankfulness. You must write these three words upon the tablet of your heart. Love covers over a multitude of sins. It is patient, kind, and keeps no records of wrongdoing. You must love your husband this way, even when he is cross or not as loving as he should be.

"You must also recognize the power of forgiveness. To truly forgive is to live as if the offense never happened. You must always forgive any offense, immediately, even if he doesn't seek it, lest a bitter root grow within your heart and defile you and your home.

"Finally, you must be thankful. Don't focus on the little your husband does wrong or the qualities that he lacks. Instead focus on all that makes him wonderful and all in him that blesses you. I know wives who have husbands who lack much, and yet, they are more joyful than wives whose husbands lack little, simply because of the power of thankfulness. All that I have told you is powerful, and as you likely know, it is all commanded in the Scroll."

"That is very insightful!" Rachel exclaimed. "Please tell me more."

"Be joyful," Leah replied with a smile on her face. "Have your manner of living say to your husband, *I am blessed to be your wife*. When he walks into your home, smile and embrace him. Tell him how wonderful he is. Look your best and manage the affairs of his home well, as unto the Great King. In doing so, you will have a husband who embraces his role and who is bold and confident in his leadership. If you don't follow this counsel, you will have the opposite."

* * *

That evening, after the ceremony and festivities, I heard Rachel say to Leah, "I go now to enjoy the love of my husband. What precious grace is given to us by our Great King." She then looked at me. "May you also experience such a love, my friend. You are blessed to have Leah as your companion. Listen to her wisdom."

On the following morning, I began my journey back to Ravenhill. Our party was six: Nathan, Leah, Levi, Ruth, Jonah, and me. The trip home was such a delight, for I loved my friends. I had missed Hannah, but I realized that I had a greater fondness of friendships with people older than I, for I was able to learn from them how to mature and grow.

On the day of our arrival, I found my father, Martha, and Hannah all waiting for me at my home, for Jonah had scouted ahead to inform them of our arrival. It was so good to be back home, and I quickly fell into old friendships and old routines.

It wasn't long before we all heard the news that Leah was pregnant. I loved watching her belly grow during the following months and enjoyed our conversations about what it was like to have a human growing within you. Hannah and I remained busy working in the market, helping our fellowship, and training with the Scroll and bow. I did notice, however, a slight change in her. At first, I thought it was simply because of our time apart, and that perhaps I had changed a bit, and this made her seem different. But as I spent more and more time with her it seemed to me that she had changed for the worse. Not only was her attitude with her parents worse than normal, but so was her attitude toward the Scroll. The change in her attitude was so subtle, however, that I never openly asked her about it but simply hoped that it would return to what it had been.

I soon turned fourteen. Martha would visit on occasion, but otherwise I was left to my chores and work in the village with Hannah, and of course, my training with Leah and Ruth. One morning I heard a knock at my door. It was Hannah.

"You didn't meet me at the road as you normally do, so I wanted to make sure you were alright," she said.

"I'm so sorry," I replied. "I didn't wake up like I usually do. I was up late speaking with my father. He was leaving early this morning, and I wanted to visit with him before he left."

"I wish my father and I still spoke that way," she said with discouragement in her voice. I was going to ask her about their relationship, but she quickly changed the subject. "Guess who's going to be waiting for you today in the Market?" she remarked with a smile. I knew she was speaking of Troy. He had been speaking with me for nearly a year now. He was a few years older and handsome, but not a man of the Scroll.

"It doesn't matter," I said to Hannah with a bit of frustration in my voice. "He doesn't follow the Scroll."

"Does that even matter?" she asked with similar frustration. Her words shocked me.

"Does that even matter?" I repeated. "Of course it does. The Scroll forbids us to be with others that don't share our passion for the Great King. Troy isn't reborn. He doesn't know how to fight dragons. Why in the world would I want to be with him?"

Hannah remained quiet. We walked along for another moment until she broke the silence. "Do you ever think we're missing out on something big?" she suddenly asked.

"What do you mean?" I replied.

"I don't really know," she said. "I just wonder if there's something out there that we're missing."

"We are followers of the Great King," I responded with conviction. "We have the Scroll and the fellowship. What else could there be?"

"Don't you wonder if there's more for us, especially us girls? We help out our families, get married, have kids, and then get old. What if there's some secret that's being kept from us?"

"I haven't really ever thought about it," I said. "I honestly couldn't imagine what else there is. Aren't you still excited about getting married someday and being a mother?"

Hannah sighed. "I'm not as sure as I used to be. Wifehood and motherhood used to be something I looked forward to, but what if it's all blown out of proportion? What if being a wife and a mother isn't all it's cracked up to be?"

I was so shocked to hear Hannah's words. It was the first time I had ever heard a girl from the fellowship question or doubt the Scroll. I had noticed a change in Hannah since my return from Anthropolis, but it was so gradual that I had underestimated how bad it truly was. I reasoned that it was mainly based on her frustration with her parents, but something else was happening, for Hannah's words were outright denying the Scroll.

"Hannah," I said with compassion in my voice. "What's happening to you? You've never said things like this."

She remained quiet for a time, looking out upon the rolling prairie as we walked. "I don't know if I can tell you," she said at last.

"What do you mean?" I asked curiously. "Why not?"

"Can I trust you not to betray me?" she asked directly.

At first, I wasn't sure how to respond. I had been taught by my father to entrust all things to his care and to never keep secrets, but I was also faced with the idea that Hannah might be in trouble and wouldn't open up to me unless I gave her my pledge of confidence. I knew that I should have refused her, but my heart gave into folly.

"Of course you can trust me not to betray you," I said. "I can keep a secret."

Hannah stopped and looked at me closely. "Are you sure?" she asked.

"Absolutely," I responded.

"I was approached a few months ago by a woman in the marketplace," she said, as we turned and continued to walk down the gentle slope. "She is an amazing woman, Elizabeth," she continued. "A woman like no other. She knows more than any of our elders, and she has shown me a better way."

"A better way?" I asked. "A better way to do what?"

"To live," Hannah replied.

"A better way to live?" I repeated. "Better than what? Surely not better than the Scroll?"

"In addition to the Scroll," she replied. "This woman has progressed beyond the wisdom of our forefathers. She has discovered truth, especially regarding womanhood, that is setting women free like never before."

"Setting women free?" I asked. "What do you mean? Free from what?"

"Free from the dominion of men," Hannah explained. "Women are breaking their chains. They are now able to pursue their own dreams and happiness instead of being forced into a lifestyle that might sound glorious but is actually a trap."

"A trap?" I asked. "Surely, you aren't talking about being a wife and a mother?"

Hannah remained silent.

"Who is she?" I asked curiously.

Hannah exhaled and bit her lip. "I'm not sure I want to tell you," she said. "Forgive me. Come with me tonight and you will meet her."

"Meet her?" I asked. "You mean a meeting in the town square?"

"Oh no," she replied. "It is a secret meeting. But I am allowed to bring a friend. You will love her."

I knew that my father wouldn't approve of me going to a secret meeting of people who are speaking against the Scroll. I knew I should refuse, but I couldn't. I wasn't sure if it was my curiosity, my love for Hannah, or something else that made me justify my actions, but I felt that I couldn't resist.

"So when exactly is this meeting?" I asked.

"It is an hour after sunset," Hannah replied.

"Where is it?" I asked.

"You promise not to tell anyone?" she pressed me.

"I promise," I replied.

"It's in the forest," she said.

Chapter 14

I looked at Hannah with a look of fear, frustration, and anger mixed together.

"Hannah," I said solemnly. "You actually go into the forest at nighttime?"

"It is safe," she said. "Trust me."

I took a deep breath and closed my eyes, trying to regain my composure. What had begun as an ordinary walk to the marketplace had now turned into a nightmare. I had learned that my dearest friend was entertaining ideas that seemed to be radically opposed to the Scroll. She had been meeting with a group of dangerous thinkers in the midst of the dragon's dominion, and I had promised not to tell anyone while giving the impression that I might possibly attend!

"You will come with me, won't you?" she asked longingly.

"Why would I want to?" I asked, mainly thinking out loud.

"Because you want to hear the truth about your future," she said. "You want to accomplish more than our foremothers achieved."

We were now entering the marketplace with its usual activity and commerce. At last I made a resolute decision. "I'm sorry Hannah," I said sincerely. "But I will not attend such a meeting."

Hannah scoffed, breathed deeply, and went straight to her work. We didn't speak for most of the morning, and my soul was in turmoil. About midday I heard a familiar voice call my name. It was Troy.

"Hello Elizabeth," he said.

I replied cordially, and then continued my work in a way as to not have to look at him.

"I was thinking that maybe we could go for a walk later today down by the creek," he said kindly.

I looked at him with a polite smile. "I'm sorry, Troy," I said, "but as I've told you before, if you want to spend time with me or have any real conversation with me, you must first speak with my father."

Troy sighed. "Yes, of course," he said, trying to be obliging. "I will try and do that soon I think. Farewell." He soon wandered off and was gone.

"You see?" Hannah said coming over from her booth. "This is exactly what I mean. Troy is a good boy, and he is attractive, and he likes you. And yet you don't even give him a chance because of teachings you've heard from people who supposedly have the truth."

"It is the truth," I told her. "And the truth always brings blessing."

"Tell that to my parents," she replied with pain in her voice. "They've been following the Scroll for years, and look at where it's gotten them."

I sighed deeply at the pain that my friend carried from her family experience. Her parents claimed allegiance to the Great King but for some reason didn't seem to have a blessed marriage.

"Listen to me, Hannah," I said. "My father has always told me that we can't base truth on experience, but on the Scroll. Experience can be deceiving. The Scroll, when interpreted properly, is always correct."

Hannah gathered up her things. "Then maybe you need to hear a better interpretation," she said, and she walked back toward her home. I stood there, in the midst of the marketplace and yet all alone. My mind was racing.

'What if I have been told a lie?' I asked myself. Or, perhaps I hadn't been told a lie but only something that wasn't completely true? The Scroll is truth, but as I had just declared, it must be interpreted properly.

Soon I headed back to my home. There I enjoyed a wonderful dinner with my father who had returned from his trip. Martha, along with Captain Benjamin, had also come to visit and soon there was a wonderful gathering of the aged around our campfire. As was their custom, they spoke of the Scroll and the Great King. Their words were both comforting and unsettling. A seed of doubt had been sown in my mind, and it frustrated me greatly. Usually I would have loved just to sit and listen and ask questions at such a gathering, but I was unable to do so. There was a curiosity and suspicion in my soul that had to be resolved. The sun was now setting. I asked my father for permission to take a long walk. He gave it, and I headed towards the edge of the forest.

My heart was racing, for I knew that I was doing wrong, but I was concerned for Hannah. Not only that, but a part of me wanted to hear the words of the woman. I wanted to hear her words and to see if I was indeed deceived as Hannah had claimed.

I soon saw two figures walking up to the forest's edge from further ahead of me, and it seemed that they were unaware of my presence. The two figures came to the tree line and began speaking quietly. I then noticed a third person, likely a guard of the meeting, who allowed them to enter. Suddenly, without forethought, I entered the forest from where I was and began to make my way toward where I thought they were meeting. I knew I was in the forest, in dragon territory, but I didn't think of this much, likely because other humans were nearby. I soon saw the glow of the fire and heard voices. I came as near as seemed safe, and then climbing a large birch tree, I made my way up to where I felt completely concealed.

Six figures, all women, were around the campfire. They had all been cloaked but were now unveiled and speaking softly to each other. It was clear to me who the leader was. Even amongst the dim light of the fire I could tell that she was the most beautiful woman I had ever beheld, and everyone seemed to be drawn to her. Suddenly I blinked, squinted, and looked again. I recognized her, but I couldn't tell from where. Then it hit me. She was the woman I had seen two years earlier in the marketplace who had come to my rescue with the shop owner.

A cloaked figure then entered the circle. "Ah, and here she is!" the leader spoke. "Hannah, how wonderful to see you. Is your friend with you?"

Hannah removed her hood and sat down. "No, Vashti," she said. "I'm sorry but she isn't. I had hoped she would join us."

"It is of no consequence," she said, though I thought I saw a measure of disappointment in her eyes. "The faithful will be gathered in their own timing."

As Vashti spoke, I was taken aback by her charisma. I guessed her to be about twenty-three years of age, and yet she spoke with the skill of one of the elders.

"It is time to begin," she said solemnly. "Listen clearly. You are the foundation. Upon you and your sacrifice and allegiance, a new day is dawning, a day within which women will rule." The ladies around the circle nodded in agreement, though Hannah did not. I could tell that she was inspired by Vashti, but not yet completely loyal.

"Hannah?" Vashti commented suddenly. "Why do you tremble? You don't look well."

"It's the forest," Hannah replied. "It frightens me to be here, for this is where dragons prowl."

"I'm not afraid of dragons, my sister," she said. "For they run from me. I have power over them."

"Power over dragons?" Hannah asked. "You mean to say that you fight them? We train to fight them."

"Fight them?" Vashti asked. "I could fight them, I suppose, if I wanted to. But I don't need to fight them. As I said, I have power over them. They submit to me. Why else do you think I am able to sit within the forest unafraid? I know they won't hurt me."

"But how?" Hannah inquired curiously. "How do you keep them from attacking you?"

"Your question is a good one, child," Vashti said. "The answer is simple. The dragons will not attack something more beautiful than themselves." At these words, the other women present made sounds of amazement.

"There is a power available," Vashti continued, "a power that can make you the most dominant force on this planet. You follow the Scroll, don't you Hannah?"

"I do," Hannah said hesitantly.

"You don't need to be ashamed," Vashti said encouragingly. "The Scroll has many wonderful insights for us; yet there is more to discover. You must progress beyond the reaches of the Scroll. There is power there, but the greatest power is within." I found these words to be dangerous, yet I was so enraptured by her beauty and charisma that I continued to listen with interest.

"So, you are saying," another woman began, "that eventually you stopped following the Scroll?"

"I wouldn't say I stopped following it," Vashti said. "Only that I found something better."

"Better?" Hannah mused, seemingly inspired by the notion. "But what would be better than the Scroll?"

"Freedom," Vashti replied. "That's what is better than the Scroll; a life where you make your own rules instead of fitting into a mold that another makes for you. Trust your own hearts, and trust your own beauty. You were made beautiful for a reason. Truth be told, there is a beauty that you haven't even tapped into. There is a power that you haven't yet realized."

She then motioned to another woman in the circle. "Why, just look at Tabitha?" Vashti said with a smile. "She is very active in the Castle here in Ravenhill. She loves the Scroll, and yet, she has found through us a better way, haven't you, Tabitha?"

"I have indeed," Tabitha said with a smile. "For so many years of my life I was indoctrinated to believe that the only authority was the Scroll. Those years were oh so dull and enslaving! Don't get me wrong. The Scroll does have some good things to say, and I adore the Great King. And yet, the Scroll is, after all, just a scroll. It is a piece of paper. The Great King was a man, flesh and blood, and He taught me to love life and believe in myself. The Great King, therefore, is really an idea when you think about it. He symbolizes for all of us what we can accomplish when we believe in ourselves, just like He believed in Himself.

"Before my eyes were opened, I was so bored, just being a wife and a mother. But now that I have found the truth in my heart, not on just some old piece of paper, now I have true freedom and life. And it is all thanks to Vashti. I am now able to help other women find freedom. There are so many young wives in our Castle that are stuck in the same trap I was years ago. But they won't be for long. I'm going to show them how to find their own truth and to live life to the full."

As the woman spoke, Vashti's face was full of ecstasy and excitement. The woman continued. "Do not underestimate this movement, ladies," she said. "Nothing is impossible for us. Why, our own Castle here in Ravenhill has just elected its first female captain." At these words all of the women present gasped in unbelief and joy.

"She is only one of the lesser captains," Tabitha explained, "but I have no doubt that soon Castles will employ lead female captains, for this is the way of the future. Already many of us are wielding the sword. Oh, who would have thought that we would see such days! When I was younger, I would have never dreamed of being able to wield a sword, and now, I own four of them. And when I grip them, I feel like a woman with power!

"At first, many men, and even some women, opposed such things. But all I had to simply say was, *'This is what I feel in my heart is the right thing to do.'* That always makes them stand down, and it is the truth after all. So take heart, my sisters. There is no institution that exists that isn't going to be infiltrated by this revolution."

"Well, isn't that wonderful?" Vashti asked with a laugh of jubilation. "We will indeed bring this into every realm of our society: the schools, the marketplace, and even the Castles. Thank you, Tabitha, so much for sharing. The beautiful reality that Tabitha has discovered is that the truth can be different for each of us. It can be exactly what you want it to be."

I had never heard anyone speak in this way, and even though I thought it to be incorrect, it moved something within me. A part of me wanted to believe it. I wanted to believe that there was something more.

"Well," Vashti said at last. "It is now time for a more secretive conversation that only those who have pledged their allegiance can attend." She then looked at another woman sitting with her back to the depths of the forest.

"Do you have them?" she asked. The woman nodded, and then revealed a bag from behind her.

"Excellent," Vashti said and then turned to Hannah. "Forgive me, sister. But you must leave now. But don't worry. I will see you again soon. And I am still very eager to meet your dear friend." Hannah stood to her feet.

"Thank you," she said.

"Of course," Vashti replied. "You are a beautiful young woman, though your true beauty is only just beginning to emerge." Hannah then bowed and left the group.

All was quiet. I remained in the tree, as still as possible, eager for what was in the bag. As the woman removed them, they looked like stones, painted different colors and smooth. I then discovered the truth. They weren't stones. They were dragon eggs. I tried not to gasp aloud. I had heard of dragon breeders who would plant eggs upon the edges of the forest and sometimes would even raise baby dragons for a time and then let them go. I was appalled and a sudden terror came over me. I quickly slid down the tree and exited the forest. My dreams that night were uneasy. The next morning, as I met Hannah on the way to the marketplace, I was still shocked and confused by everything that was happening.

"The meeting was wonderful," Hannah said. "I wish you would have been there. Everything the woman said was amazing."

"But she is wrong," I said, trying to bring myself back to what I knew I believed.

"How would you know?" Hannah retorted.

"Because I was there, hidden and listening," I confessed.

"Seriously?" Hannah exclaimed. I thought she would be mad at me, but she was actually happy at the news.

"Have you ever seen such a beautiful woman?" she asked. "I've never seen any woman in our fellowship as beautiful and free as Vashti. She seemed completely unbound from anything, without a care in the world."

"Vashti's words are blasphemy," I said. "They may sound good, but they are wrong, so wrong." We then arrived at the marketplace and began to set up our shops.

"You should see the way she dresses," Hannah replied, taking no note of my earlier remark. "Her clothing is so amazing. I wish I dressed like that. People look at me in the market, for a different reason, because my dress is so peculiar. But dressing and acting like Vashti would turn heads for a different reason."

"Hannah!" I said in frustration. "I'm shocked by your words. Why would you want to turn such heads in your direction? They would be the heads of those aligned with the world and opposed to the Scroll."

"Once again," she said. "How do we know that is true? What if it isn't? What if we are the ones deceived and everyone else is correct?"

This last question penetrated my heart and mind profoundly. *'What if we are the ones deceived and everyone else is correct?'* The thought terrified me. I stopped my work and stood still. Hannah seemed to see the wheels turning in my mind.

"I'm not going to be tricked any longer," she said confidently.

"I must return home," I said, confused and frustrated at the circumstance. I was upset by Hannah's words, as well as my lure to Vashti. Deep down, I believed her words were wrong, but at the same time, I couldn't deny that I could be completely deceived. And deep down, I couldn't hide the fact that I found something in Vashti to be very attractive, and it challenged my whole way of thinking.

"Don't misunderstand me," Hannah said. "I'm not denying that the Great King is real. I'm just saying that maybe He's misrepresented. Maybe our fellowship and teachers have things wrong. And maybe, just maybe, Vashti is an answer to prayer."

"I'm sorry," I told Hannah with a forced smile. "I just can't talk or think about this anymore. My mind is too confused. I will return shortly. I just need some time."

I walked away and within a few seconds was crying. As I rounded the corner, I was sobbing uncontrollably. In only one day, all that I believed was dashed to pieces in my mind and I didn't know how to correct it. I suddenly felt all alone and hopeless. I rounded another corner of the busy market and found a place to sit down. My tears continued. I then felt a hand upon my shoulder. It was Troy's.

"What happened?" he said in a kind voice, and sitting down next to me continued. "You look like you need someone to help you, to comfort you. I am here." He then took my hand and raised my chin up to his with his other hand.

"You are so wonderful and beautiful," he said to me, and I felt my heart flutter. "Tell me what is wrong, and I will comfort you. I will protect you and shield you from all harm. Be my girl, Elizabeth, and you will never hurt again."

Chapter 15

At that moment I felt myself on the edge of a precipice. I could either remain strong emotionally, or I could fall into the arms of this young man. He was handsome indeed, and strong. I thought of how good it would feel to let him hold me and cherish me. I would be his girl, and everyone would know that he only wanted to be with me. I would be his girl, and it would make me feel so valuable and beautiful.

I felt myself beginning to fall. His touch was so comforting. But then something happened; something deep down in my soul came to the surface. They were the words of Leah: *'Your heart is a precious jewel, Elizabeth, and it's reserved for your future spouse. You must give it to no other.'* More tears welled up in my eyes, and for some reason, Caleb came to my mind. I quickly stood to my feet, Troy's grip was removed, and I felt a new clarity of thought.

"I'm sorry Troy," I said plainly. "I cannot accept your invitation to be your girl. I've never linked, and I never plan to."

He started to speak, but I had already turned and was walking away quickly. As I rounded a corner, I saw Martha, sitting upon a stool with her quilts displayed for people to buy. I was nearly tempted to fall into her arms from emotional exhaustion and confusion. Despite my effort of restraint, she seemed to read my expression, likely from my blood shot eyes.

"Come sit with me awhile," she said kindly. I gladly accepted the invitation.

"You seem worn down, child," she said. "And I see the marks of tears, as if you're carrying a heavy burden."

For some reason, I didn't want to speak of Vashti or of my conversation with Troy. I wasn't sure if I was trying to hide something or if I was simply embarrassed or if it was all just too much to share. And so I told her of Hannah, the changes she was feeling and the shocking words she told me. Martha sighed.

"Such consequences I've feared for some time," she said sadly. "The spirit of maidenism is seeping in and doing its work."

"What is maidenism?" I asked.

"It is a spirit that the Great Dragon has woven into the hearts of both men and women," she replied. "It is a spirit that destroys women, destroys men, destroys marriages, destroys families, and destroys the next generation. At first it sounds good, like something that is pure. But it is a guise for the plans of the enemy. People, especially women, drink it to the dregs, thinking it is good medicine, but they are actually consuming poison."

"But how is it in Hannah?" I asked with sincerity and amazement in my voice. "She's one of us!"

"No one is immune to the wiles of the enemy," Martha explained. "I will explain to you how this has happened. There are a handful of ways that maidenism enters a person's heart. Too often it is the example of the mother that corrupts the daughter. A mother's example is strong, in particular with how she treats her husband. If a daughter perceives that the mother is disrespectful, controlling, or unaffectionate with her husband, then that daughter will be poisoned and corrupted, usually without knowing it until it is too late."

As Martha said these words I instantly thought of Hannah's mother. She dressed like a follower of the King and was very cordial with the fellowship, but I witnessed, more than once, her disrespectful tone to her husband. I had also remembered how I often wondered whether she or her husband was the head of that family. I thought of Hannah's father and realized something I had never before noticed. Of all the men in the fellowship, he seemed the least engaged, or that is to say, the least bold and gallant. It was as if the attitude of his wife had turned him into a man without confidence, a man who lacked any ambition in life. My perception was quickly confirmed as Martha continued.

"The mother's lack of belief in her calling as a wife becomes the hinderance of the father as well, for the Scroll speaks of the woman being the helper and completer of the man. And therefore, since the woman isn't focused upon the needs and vision of her man, the husband is slowly tamed from a lion to a lamb, from a man whose goal in life isn't to do great things for the Great King but to simply keep his wife happy. He is no longer confident in his role as leader, warrior, and teacher. He becomes like a needful puppy at the heels of the wife, always begging for her approval, always feeling empty of all true motivation and initiative.

"The ironic reality is that such a wife will never be happy, for she likewise has forfeited her role and mission. The daughter sees all of this and concludes that the words of the Scroll are empty of true power and purpose. The sons also, by extension, grow up like the father, effeminate and void of any traces of manliness. They perpetuate the curse that began with the mother. It is a sad and tragic disease, this maidenism."

As Martha explained the scheme of the enemy in regard to destroying both women and men I was overcome with sadness. I looked about us at the business of the market, my eyes beholding different people going about their day, and I wondered how many of them were infected with the disease of maidenism. Before Martha's explanation I would have guessed few, but now my eyes seemed opened. I suddenly saw the toxin of maidenism flowing through the veins of the populace.

Martha put her hand upon my shoulder as we sat together. "The Great King is calling you, Elizabeth, to be set apart from the lies and destruction of this attitude. He is calling you to be a true daughter of Zion." She then pulled me close.

"Do you remember that vision I showed you years ago," she said, "the story of those two people who were in love?"

"Of course I do," I said, the joyful memory bringing relief to my mind.

"Close your eyes and I will show you more," she said.

I quickly obeyed and my mind soon beheld the couple, happy and content as the last time I saw them. To view their faces again was such a pleasure and comfort, for I had fallen in love with them when I first beheld them years earlier. They were now parents, for a young son was playing upon the green grass around them, and the woman was again with child, but something was different. Their hearts didn't seem to be as interwoven as before. The joy was fading. The man seemed to be burdened and weighed down, as if every day was a labored endeavor. Then I beheld them speak to each other. It wasn't clear what the context was, only that his wife, that beautiful woman I had fallen in love with, had taken the reins of their family that were rightfully his.

He came in from a day of working the fields and sat at the table. "Well?" she said with an unpleasant air. "Is the crop going to be ready in time for the shipment next week?"

As the man spoke, he didn't even look his wife in the eyes. "It should be," he said with a downcast expression.

"It should be?" she repeated. "It must be. Do you realize how much this has been a burden to me? I already have one child to manage and another on the way, and now I have to worry about the fields which should have been your area of expertise."

"I tried to," he began.

"Don't interrupt me!" she snapped. "This is all your fault! If you had just listened to me in the first place, we would have had the harvest ready a week ago at least. But no, you had your crazy dream of half a dozen different vegetables when the whole time I told you it wouldn't work. Do you think I'm going to let you risk our family's security for your ludicrous fancies?"

As she lectured him, his eyes remained fixed upon the floor. His expression was one of a man who had no drive, no purpose. He was a man deflated and defeated.

After she finished, he slowly rose from his chair and walked outside, leaving the woman all alone. I watched her sitting there, her expression one attempting to justify an attitude she knew was wrong but couldn't seem to overcome. The guilt came upon her conscience, but she then shifted it back upon him. *'If only he would listen,'* she would say to herself. *'As long as he listens, we will survive.'* The vision began to fade, the last image of her all alone, her only company being her bitter and domineering personality.

"But I don't understand," I said to Martha, so saddened by what I had seen. "They were so in love, so beautiful. They still seem to have love, but it isn't the same. What happened?"

"You must understand," Martha said, "that a wife is a powerful force. She can make her husband, and she can break him. It's all contingent on whether or not she honors him. Is she going to follow his lead? Or is she going to take it from him? The Scroll is clear: The woman was made for her husband, as a helper, and is called to submit to him and to revolve her life around completing his vision for their family.

"There are three ways that women respond to this teaching. First of all, there are those women that outright deny it. To them, the command to submit to your husband is utter folly and is to be discarded and loathed as being absolute rubbish. The majority of women in this modern era hold to this view. They ignore the clear reality that in the beginning man was put in charge and the woman was made as a helper.

"The second way they respond is to accept that such words are indeed the words of the Great King, but deep in their hearts, they don't rejoice in the truth. They believe that the Scroll is true, and that the Great King made women to be helpers to men, but they hate it. They wished the Great King had done something different. This second view, my dear, is the view that this woman in the vision had. She believed the words were true, but she despised them, and in the end, it poisoned her marriage."

"Did the marriage ever improve?" I asked hopefully.

"You will have to wait and see," she replied.

"And what is the third way to respond?" I asked.

Martha smiled. "It is to not only believe that such instructions are the infallible words of the Great King but to also embrace such words."

"And is that your response?" I asked.

"Absolutely," she declared. "And you?"

"For certain," I said, and yet, even as I said the words, I knew they weren't exactly true. Doubt was plaguing my heart.

"Most women respond in the first way," Martha said. "They outright reject the Scroll. The next largest group are the second kind, who accept the words but inwardly abhor them. But the third kind of woman, who embraces and adores the words of our King, she is a rare jewel. Such like her are few. You must always be this woman, Elizabeth."

***

In the weeks to come, I noticed a continual change within Hannah. There was a battle raging within her. On certain days, she was a girl that loved the Great King. On other days, she was a girl walking in the philosophies of maidenism. I

had to admit, however, that the battle was not only raging inside of her, but in me as well.

I began thinking more and more of Troy. At first, I didn't think twice about him. He wasn't even an option. He had little to no characteristics on my list that my father encouraged me to write out of what I wanted in a spouse. But now, more and more, I began to think that he was a boy worthy of my heart. His words and his touch seemed to penetrate my heart and mind. I was crushed in spirit and sad, and Troy cared. He really cared about me and my feelings, or so it seemed. I pictured him one day being a mighty man for the Great King, much like Nathan.

I was worried, however, as to what others would think. I knew that Leah, Martha, and my father wouldn't approve, and yet, I more and more believed that it didn't matter. If Troy was the one, all that mattered was the approval of the Great King. I wanted so badly to open up and bare my soul to my father, but I was scared. In the end, I decided to speak to him, but to not fully disclose all my thoughts. The opportunity came the next morning, around our small breakfast table.

"Father?" I said. "How do I know when I've met the right young man to marry?"

"What a beautiful question," he said in response. "I've been hoping you would ask. The answer isn't as complicated as most would presume. First, the boy must be aligned with the Scroll. No one is perfect, of course, but this young man must truly long to obey and serve the Great King. And second, you know he is the right young man when you don't want to go on living life without him. You could live without him, of course, but you don't want to. Your heart has become knit with his, and you want to serve him for the rest of your life. You must see in him a man with a vision for his future that you want to assist, for his plan will become yours. And if your father agrees, and the captains in your fellowship approve, then you move forward."

I remained still. I was inwardly frustrated at the fact I knew Troy wasn't a boy who was aligned with the Scroll. "What if," I began slowly. "What if the young man isn't aligned with the Scroll but will be one day?"

"If the young man isn't aligned with the Scroll," my father replied, "then he isn't ready to lead a woman in life, and therefore isn't ready to get married. Many a woman has fallen into the trap of believing that the man will one day become a man of the Scroll only to experience a lifelong disappointment of never being married to the man she thought he would become."

"Why would a girl marry such a boy?" I asked, curious at my father's answer.

"It is simple," he answered. "She gives her heart away, and so it is too late to turn around. She allows the boy to capture her heart and mind, and once her heart is his, she will look beyond any barriers in order to be with the boy who has her heart. This is why, my dear, linking is so dangerous. When parents allow their child to link, they are doing just that; they are linking their child's heart to another's prematurely. And very often their bodies soon link as well. That is why you must follow the teaching of the Scroll and guard your heart above all else."

Our conversation was interrupted by a knocking at the door. It was Leah and Ruth.

"Forgive our intrusion," they said with bows in hand. "But we were wanting to train with Elizabeth if she's available."

"Always!" my father said with thanksgiving in his voice. "That is, of course, if she wants to."

I quickly grabbed both bow and quiver and followed the ladies outside. The morning air was cool and the birds were singing. My heart was still heavy with the last words my father had spoken to me, *'you must guard your heart above all else.'*

Leah's belly was beginning to show her second pregnancy. It was comforting to be near to these two women who were so dear to me. They exhibited the quality of womanhood to which I wanted to attain, and yet, Vashti's face was also present in my thoughts.

"So," Ruth asked, "how is my dear friend doing today?"

"Very well, thank you," I replied, trying to hide my inner struggles.

"Good," Leah replied. "Today you will train in a way you have not yet experienced."

We were walking toward the forest's edge, and my heart began to grow anxious. "What are we doing?" I asked, unable to hide the fear in my voice.

"Don't fret, my sister," Ruth said. "You are ready for this."

"Do you remember the serpent that lured you from your window that night that the village burned?" Leah asked.

"Of course," I said. "Why?"

"Look ahead," she said.

My eyes raised upward, and what I beheld caused my heart to tremble within me. I dropped my bow to the ground and put my hand over my mouth.

Chapter 16

There before me, upon the outer edge of the forest, was the dragon that I first beheld six years earlier. Its long serpent body had doubled in length and was now around thirty feet long. Its four long and skinny legs made my skin crawl. It was a formidable creature. My first inclination was to turn and run, but my training took over, and I stood my ground.

"Remember," Leah said calmly. "It can't hurt you. It is all illusion and deceit. It can only have power over you if you allow it to."

My body was shaking, and my breathing was labored. I reached down and retrieved my bow.

"It's alright," Ruth said. "You've got this. You are a woman of the Scroll."

I could tell that Leah and Ruth were somewhat surprised at my fear and apprehension, but I wasn't. My heart, which used to be a place of purity, truth, and confidence, was now a place of doubt and distress.

"Well," the dragon spoke, its voice making my heart tremble. "Has the Great King really said that you can't live your life the way you want to?"

I took a few deep breaths and pulled from deep within me the faith I still hoped I had. "I can live my life," I replied. "I am free to live my life and pursue my dreams, but the Great King has told me that I cannot be the leader, and ultimately, that I must yield to the Great King Himself."

"So then," it replied, "you are not free."

"I am free," I insisted. "The Great King gives me rules to live by, but that doesn't mean I'm not free."

"You foolish child," the serpent retorted as it stepped closer to me. "Even if you had the entire garden of life at your disposal, if the Great King forbids you to eat from even one tree in that garden, then you are a slave and not free."

My heart wavered and my mind was puzzled by the serpent's words. Something in me agreed with the serpent. How could I be free if the Great King dictated even one area of my life? A voice within me brought me aid, *'The Great King is Lord of all and worthy of your life. The Great King knows better how to live your life than you do.'* A measure of confidence returned.

"I am His servant," I said after a moment of silence. "He leads me, and I follow."

"And what will happen to you if you don't follow the Great King?" the dragon asked. "What will happen if you do what you think is best?"

I thought of Troy, and I was reminded of Vashti's words. She claimed to have a better way.

The serpent now began to encircle me.

"Answer me," the serpent said slowly. "What will happen if you reject the Great King?"

I replied slowly and articulately. "If I do not follow the Great King, then I will die."

"You will not surely die," the dragon said with a smile.

"I will die," I replied with anger in my voice.

"No," the serpent replied slowly with confidence. "That is not true. You have been deceived. Think of others you know that have lived their lives the way they thought best. Have they died? Of course not. You will not die."

"I will die!" I screamed, tears flowing down my cheeks.

"No," it repeated peacefully. "You will surely not die. Instead, you will live. Indeed, you will become like the Great King Himself. You will be truly alive, with the wisdom to make your own choices, to choose your own destiny." The serpent then extended its hand to me. "Come here, my child," it said. "All freedom and beauty and pleasure are with me."

As I looked at the serpent, I suddenly felt the same emotion I felt with Troy and also with Vashti. I took a step forward.

"Elizabeth!" Leah shouted, and I could sense in her voice both her shock and her disappointment. "You must be strong in the Great King. You are better than this!"

I stopped, hesitated and tried to step back. Tears continued to flow down my cheeks.

"Don't listen to them," it said. "They are holding you back from becoming the real you. Don't you want to be beautiful? Don't you want to be loved?"

My mind was in torment. I simply wanted everything and everyone to go away from me. "Go away," I said at last. "Go away and never come back." The countenance of the serpent changed. Its face grew fearsome. It uncoiled from around me and slithered back and forth in anger.

"I'm not going anywhere," it said. "Not without your corpse in my gullet."

"You can't," I said trembling. "They told me you can't touch me."

"Another lie," the serpent said, and I noticed smoke coming from its nostrils. "You believe all of their lies, and therefore, you are not worthy to live." The creature made a cough-like sound, and a ball of fire about the size of an apple flew towards me and struck me in my chest, knocking me to the ground.

"Stand up!" Ruth shouted. "Don't believe its lies! Hold on to the truth of the Scroll!"

I stood to my feet. The beast was coming nearer. "But you said it couldn't touch me!" I shouted.

"They lied!" the serpent interjected.

I turned to run. The last thing I remembered hearing was the cries of Leah and Ruth. "Never turn your back to the enemy!" they shouted with fear in their voices.

I then heard the serpent project another fiery dart which struck me in the back. I landed upon the ground, and all consciousness left me. The last thought in my mind was the echoing words of the serpent. *'They lied to you. It's all a lie.'*

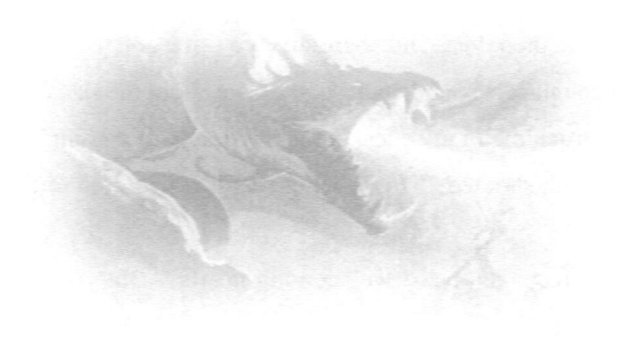

Chapter 17

I woke up on the ground, my chest and back both in pain and my stomach in knots. Leah and Ruth were standing over me, their heads turning side to side as lookouts. I slowly sat up.

"Is it gone?" I asked.

"It is," Leah said. She then looked at me with a sorrowful expression. "Forgive me," she said. "I thought you were ready for this. I was mistaken."

I hung my head down and wept. I wanted to tell her that it wasn't her fault. I wanted to tell her about all that had happened. "I'm sorry," I said sobbing. "I've failed you both."

My two sisters embraced me, also weeping. "You haven't failed us," Ruth declared.

"No indeed," Leah testified. "Do not worry, my dear Elizabeth. You have fallen, but you will rise stronger than before."

But will I? I thought to myself. Was this end of my pilgrimage as a daughter of the Great King? What if the serpent and Vashti were right? What if I was missing out? What if the Great King was good, but something out there was even better?

I went home defeated and dejected. And for the many months that followed, I continued to struggle with the question of what was really true. Troy continued to speak kind words to me and give me gifts in the market. My training almost ceased completely, for I lacked the motivation. I assumed that Martha could sense what was happening, and so I began to avoid her, along with everyone else, preferring to be alone.

One evening, deep in the dead of night, I was suddenly awakened from my sleep. At first, I was a bit disorientated, and I tried to fall back asleep. But then I realized that I heard voices. One was that of my father, the other of a man I didn't know. I slowly tilted my head to the side and slightly opened my eyes.

There, seated around our tiny table in the middle of our cottage, were my father and a man I'd never seen before. He looked much like my father, yet was older, much older it seemed. The only light was from the candle that burned upon the table, lighting the faces of the two men as they spoke long into the night.

"So, you are telling me that there is a new enemy?" my father asked.

"Not a new enemy," the man answered, "but a new scheme." His aged voice was strong and formidable, even when gently spoken.

"The Scroll commands us to not be ignorant of the enemy's schemes," my father said. "Please tell me what you know."

The aged stranger lowered his voice. "There are folks about," he said slowly, "some of them agents of the Great Dragon and most of them his useful fools. They are going after women."

"What do you mean?" my father asked. "As slaves?"

"Not physical slaves, but slaves in their minds and souls. The enemy is trying to pull all women away from the ways of the Scroll. His strategies are many, and they are brilliant."

"What strategies?" my father asked, his face filled with terror.

"There are many," the aged man began. "One strategy of the Great Dragon is to darken the hearts of women. He knows they are powerful and can make or break future generations. His servants are trying to get women so involved in things that seem good that they avoid their roles in the family. Married women are now looking for a different identity than that of wife and mother. They are seeking power, influence, and purpose in the marketplace. Many single women are avoiding marriage, and especially children, so they can make a name for themselves in the same way."

"Surely you are misled," my father said. "Surely women haven't been convinced of such an empty exchange: the joys of the home for the burden of the workplace!"

"They have indeed," the stranger said. "Some pursue such ends deliberately, having been deceived by modern philosophy. Others are innocently trapped."

"Innocently trapped? How?"

"I am now seeing this happen often," the man explained. "I have been traveling much and have even seen this with Scroll-followers, I am sad to say. Women are being convinced that being with child ruins their lives and their bodies. So they enter into marriage with an idea to wait a few years before they have children. At first it was a year or two, then three. Now many are waiting five years or more."

"It perplexes me as to why people would wait to have children," my father said.

"It is the philosophy of the time, the *youngling* philosophy," the stranger explained. "Children aren't growing up, and so, even in marriage they desire to be without responsibility for an extended time."

"How shameful," my father said, "to go into marriage with such selfish, childish thinking!"

"And so," the man continued, "the scheme of the Great Dragon is working and taking hold. This is how the woman gets innocently trapped into being a woman of the marketplace instead of the home and Great King. During the first five years of the marriage, the woman is working as hard as the man in commerce and in the marketplace. As you would expect, the couple enjoys a double portion during those years, matching their lifestyle with their income. Then, when the woman is eventually found to be with child, she is suddenly faced with a difficult choice: to either relinquish her profession, duel income, and magnificent lifestyle so she can devote herself to being a wife and mother, or, to find someone to care for her child while she continues to share in Adam's curse.

"As you can imagine, few are willing to sacrifice all the material possessions, power, and prestige they have grown to love so dearly. Others are trapped because of debt with the bankers, a debt which enslaves them to a duel income. Few of these women are able to return to the ways of the Scroll. They had dreams of motherhood in their youth, but now such dreams seem utterly impossible and unrealistic."

"That is a trap indeed," my father said. "I can see very clearly how basic misunderstanding can lead to such devastation and enslavement."

"Times are changing," the stranger testified, "and they will only continue to drift away from the ways of the Great King, for the enemy's hold on these people is strong. The foundations of our forefathers have crumbled. Society has lost the ancient path. Even non-Scroll followers, in our youth, were very much aligned with the Great King. But now, the philosophies of the Great Dragon have taken hold like never before."

My father hung his head in dismay. "This is grave news, my friend."

"It gets worse," the man said. "The enemy is also trying to convince women that the ways of the Great King make them inferior."

"Inferior?" Samuel repeated. "That is absurd! According to the Scroll, they are the treasured gender, the sacred gender, the lifegiving gender."

"Amen," the man declared. "But you know how the Great Dragon operates. He is a liar. All of his strategies are rooted in deceit. And so now, you have girls who grow up believing that marriage is slavery and that to be a mother is a burden. And so, as they blossom into young women, they come to despise themselves."

"That makes sense," my father said. "For as they look at their bodies, they will see the blessings of wifehood and motherhood within their very nature. And since they have learned to associate femininity with captivity, they will renounce it. This is most dire, my friend. For me, it is unthinkable!"

"It will soon come here, to Ravenhill. It was birthed in the academies of Anthropolis. It is spreading now through the theaters, the academies, and even the Castles."

My father breathed deeply. "Good heavens," he said with pain in his voice.

"Sadly, there is more," the man continued. "With the death of femininity, we are also witnessing the abolition of men. For as women no longer look to men to lead them, to protect them, and to provide for them, men are slowly losing their manliness. They are not growing up. Their courage, resolve, and responsibility are all fading away. They no longer know how to think. They are men without chests!"

My father shook his head in disappointment.

"There is much more," the stranger replied with heaviness in his voice, "too much to tell. The ripple effects are boundless. I will burden you with only one more result of society embracing such philosophies."

The stranger then took a deep breath. "Women are now playing in the games," he said.

My father sat upright, looking at the stranger with a look of confusion, shock, and unbelief. "The games?" he said. "What games do you mean? You don't mean the games of the coliseum, do you?"

"I do," the man said.

My father still looked perplexed. "You mean to tell me," he began, "that women are running about doing mock combat, all for the amusement of others?"

"Indeed, they are. The philosophy of this age teaches that *what men do, women should do*, and so women are being led away from the Great King's true purpose for them."

"Then we are doomed," my father said quietly as he sat back in his chair. "If what you are telling me is indeed true, that women are being convinced to do all that men do, then our way of life, our faith, all of it will soon be swept away."

The old stranger smiled. "You forget one thing, Samuel. You forget the most important thing. It is this: The Great King is in control. He knows all of this is happening. He is allowing it. This should comfort you. For even if this is His judgment upon this land, we still have His promise."

"What promise?" my father asked.

"That He will build His Castle," the man answered passionately. "Do not fear, my friend. The Great King promised to keep a remnant. We have all the hope and power and opportunity possible at our fingertips."

My father again sighed deeply. "Tell me, my old friend. Please tell me. In response to this coming aggression, what should I do?"

"Preach the Scroll," the man answered, trembling with righteous fury, "and inform your flock. There is no doubt about it. The enemy has realized the power of gender, and so he has fixed his sights upon it. He knows that if he can get women to become more like men and men to become more like women they will fail. He knows, rightly so, that the Great King made us male and female and that within those words is immeasurable power."

"But aren't at least some of the Castles standing against this philosophy?" my father asked.

"Some are, the Great King be praised. But many which began bold and honest, are now giving in. Some are just truly deceived and believe it is right. Others are giving in to the fear of man. They are being convinced that it is the intentions of the heart that matters, not the truths of the Scroll."

"What nonsense!"

"That is why, Samuel, you must teach your flock that gender is paramount. You must teach them that, as parents, they have only this one strategic goal: to raise their sons to be true men, according to the Scroll, and to raise their daughters to be true women, according to the Scroll. If this is their goal, then you must convince them that they will most assuredly succeed."

My father then smiled. "That almost sounds too simple," he said, "doesn't it?"

"It does sound simple," the stranger said, "but simplicity is not opposed to power. Think on it, friend. What does it mean for a son to be a true man? It means that he is honest, hardworking, educated, and a provider and protector of women and children. It means that he is holy, that he walks in the ways of the Great King. Do you not think that is equivalent with success?"

"It is indeed," Samuel said.

"And what does it mean to be a true woman of the Scroll?" the stranger continued. "It means to be a woman of gentleness, propriety, submission, and truth. It means to be a woman of purity, devoted to the Great King, and if called to marriage, zealous for the vision of her husband, and dedicated to the sanctification of her children."

My father sat back in his chair and laughed. "Well," he said. "These are simple truths, yet powerful beyond words."

"And that is why," the man concluded, "we must preach the truth. The Great Dragon is taking hold of the Castles more than ever before. He is convincing the leadership there to avoid subjects that are too *'controversial.'* They no longer teach the full counsel of the Great King."

"In that case," my father said, "we are going to witness the death of true manhood and womanhood."

"We are indeed," the man said. "Though, not completely, for our Great King promises to always keep a remnant. And so, we must fight the good fight of faith. We must shepherd our sons and daughters and keep them from conforming to the patterns of this world."

My father leaned forward and sighed, and even in the dim candlelight I could see the sadness in his eyes. "Something else troubles you," the man said. "Something beyond this tragic news I have brought you tonight."

"It is my daughter," my father said. "I fear that she isn't well. I fear that she is drifting. I plan to speak with her in the morning. I have waited a few weeks, hoping she would come to me, but she hasn't."

He then looked up at his friend and smiled. "I wish you could see her," she is a beautiful girl.

"Even a blind man can see beauty," the visitor said. "I can see even more than you do."

"And what do you see?" my father asked attentively.

"I see a precious jewel," the man replied, "a jewel that the Great King created to shine like the stars in the heavens. And yet, her light is fading. The very question of our conversation is the battle raging within her. The subject of womanhood has been brought to prominence in her mind. She is at a crossroads, looking to the left and to the right, and soon she must make her choice."

"I will speak to her in the morning," my father replied.

"I pray that you are able to connect with her," the stranger said. "I pray that you still have her heart."

"Thank you," my father said. "And what about you, my old friend? What is your next move?"

"I must go to the mountains for a time," the man replied. "There is something awaiting me there."

The men talked on late into the night, and I soon drifted back into sleep, but not before I said a prayer to the Great King. "Help me," I prayed. "I'm not sure if you're real."

I was suddenly stirred again, this time by my father's hand upon my shoulder. "Wake up," he said. I arose and looked about me. The light of the morning sun was shining into our home, and the stranger was gone.

"What's wrong?" I asked.

"It's Leah," he said with a smile. "Her water has broken. The baby is coming soon!"

I quickly jumped out of bed and made myself ready. I was then out the door and hurried to Leah's home. I was so excited and happy for her. There were few women that I loved and respected as much. There was already a crowd gathered around her cottage. Martha, who was the chief midwife of our fellowship, was inside. I could also hear Nathan and Ruth encouraging Leah as she labored and breathed and groaned.

The anticipation that was building in my mind seemed to spur my desire to be a wife and mother. I felt a warmth within me that I hadn't felt in many months. I longed to hold the child, to see Leah smile upon the life she had birthed.

I suddenly heard Leah burst out in tears. *Tears of joy*, I thought to myself. Oh, the moment had come! But I then heard her scream. "No!" she shouted, and violent sobs followed. Ruth then came out of the tent, and all flocked to her.

"What's wrong?" Captain Benjamin asked.

Chapter 18

Ruth's face was flushed, and tears began to stream down her cheeks. "It's a stillbirth," she said. A cry of anguish and pain went up from all those present and many wept aloud. I couldn't believe it. Why did this happen? Why did the Great King do something to such an amazing follower of the Scroll? Everything seemed empty and hopeless. I wept for nearly an hour.

That evening, at dusk, we buried the child. It was a girl. They named her Naomi.

"The loss of a child can never be measured," my father said as he gave the eulogy that evening. "Naomi was beautiful, and indeed, she still is, for she is with her Creator. And though we will miss her dearly, we trust that she is at peace and that joy is all around her as she basks in the glory of the Great King."

As my father spoke, both Leah and Nathan wept. For me to see that mighty man and warrior cry was so humiliating and difficult. With every tear I felt the hope and life draining from my body. What had once been a joyful anticipation, having children, was now a dreaded fear. I didn't want it at all. Too much burden, too much pain. After the funeral, I wanted to go to Leah. I wanted to comfort her and Nathan, but I couldn't, seeing them there, weeping and holding each other, with little Levi beside them. How could I comfort them? What could I do?

I left the funeral feeling emptier than ever before. I didn't want to talk to anyone. I didn't want to be around anyone. I didn't want to wield the bow. I simply wanted to sleep and forget. I quickly put myself in bed before my father arrived at home and acted like I was asleep. I knew he intended to talk to me, and I was afraid of the conversation. Silent tears seemed to drench my pillow long into the night, for I was heartbroken at the wall that had been erected between my father and me. He had been my savior, provider, and protector, and now I was avoiding him.

I awoke the next morning exhausted. I quickly arose and left for the marketplace. My stomach was aching from hunger and anxiety. I arrived before Hannah and began getting my things in order. A voice awoke me from my depressing reverie.

"It's you," the voice said, longingly and kindly. It was the voice of a woman.

I looked up and recognized the person at once. It was Vashti. She was accompanied by two other beautiful women. "Hello," she said with a kind smile. "Your name is Elizabeth, right?"

"Yes," I replied, excited that she remembered me.

"You see, ladies?" she said referring to those with her. "This is the young lady I was telling you about. Isn't she beautiful? I came to her rescue a few years ago." The two women looked upon me with kind affection as they nodded their heads.

"I've been so looking forward to seeing you again," Vashti said. "It has been too long. I just recently returned, and it seems like fate has caused our paths to cross once again. Have you thought about our conversation that day? Did it make any impression upon you?"

I didn't know what to say. Had I thought about it? I had every day for the past few months. Did I know what was true and what was false? Not at all.

"I have," I said. "I still don't really know what to believe."

"Believe in yourself," she said. "Believe in what you can see and feel inside of you."

I remained quiet, not sure what to say. "What are your goals in life?" she asked.

"Well," I began carefully, "I do plan to marry someday."

"Marry?" she repeated. "That's no surprise to me. A beautiful girl like you will have many suitors, but why marry?"

This question took me off guard. "I don't understand," I said.

"Let me help you," she said patiently. "You have a desire to be together with a man. Like I said, I have no doubt that many men already like you. That's all good, but why marry?"

"What's the alternative?" I asked curiously.

"Just being together," she said plainly. "What's the point of putting a fancy title on it or of having a ceremony? Do you know where the idea of marriage came from?"

The answer seemed to come right out of me. "The Scroll?" I replied.

"You are correct," she said. "Though it was also in ancient history before the Scroll was written. It was invented by men. And do you know why they invented it?"

I shook my head. "They invented it to have domination over women," she said. "They wanted to keep us quiet, submissive, and enslaved."

"But," I said hesitantly, "it's in the Scroll."

"And who wrote the Scroll?" Vashti asked with a smile.

"The Great King," I answered.

"That's what your people believe," she answered. "Yet it is a metaphor. By faith, you take it as the words of the Great King, but in fact it was written by men.

And these men had agendas, namely, to dominate women, so as to fulfill their lust, power, and greed."

I was speechless.

"You must progress, my sister," she said. "You must progress beyond such narrow-mindedness. I know this is hard for you to accept, but it's true. The men in your fellowship want to use the women to simply cook for them and breed offspring. They breed their women like cattle, not at all concerned about their health and welfare."

I immediately thought of Nathan and Leah. Did he care about what the pregnancies had done to her body? Or about what the stillbirth had done to her emotionally?

"It is also the same with headship," she continued. "This idea that many accept that the husband is supposed to be the leader, or the 'head' of the family, why do people believe this?"

"It is also in the Scroll," I answered.

"Indeed," she said. "And once again, who wrote the Scroll? It was written by men. This will be hard for you to hear because of how much you've been indoctrinated. I can tell by how you dress that you belong to a fellowship of Scroll-followers. Listen to me, sister, for I tell you the truth: Freedom for our gender cannot be won without the abolition of both marriage and the patriarchal society."

I was again silent, not sure of what to say. I still wanted to believe in the Scroll and all that Martha, Leah, and my father had taught me, but I was also attracted to the gleam in Vashti's eyes. She seemed free in a way that I had never experienced within my fellowship, and she seemed more beautiful than any of the women I had ever known.

"You think on these words," she said with a smile. "A new day is coming. Our kind, women, will soon rise, and I hope you are one of the women leading the charge." She and the women with her gave me hugs and kind words of encouragement, and then walked away.

I was overcome with emotion and ideas. There was so much to digest. I decided to return home. I was only halfway through the market when I came face to face with Troy.

"Greetings Elizabeth," he said. "It's good to see you."

I returned the greeting, smiled, and tried to hide my turmoil. A part of me wanted to talk to him unreservedly, but I suddenly remembered the words of my father. I remembered that when a woman gives a man her heart, she shuts her eyes to all of the reasons that she shouldn't be with him.

"Have you thought about my request?" he said. "I had asked you to be my girl, and that is still what I want."

I shook my head slightly. "I'm sorry, Troy," I said. "I just don't think that's a good idea."

"What if I told you that I thought you were beautiful?" he asked. "And what if I even said that I thought I was falling in love with you?"

These words had a strong momentary effect on me. The first emotion was to want more of such words, to feel loved and protected, and to feel wanted by a handsome man. Something within me, however, kept me aware of my father's wisdom. It was as if he was there with me, speaking to me.

"You are kind, Troy," I said, "but my heart is reserved for another."

"Another?" he repeated "Who?"

"I don't know," I answered. "But it will be a man who loves the Scroll and who follows the Scroll."

"I like the Scroll," he said smiling.

"You do?" I asked, seemingly drawn to such a confession.

"Absolutely," he said. "It's an amazing manuscript."

"But do you believe it?" I asked.

"With all of my heart," he replied.

"And so," I continued, "you are a follower of the Great King?"

He hesitated, and the pause seemed to awaken me from my slumber. "I think I am," he said. "Well, I want to be. Maybe you can show me how."

My heart was pounding within me with so much emotion! I felt like falling to my knees and sobbing. I opened my mouth, but all that came out was, "Excuse me a moment." And I turned and made my way quickly through the crowded lane. Soon I was running across the small bridge and up the hill, toward my cottage, and then near the forest. I turned. No one had followed me. I fell to my knees and wept.

I felt so alone. I felt that no one understood me, and that no one was with me. The Great King didn't at all feel near, or even alive. I was attracted to Troy and to Vashti, but that all seemed so uncertain and confusing. I wept so long that I nearly fell asleep there on the prairie. Eventually my eyes dried and I sat up. The sun was in the West; the evening breeze was blowing; I looked up at the sky.

"Please give me love," I said, not even sure who I was addressing. "Give me someone to love. Give me someone who will love me."

I looked toward the forest, and something caught my eye. I couldn't make it out, only that it shined, sparkling in the light of the setting sun that shone under the brush. As I approached the edge of the forest, a voice inside of me said to go no further. I knew that wisdom would have me deny my curiosity and flee quickly in the opposite direction. I hesitated. I took what I thought would be one last glance at the mysterious object.

It sparkled again. I could no longer resist. I quickly and quietly made my way to the object. I took my eyes off of it for only a second to scan the tree line in front of me: no dragons. I then reached down and moved a leaf that was obstructing my view and beheld that which was pulling upon my soul. At that point I realized what it was. I breathed heavily, and my eyes opened wide. I knew I should turn and run. But I felt like I couldn't. I reached out and took hold of it. It felt pleasant to my skin. I cradled it near to my chest and was instantly attached to it. I knew I would never forsake it. It was at that moment my most secret and most sacred possession. It was a dragon egg.

Chapter 19

I knew I couldn't take it back to the cottage with me. I also knew that I would soon be sought after by my father. I quickly dug a shallow hole, placed the egg in it, and covered it with leaves and sticks. I just wanted to keep looking at it, but another part of me was screaming at myself about how wrong my actions were. *'I will leave it here and never come back,'* I told myself. But inside I knew, and feared, the truth. I would soon be drawn back. I tried to bury such thoughts far away from me and quickly hurried back to the cottage. My father was waiting at the table.

"Are you alright?" he asked. "You look a bit shaken."

I quickly sat at the table and forced a smile. "I'm fine," I said. "Just excited to eat and get to bed."

"Elizabeth," he said gently. "Have you been alright? I've noticed that you seem to be withdrawn, and I just wanted to see how you are doing."

I knew that this was the time he had been waiting for. I wanted to tell him so much, but I just couldn't. I feared his disappointment and shame. Confusion and temptation seemed to be pulling me in multiple directions.

"I have been a bit withdrawn," I confessed, unable to look my father in the eye, "and I have been struggling with some things, but I'm not sure that I'm ready to talk about them just yet."

My father paused.

"Well," he said at last, "I understand, and I just want you to know that I love you dearly and that the Great King is with you. I hope we can talk more very soon. I long to know your thoughts, for you are very dear to me."

He then took a deep breath and smiled as he looked within my eyes. His expression was so sincere and loving that it made me ashamed of my deception.

"Just remember this," he said gently. "Remember the words of the Scroll: '*The Great King is always near to the broken hearted. He is the way, the truth, and the life.*' If you will remember these words, my daughter, they keep you from stumbling."

I thanked him for his kindness, and we ate together in silence. His words had pierced my heart and soul, and it took all of my energy to not break down weeping at what he said. As I lay in bed that evening, my thoughts quickly turned from my father to the egg. I couldn't stop thinking about it. From the moment I saw it, and especially touched it, something happened inside of me. It was like I was attached to the life inside of it.

For the following three weeks I took care of the egg, always making sure it was covered, enjoying above all else to look at it. I would check on it early every morning and then again before bed. Upon one such morning I was at the breakfast table when my father broke the silence.

"I'm not sure if you've heard," he said, "but Leah is pregnant."

"Pregnant?" I repeated. "So soon?"

"You seem upset," Samuel said in surprise. "I figured that you of all people would have been excited at such news."

"Well," I said, choosing my words carefully. "I am very pleased at the news; it just took me off guard."

I couldn't bring myself to tell the truth. Oh, how dishonorable was I to lie to my own father! In all reality, and to my own surprise, I was shocked at the news and found myself angry at Nathan. Didn't he care about his wife? Didn't he want to protect her body and spirit?

My thoughts were interrupted by a knock at the door. It was Hannah. "I made you breakfast," she said. "I thought maybe we could have an early picnic, maybe even train a little bit."

This random act of kindness was a great blessing to me. I had felt that I had been drifting away from Hannah, and such an invitation was perfect timing. I gladly accepted, grabbed my quiver and bow, and traveled with her atop the gentle rise in the hill.

The breakfast she made was delicious, and as we ate, we spoke about many things. "Vashti visited me in the market," I said.

"Me too," Hannah replied. "Did she share with you her views concerning marriage?"

"She did," I replied. "Do you think that what she says is correct?"

"I can't believe I'm saying this," Hannah replied, "but I actually tend to agree with her. Much of what she says makes sense to me and lines up with my experience. You've seen how my mother treats my father. She often orders him about and tells him what to do. He is continually trying to make her happy, almost like a slave seeking to please his master. It used to bother me, but more and more I'm thinking that it is the best way. I don't think my father could run our family half as well as my mother does."

Her words stirred a deep feeling in the pit of my stomach. "What do you think?" she asked.

"I don't yet know," I said, and desiring to change the subject, I suggested that we train. We made our way over to the archery targets. "Best of ten?" I suggested.

"I don't really feel like shooting after all," Hannah said. She then reached down and took hold of an old sword that lay against an old wooden bench. She picked it up and began to slash it to and fro.

"What are you doing?" I asked with concern in my voice.

"What does it look like?" she said sharply.

"You can't do that," I insisted. "It's wrong."

"Says who? Oh, that's right," she continued sarcastically, "the Scroll says it's wrong. And who was the Scroll written by?" She then extended the sword to me. "Here," she offered. "Take it."

"I can't," I said.

"Sure you can," she insisted. "Take it. It feels wonderful."

I paused, my mind weighing up the situation. Something inside of me suddenly sprang to the surface of my mind and attitude. It was a sense of rebellion that I had never before experienced in my life. I reached out and took hold of the hilt and began swinging the sword around me. I suddenly sensed a power within me. It was as if I had found something that was either forbidden or forgotten but was sweet to my flesh. Something in me began to change. I had previously always seen myself as a woman who would, one day, be under the leadership of another. But as I held the sword, my mind began entertaining thoughts I had never considered. What if I, instead of my husband, had the vision? What if I was the great warrior and my husband assisted me in my vision? What if I was a better leader, a better visionary, and a better warrior than my husband? I would be the one everyone looked at instead of someone working in the background to make my husband successful. I would be the Captain.

A voice broke the silence of my thoughts. "What are you doing?!" It was Leah. I was ashamed, and yet I didn't want to drop the sword. In my periphery I saw Hannah turn and leave. I stood my ground, still holding the sword.

"I'm training," I said, trying to be confident.

"Elizabeth?" she said. Her voice was so gentle, so caring, and so sincere, that it cut within my soul. I slowly put down the sword as tears began to form. "What's happening inside of you?" she asked.

I looked at this woman that I loved so dearly and admired so much. A battle was raging within me. It was as if part of me saw my dearest friend, another part of me, a potential enemy. My breathing grew in intensity as I began to speak.

"Why?" I asked, and as I spoke I began to weep. "Why did Nathan get you pregnant again? Why does he want to bring you so much pain? Why is he using you? Doesn't he care about you?"

"What?" Leah said with surprise in her voice. "Who have you been talking to?"

"I've been talking to people who know things," I said, "people with wisdom."

"Not the wisdom of heaven," Leah countered. "My dear sister, I know it was hard for you to see me hurt as I did at the death of my child, but you must understand that those tears were also tears of thanksgiving, joy and praise. Thanksgiving that the Great King allowed me to bear a child. Joy at the thought that my child was with the Great King. And praise to the Creator who had given me a daughter who I will one day know and have a relationship with."

Leah's words increased the battle within me. It was as if Vashti and Leah were battling within my soul, both trying to win me to their way of thinking.

"It wasn't Nathan who pushed me to get pregnant again," Leah explained. "It was my desire above all else. I am a woman of the Great King. I am a wife and a mother. My children are warriors of the Great King. This world will bring us heartache and trouble, but the Great King has overcome this world, and His mercy is new every morning. I wouldn't want to not be pregnant. It is such a blessing of the Great King."

I was again emotionally and mentally exhausted. I felt like I was spinning in circles. I still found Leah wonderful and beautiful, and deep down I still wanted to be a mother. An idea then flooded into my mind that brought me such immediate joy. Everything became crystal clear. I knew what I needed to do, and no one would stop me. There was no need for deliberation. I ran toward Leah and we embraced, both weeping.

"I'm sorry," I said.

"Don't worry," she encouraged me. "The Great King is with you."

I thanked her and excused myself. I turned and walked away. "I will be a mother," I said to myself. I knew what to do. The Great King, or fate, whichever one didn't matter, had already provided to me a child. I had a dragon egg. And the life within it would be my offspring.

Chapter 20

I acted like I was making my way back to my home until Leah was out of sight. I then sprinted to the forest's edge and looked within for dragons and then around me for humans. No beast or person was in sight. I searched within the hole I had made and found the egg. Its touch was soothing in a way that I couldn't explain. I felt that I could feel the life within moving about, being formed, and I felt that it sensed my presence. I knew that dragons were all evil and only good for being destroyed, but I felt that this dragon was different, that it was special, that I was *meant* to find it. I began to dream of taming this dragon and training it to fight for us. It would be the most powerful dragon, and it would fight for the Great King.

For another four weeks I tended to the egg, keeping it warm and dry. All I thought of was the egg and the life within, as well as Vashti's words about progressing to further discoveries of how to live. I still went about my daily chores and fellowship with our gathering every King's Day, but I felt distant from them all. Less and less I saw them as attractive and as people to look up to. I still loved them, and I still believed in the Great King, but my understanding of Him was changing. The Scroll was becoming something that had very little true authority. It was a story, and whether it was true or false didn't matter. I began to see it as a collection of fables, meant to teach life lessons.

Every evening I dreamt of the dragon that would be mine. I thought of how I would amaze those I loved, such as my father, as they saw me do things they had never dreamed were possible. I would start a new kind of Castle, one within which all were accepted for what they individually believed. Our unity would be our diversity of thought. No one would be turned away for what they believed. Love and acceptance would bind us all together. I would raise up an army that would be more of a threat to the Great Dragon than ever before.

I was checking on the egg one morning when I thought I heard something. I looked closely at the egg and noticed cracking. I couldn't believe it was actually happening! The dragon was hatching! A claw emerged. I reached out and touched it, and as I did, the sensation I felt by holding the egg was magnified. I just knew that the creature knew who I was and was waiting and longing to meet me just as I was to meet it. The egg now split in two, both ends falling to the ground, and there in my lap was a newborn dragon. It looked up at me with eyes that strained within the new light. It was a red dragon, its crimson skin lined with purple streaks. It nestled its head within my bosom and seemed to purr as I caressed its neck. I wept tears of joy, for I felt so much love in that moment, and I was sure that this dragon was an answer to my prayers.

I then realized that it needed food. I wasn't sure what dragons ate, so I put the dragon back in the hole and ran to the cottage, retrieving vegetables and meat. I quickly went out and fed my child, who quickly devoured all that I had prepared. I put the dragon back within the nestled hole and ordered it to stay there, certain it understood me.

I knew at that moment I would have to live a duel life. My dragon would have to be a secret until it was ready to make itself known to the world. I also realized at that moment just how powerful my attraction was to Vashti. I loved my father, Leah, and Martha dearly, and I also longed to be with them, but this desire regarding Vashti and her companions was different. There was something in them, or perhaps in me (I wasn't sure), that was drawing me. Oh, to just have Vashti and the girls look at me and smile! To have them esteem me! This brought such a feeling of love and belonging to my soul.

For the next few weeks I fed my dragon twice a day and taught it as I would my own child. Our time together was brief, out of a fear of being discovered, but I was pleased to find out just how much I could teach the dragon in only a few minutes a day. It was brilliant. I began by making sure it knew I was its mother and that it was my child. I then began to teach it the Scroll. It was able to memorize after only hearing the passage one time! It asked me what its name was, and I chose to call it, Beautiful, for that is what it was.

My life revolved around these brief exchanges and they brought me such joy and hope for the future. I explained to Beautiful that it would be a good dragon and that it would help me fight the forces of darkness. Beautiful was so committed and excited for my vision! In the meantime, I kept mainly to myself, not even disclosing my secret to Hannah, though I thought she would likely approve. I longed to see Vashti, however, and was anxious for that day to come.

As I came down the village road to the market one day, I noticed a small gathering of young ladies around Vashti, who had elevated herself upon a wooden box. My heart jumped and I hoped I hadn't missed anything. I quickly made my way to the gathering, and placing my produce and quilts just outside the circle, I promptly immersed myself in her words.

"You've been deceived, ladies," she was saying, her alluring eyes piercing our souls. "You've been tricked, and for generations now, you and other women have been slaves without knowing it."

All of the other young ladies around me stood silent, their eyes fixed upon their leader. They were disciples of this woman, and whatever words she was about to say they would embrace and follow. At that moment I realized her power more than I had before. Something within me was cautious, but something else desired to follow her to whatever end she led.

"You've been told," she continued, "that it is your duty to serve others, mainly men. *'Serve your father.' 'Serve your husband.'* These are the words that you were likely told when you were young. But step back and think for a moment. What is that actually called?"

Everyone waited for the response, mesmerized by the beauty of this woman.

"It's called *slavery*," she replied with a voice of hatred. "You've been tricked into slavery without even knowing it. Listen to my words, sisters, for they will set you free. You must no longer serve the men but yourselves. You must be your own masters. You must make your own destinies. To put your life and calling and path into the hands of men is foolish."

I felt tears coming to my eyes. Her words sounded so good, so inspiring. And yet, I thought of my father, the man who had broken into darkness, cut my chains, and set me free. Wasn't it right that I follow him? My thoughts were cut short by Vashti's words: "Do you want to know what it is?" she asked mysteriously. She paused to intensify our suspense. "Do you want to know what it is that brought about such deceit and slavery for women? It was this." She then held up something. Everyone, including myself, gasped at what we saw. It was a Scroll.

"This scroll, commonly referred to as *The Scroll*, is one of the most brilliant strategies of those who wish to enslave us. Its claim is that it was written by some Great King who actually never existed. This scroll was written by mere men who wished to deceive the world. Their main area of deception was to remove women, the wiser and nobler gender, from a place of superiority to that of inferiority. And it is all wrapped up in one word: *yield*. Listen, my sisters, to these words."

She then unrolled the Scroll and began to read. *"Wives, yield to your husbands as unto the Great King."* Many ladies around me gasped. Vashti continued. *"Wives, this is how you make yourself beautiful and radiant...."* At this point she raised her voice and shouted the words in anger, *"by yielding to your husbands, regarding them as your masters!"*

The women around me began to shout in disapproval and disgust of the words she had read. "That's horrible!" one said.

"Away with the Scroll!" said another.

"We will no longer yield to men!" said a third, and my heart seemed to stop within me, for I recognized her voice. I turned and looked in shock. It was Hannah.

Chapter 21

The women all continued their shouting. My eyes stayed fixed on Hannah. Her countenance frightened me, for her eyes were filled with what seemed to me to be hatred and anger. I found within myself a mix of emotions. I was drawn to Vashti but afraid for Hannah and myself. I then thought of the Great King. Was He real or just a made-up man like Vashti was saying? Was the Scroll real or just a deceitful writing used to control women? I thought of my dragon. The Scroll said it was evil, but I knew in my heart that it wasn't. Perhaps the Scroll wasn't perfect after all? My heart was burdened with doubt and pain. Vashti then called for silence and continued.

"This word, *yield*, is ugly and destructive. It makes us weak, mere doormats to be walked upon! We must stick together, sisters. The opposition against what we stand for will be great. We must stand together and recruit some men to be on our side. Yes, even the men, despite their shortcomings, should be on our side. They are weak and easy to turn around," she said with a wave of her hair and a smile. "We must take back our freedom. I will return to you soon. Until then, spread our message and take control of your lives."

She then got down from her box and many embraced her, Hannah being one of the first. I also wanted to embrace her. I wanted to be noticed by her, but I was afraid of Hannah seeing me, and so I quickly took hold of my things and continued on to my usual place in the Market.

After a few minutes, however, and to my secret delight, Vashti soon passed by me. She noticed me and turned from her current course and came my way. My heart beat with excitement. "Ah, my dear Elizabeth," she said lovingly. "How are you?"

"I am well," I replied with a smile.

"I noticed you at my rally just now and wanted to speak with you," she said. "I'm sure these vegetables you're selling belong to your father, yes? Well, those days are coming to an end, make no mistake about it. We will liberate all of our sisters and put men in their rightful place. Yes, yes. There is more to say, but you are still quite young. The time will come soon. We will all unite. No more yielding for us.

"But the main reason for my visit with you is this: There are many ladies who want to be leaders in our movement. They hang around me like leeches, trying to win my approval," she said with flattery in her voice, "but I am truly impressed by very few of them. They aren't strong, not strong like you. I want you to join with me, to be my right-hand woman, to eventually lead our sisterhood. What do you say? Are you with me?"

I paused, not even able to breathe. It seemed liked time stood still, and everything was before my eyes: Vashti, my father, the Great King, and the Scroll. I thought of my dragon. I was sure Vashti would praise me for such things. I pictured me, standing beside her, my dragon at my side. I would be beautiful like Vashti. I opened my mouth to speak but nothing came out. I licked my lips and took a deep breath. Vashti looked at me with a raised eyebrow and a serious look upon her face. It wasn't attractive.

"Of course I'm with you," I finally said.

Her face then lit back up and became beautiful again. "Oh, that's my girl. What a powerful soldier for our side you will make, such beauty and charm. You will be able to turn the minds of anyone, especially the weak men that pollute such villages as this one. This is just the beginning, Elizabeth. We will bring such change as the world has never seen. I will return in a few weeks and seek you out. Until then, break off the yoke of your oppressors."

I smiled and nodded as she turned away and continued on. She walked with such confidence and strength. My heart was still racing. I felt like I was a part of something special, and that I was now important, and wanted, and free. Vashti wanted me to be her second in command! My thoughts were quickly interrupted by Troy. He was before me, looking at me as one who is proud of his friend.

"You know her?" he asked. "She seems like a powerful woman."

I suddenly felt great pride swell up in my soul. "I do indeed," I replied haughtily. "She has asked me to be part of her team, and not only a part of it, but a very special part."

Troy smiled. "That doesn't surprise me," he said. "She needs women of beauty to stand with her, and your beauty surpasses them all." At these words, I felt my heart slip from my grasp, straight into Troy's hands.

"I love you," he said to me.

"You do?" I asked.

"Yes," he replied, "and I will love no one else but you forever. Trust me."

"And you will follow the Great King?" I asked.

"Absolutely," he answered.

I was breathing heavily, and my heart pounded within my chest.

"I want you to be my girl," he said.

144

I wanted to say yes. It was on the tip of my tongue. He reached out and took my hand. So badly did I want to just give in and trust him completely, but something deep within me forbade it.

"Give me a day to think it over," I said. "Then I will let you know."

"Take as long as you want," he said. "I just hope it isn't too long. I'm too in love with you."

I ran home, and by the time I arrived, I convinced myself that tomorrow I would tell Troy that I would be his girl. Not only that, but I was convinced that Vashti was the best woman in my life to follow. She was beautiful and wise and popular. Everything in my life was aligning itself perfectly. I was going to be a woman of power and beauty and influence. I was going to have a man that would love me faithfully and adore me. I had a dragon that was going to be the first of its kind. And I still had the Great King in my heart. Hannah had been right all along. There *was* something I was missing! There *was* truth beyond the Scroll, and I had found it. I had finally found my true life purpose!

I arrived home and found the house to be empty. I quickly took food to Beautiful. It was hiding just inside the forest's edge, just as I had trained it to do. Beautiful was now no longer a baby dragon and was about ten feet long, from snout to tale, and stood around five feet above the ground. We had spoken, the day before, about beginning to let me ride upon its back, and I was hoping this might be the day.

"Hello Beautiful," I said happily.

"Hello Mother," it said with a bow. "How are you?"

"Better than ever!" I exclaimed. "There are great things ahead for us! The Great King is making everything wonderful and clear!"

"How exciting!" it said with a smile. It then hesitated. "Mother?"

"Yes?"

"I have something I want to show you."

"What is it?" I asked curiously.

"It is a surprise. Well, actually I'm not really sure how to describe it, but I think you will like it."

"Alright," I said with a smile. "Do I need to go somewhere to see it?"

"Only into the forest a bit," Beautiful replied. "I put it over there."

"You know I can't go into the forest," I said with a tone much like a mother would use on a child who is asking for something they know is wrong. "You will have to bring it here."

Beautiful hung its head with a look of sadness. "I suppose I could do that," it said, "but I think you will like it better if you get it. It's hidden, and it's a surprise."

"Well," I said slowly and with a tone of disapproval, "how far away is it?"

"Not far at all," Beautiful said with renewed excitement. "It is only a short way in. I can see the spot, but I won't tell you. It's a surprise, and none of those evil dragons are anywhere nearby. I would know if they were."

I looked around to make sure no one was about. "Well, alright," I said at last, "but it must be quick. You will protect me, won't you?"

"Of course, I will," it said. "You are my mother."

I grabbed my bow and entered the forest slowly, stooping down low and scanning the trees for any sign of dragons. The forest there wasn't as dense as most other parts, and so it was easier to detect danger. All seemed clear. I stood up now, more confident and walked further.

"Tell me when I'm close," I said.

"Oh, don't worry, I will."

I stepped over a few fallen trees and then circled a small boulder only four feet high. I expected to find something, but nothing was there. "I give up," I said playfully. "Where is it?"

I felt Beautiful shove me, quite forcefully. The nudge was so strong that it caused me to fall forward.

"Beautiful!" I said, trying not to be too upset. "That hurt. Don't play so rough."

I heard its reply, and the voice was the same but in a tone I had never before heard. "I wasn't playing," was the reply.

I then felt something grab onto my lower leg, and fling me deeper into the forest with such power that I was nearly knocked unconscious. I strained to look behind me. I was horrified at what I saw. Beautiful was marching straight towards me, its eyes fixed upon mine, with a look of absolute evil marked upon its face.

Chapter 22

The dragon was nearly upon me. I rolled to one side and tried to stand up. Beautiful slashed at me, its claws cutting into my shoulder like four sharp daggers. I cried out in pain and turned away, running deeper into the forest.

"What are you doing?" I screamed in rage and fear.

"I'm hunting you," it replied.

"What?!" I shouted, spinning around a tree to pause and catch my breath, my shoulder bleeding and throbbing in pain. "What do you mean?"

The dragon was pursuing me slowly; a look of immense satisfaction upon its face. "I'm going to kill you," it said.

"Wait!" I shouted. "Wait! Stop!" The dragon halted, only ten yards away from me. I couldn't fathom at all what was happening. Was some inner instinct taking over and confusing my dear child? "I fed you," I pleaded. "I loved you. I was with you when you were born."

The dragon laughed. "Ha! You fed and nurtured that which has become your doom. I will now feed upon your flesh, and your last thoughts will be of the anguish that love and charity towards a dragon has accomplished for you."

"But why?!" I said. "Why are you doing this?!"

"Because I'm a dragon," it said with pleasure, "and this is what dragons do." I nocked an arrow as fast as lightning and let it fly. It simply bounced off of the dragon's hide.

"Ha," it laughed. "You can't beat me, even as young as I am. You don't have the skill or courage necessary. Your faith is gone. You are an utter failure."

Panic like never before overtook me. It was an even worse emotion than being captured by the dragon all those years back. I turned and fled with all haste. I knew I was running deeper within the forest, but it didn't matter. The dragon was no longer wasting any time. I heard its jaw snap only inches away from the back of my head. I turned around one tree trunk, and then another. I knew it was only a matter of seconds until it overtook me. In that moment one thought haunted me more than my certain death. It was that I had been so foolish as to bring it about. I was just about to stop and turn for the final encounter when I noticed a deep ravine directly before me with a fallen log over the center, joining the two sides.

The log was extremely thin and narrow, and I wasn't sure if it would hold me, or if I would have the skill to cross it, but I had no choice. I didn't even have time to think about it. I simply sprinted across it, my balance going to one side, causing me to leap for the adjacent cliff wall. My hands grabbed hold of the ground, and in a few seconds I had pulled myself up, terrified with anticipation of a sudden dragon bite to my flesh. But the attack didn't come, for Beautiful was unable to balance on the narrow pass.

I looked back across the ravine, panting harder than ever before in my life. The dragon stood upon the other side, nearly twenty yards away, clawing at the ground in anger and roaring aloud. I stood to my feet, and the beast became silent.

"The hunt continues," it said smiling. "You can't escape."

"Your name is no longer Beautiful," I said, tears of anger and sadness running down my cheeks. "It is Ugly! It is Evil!"

"Why, thank you," it replied mockingly.

"I'm going to kill you!" I screamed foolishly, not thinking of other beasts that might have been nearby.

"You can't kill me," it said. "You haven't the faith, nor the courage, nor the peace. Go ahead and try." At this it raised itself up and offered its chest as a target. I raised my bow, aimed carefully, and released the arrow. It missed. The dragon laughed. I notched another, aimed again, and fired. It hit its chest, but barely punctured the hide, only drawing a little blood.

"You see?" it said, removing the dangling arrow. "Just like I told you. Your heart isn't true enough to kill me. You fear too much. You doubt too much. You've kept secrets from your father. You've envied women who despise the Scroll. I see it all taking root inside of you."

I just stood there, helpless and empty. I looked down into the ravine. A part of me wanted to just fall to my doom.

The words of Samuel then echoed in my mind. *The Great King is always near to the broken hearted. He is the way, the truth, and the life.* Something happened. It was as if my father's words turned on a light in my soul. I was suddenly awake. I could suddenly see like I hadn't been able in many months. Everything came into perspective: all of my wrong choices and all of the empty philosophies I had embraced.

"You can't fool me," I said, coming to my senses. "I have strayed far, but no more. I repent. I follow the Great King. He is real, He is inside of me, and He is greater than you!"

The beast snarled in anger. "Foolish girl! You're alone in the forest, and you will die alone in the forest."

"I'm not alone," I replied.

The dragon then looked to its right and left trying to choose a direction to cross over. I backed away from the fallen log, as to make it think I was going to go deeper into the forest. My thought was to wait until it left and then cross back over and exit the forest. The dragon guessed my plan and cast the log to the bottom of the ravine. It then howled in a way that made every part of me jump in fear as it ran off like lightning to the West.

"Oh, Great King," I prayed, "please help me. Please guide me. I'm so sorry."

I quickly turned and ran the other direction, East along the ravine, but I realized that the dragon would anticipate this and double back to trap me when I crossed. In fear and desperation, I turned and headed deeper into the woodland. I can't remember how long I ran, but soon darkness began to creep into the forest. I knew the dragon would be able to follow my scent, and so I rubbed myself down with pine needles and crossed two different creeks to throw it off of my trail.

The constant expectation of a dragon bursting through the surrounding foliage and devouring me kept me in constant distress and anxiety. I was petrified with fear. I then came to the foot of a mountain and decided to climb it in hope of finding out where I was. By the time I gained elevation, it was nighttime.

Off to the East I could see faint lights. I guessed it to be my village, and it seemed very far away. I knew which mountain range I was on. It was completely swallowed by the forest, meaning that the only way to escape would be to go back down into the woodland below. I found a notched out covering of rock, hidden by a few trees and bushes, and I collapsed upon the hard stone, exhausted beyond description.

As I lay there, in cold darkness, I asked myself how I had come to this place. Only a day before I had security, comfort, and companionship. Now I had nothing but fear and despair. I then recalled the passage in the Scroll where it said, *'To love the Great King is to hate dragons.'* Oh, why didn't I listen?! How did I forget? What would Leah or Martha or my father say? *'It is because of my own foolishness that I am here all alone,'* I confessed to myself. I had given into a temptation I had kept secret. I knew it was wrong, and I allowed myself to be deceived. Because of my own choices I was now cast off in utter darkness with little hope of survival. I couldn't even pierce a dragon's hide with my bow and arrow. All of my skill and courage had left me.

"Oh, Great King," I prayed. "Please forgive me. Please rescue me. I have done wrong. Please show me a way to get back home to the ones who truly love me."

I barely slept at all that night, and was so haunted with nightmares that it was hard to discern reality from fantasy. The only comfort to me was that deep inside I felt that the Great King had forgiven me, just as the Scroll said He would. I was also comforted by the morning sun, shining brightly. I prayed that I had thrown the dragon from my trail, and I prayed that I could avoid it as I tried to return home. I peeked out from behind the cleft which concealed me.

The village was too far away to see. I could barely make out the grassland plains in the distance. A part of me felt that it was a fool's errand to attempt to return that way. I thought it might be better to go the long way around, though I knew that the deeper I went into the forest, the better chance I had of coming across a dragon. If I had food and water, I would have been content to simply stay hidden within the cleft I had discovered, but that wasn't an option.

My stomach was already in pain, and my throat was dry. In the end, I decided to circle around the mountain and see if there was another way out of the forest. I slowly made my way down the peak, terrified at the thought of being seen by a dragon. Occasionally I thought that I saw movement below in the thicket of trees, but I couldn't be certain. The fact that I had made it this far without seeing any dragons was only by the grace of the Great King. It took most of the morning to make it around to the other side of the mountain. The result was devastating: forest, thick and unending as far as the eye could see.

Farther off were more mountains with figures flying about them, small and unidentifiable from the distance, but I knew what they were: black dragons. I suddenly heard a sound, like that of movement coming up the mountain. I quickly ducked behind a boulder and waited. The sound was getting nearer. I tried to notch an arrow, but my hand was shaking. I tried to hold my breath. I then saw them: three figures, robed in black, walking up the mountain. I almost called out, but something stopped me. *'They aren't Scroll followers,'* I reasoned. They dressed more like agents of the enemy would dress. As they passed by, the last one brushed her face only long enough for me to see past her hood and identify her. It was Vashti.

Chapter 23

I was shocked. What were three women doing this deep in the forest? And why was Vashti one of them? Should I talk to them? What if they could help me? And yet, what if they were with the enemy? In the end, despite my fear, I decided to try to follow them. They seemed to be following a trail, but one seldom trodden. I kept my distance to such a degree that for a long time I thought that I had lost them.

I finally came upon small caves and openings in the mountain side. I guessed that dragons would be standing guard and decided to cease my pursuit. I then heard voices, coming from a narrow and tiny hidden opening in the rock behind me. I examined the cleft and found that I was able to crawl into it and that there was a red light within the narrow opening. I crawled about ten yards and came to a dead-end with a small opening at one side.

Through this tiny portal, I was able to look down into a vast cavern. It was filled with the light of a large fire, and there I beheld the three figures all standing in front of a large, black dragon. Two smaller red dragons were upon each side of the black dragon. The three figures removed their hoods. They were all women. The first woman I didn't recognize, but the second and third I did. One was Vashti and the other was Jezebel from Anthropolis.

"Report your dealings with those in your village," the black dragon ordered.

"Many ladies are coming to their senses," the first woman said. "They are taking the dominant role in their homes and are reducing their husbands to mere servants. The men are more focused on pleasing their women, at whatever cost, rather than truly leading them, serving them, or meeting their needs."

"Well done, Jade" the dragon said. "You must not relent. We must cause men to walk in fear of their wives' disappointment. This will not only emasculate the men but will also make wives think that they have found happiness, when in fact they will only find themselves more and more empty and void of joy. And thus, ever increasing darkness will follow."

Jezebel then raised her voice. "In my village, more and more women are leaving the home for work in the marketplace. And what is more, their husbands are learning to love it, for it means more silver and gold, and therefore, more material possessions. And yet, as you know, the homes are in chaos. The women are stressed and exhausted, and the children are ignored and rebellious as a result."

"Ha!" the dragon laughed in amusement. "Excellent! Our master takes pleasure in nothing more than seeing people suffer in the name of *equality* and *financial stability*. For these are the beginnings of the ever-increasing darkness our master foretold."

"What kind of darkness?" Jezebel asked with lustful eyes.

"It will be a slow fade, but it will happen nonetheless," the dragon said with a smile. "Before long, parents will seek items to distract and occupy their children, for they will be too preoccupied and drained to actually shepherd their families. Mothers will hire other people to watch their children for them, so they can engage in their own visions and interests. They will fully, and blindly, entrust their children to others, most of whom will indoctrinate and turn the minds of the children. Children will be herded together like cattle and will learn from each other how to live and think. This will, of course, cause the children to grow more disobedient than any previous generation. Many of them will become absolute monsters."

"It sounds wonderful!" Jezebel exclaimed, as she labored to suppress her overwhelming joy.

"Do not underestimate ideas," the dragon said. "They are powerful. You will convince them that motherhood is a burden, and in the end, they will not only pawn their children to others, but they will destroy the very life for which they were themselves created."

The three gasped in amazement.

"I declare to you," the dragon said boldly, "that in the name of convenience, freedom, and equality, women will do that which none could have imagined. As women, as well as men, lose the hearts of the children, and as they view children as more and more of a burden instead of a blessing, the day will soon come when pregnant women will not want the life within them. Instead of giving the baby life, they will give it death."

I shuddered in absolute horror, unable to believe what I was hearing.

The dragon then turned his attention to Vashti. "And what about you?" he asked. "What have you accomplished?"

"The women are rallying," she replied. "Many have turned to our way of thinking."

"And what of the girl," the dragon asked, "the girl we told you about?"

"She is very close," Vashti replied. "Her best friend has already turned to our side. I feel she will be next."

"Don't let up," the dragon said. "Much depends on her. She must be turned." As I listened to these words, my blood ran cold. Were they really talking about me?

"I will do the best I can," Vashti replied.

"No!" the dragon shouted in anger that made the walls tremble. "You must do more than your best!"

Vashti stood firm. "Do not worry. Elizabeth will soon be one of us. I have asked her to be my right-hand woman, and she has agreed. She is as good as ours, though the enemy's grip on her is profound."

I put my hand over my mouth for fear of crying aloud. To hear my name mentioned in such a meeting was like a nightmare. Why was I so important? It made me think back to when I was taken by the dragon those years earlier.

"Remember our strategy," the dragon declared. "We must destroy the words of the Scroll. It all comes back to the Scroll. If they deny the power of the Scroll, we will succeed eventually. Our victory cannot be avoided, for the Scroll is the constitution of our enemy's kingdom. We must make people believe that yielding is weakness and that true beauty is found in appearance and the praises of men. We must take the woman's heart away from the home, her husband, and children. We must make her think that those things lead to weakness and slavery. Without women who follow the Scroll, men are weak. Without a woman following the Scroll, all homes will crumble and be emptied of all power. This is why our Father attacked the woman in the beginning. They are the key."

The dragon then looked down upon the three women. "Will you serve a man?" he asked.

"Never!" the women replied, yelling the word with what seemed to be deep disdain and bitterness.

"Whom do you serve?" he asked.

"We only serve the Great Dragon," they all replied.

"Serving the Great Dragon comes with a reward. Name your price."

The first woman, Jade, stepped forward. "I ask for wealth," she said daringly. "I want more gold and silver than anyone I know."

"Very well," the dragon replied. He then reached behind him and handed to the woman what seemed to be a bag full of coins. She received it with lustful and greedy eyes.

Jezebel then stepped forward. "I ask for power. I want to be a leader."

"A leader?" the dragon asked. "You already are. Aren't you the governor of Anthropolis?"

"It isn't enough," she replied. "The people are mindless sheep, easy to lead astray. They already desire the darkness and are easily convinced to embrace it. I want more. I want to lead the Castles."

The dragon marveled at the request. "You are bold, Jezebel," it said with a laugh. "But you are fortunate, for your request is in alignment with the will of our master. Let me see… you will begin by leading the Great Castle in Anthropolis. In such a position you will be instructing and influencing all of the future captains of the modern Castles. Seeing a woman lead them there will prepare them for women leading in all the Castles. We already have many of the hearts in Castles, but the increase of female captains will lead to their ultimate demise, for their women will take the cue as permission to do the same in their homes." Jezebel smiled in wicked pleasure.

Vashti then stepped forward. "I ask neither for riches nor power, but for beauty. I want to be the fairest woman ever looked upon."

The dragon then stepped forward, and lowering his head to hers, he breathed upon her. Something happened, for her countenance was transformed in such a way that made my jaw drop. She looked like an angel. She was the most stunning woman I had ever beheld.

"You have been rewarded," the dragon said. "Serve diligently and faithfully, or what you have will be taken from you along with your very life. Remember also that you three know the ultimate plan of the master, but your followers must stay ignorant to the truth. They are the useful fools for carrying out our plan. Keep them passionate, emotional, but foolish, and they will bring about our ultimate goal."

"And then we will receive our ultimate reward?" Vashti asked. "We will receive the eternal inheritance the master has promised us?"

"Oh, don't worry my dear," the dragon said with a smile. "The master loves you all and will most certainly keep his promise."

As I watched this meeting unfold, I realized that these women were just as deceived as I was with the dragon egg, and even more so. They had struck a deal with someone who would use them and then abandon them. And to think that if things had gone differently, I might have been there with them!

"Now," the dragon announced. "Our time here is nearly finished. Did you bring the infant?"

"We delivered it to one of your sentinels," Vashti said.

"Excellent," the dragon exclaimed. "Let the sacrifice begin."

At this news I cried aloud. I couldn't help it. I was so utterly amazed and disgusted by what I heard, for I thought there were limits to the depravity of mankind. I couldn't imagine any such thing actually happening. My shriek echoed throughout the cavern.

"What was that?!" the dragon shouted in alarm. "An intruder! We must find her and silence her! Guards! Bring this spy to me immediately so I can dispose of her myself!"

Chapter 24

Trying to escape seemed helpless. I didn't know what to do. A part of me wanted to just close my eyes and lie still in the tiny nook I had entered and hope they didn't find me, but I knew that wouldn't work. I guessed there would be scores of dragons combing the mountain and forest, but I had to try. The Great King had been with me thus far, and even if I perished, I needed to honor Him by fighting to the death.

I quickly climbed to the edge of the hole I had entered. A dragon sprinted by, filled with hunger and lust. I decided the quicker I was off of the mountain, the better, and began to slowly descend. I heard a voice. It was low and horrifying. "Find her!" it said. "She's here somewhere!"

I thought I heard something coming closer to me, many somethings, all from different directions. I was still high upon the mountain. As I looked around me there were various portals, tiny and scattered across the mountainside. Some were only a foot wide; others were larger. I noticed a crevice around two feet wide that descended into the side of the mountain, the bottom of which disappeared into darkness. I quickly descended into it, and using my legs and back, slowly lowered myself down. Only a few seconds later, a dragon dashed overhead, sniffing incessantly, as if it was trailing my scent. I continued to lower myself into the earth. After about twenty feet down, the small chute opened up to what seemed to be a tunnel. I hesitated, listened, and concluded that I was safe for the moment.

The tunnel was only about five feet in diameter and was heading in two opposing directions. I followed the route which seemed to lead further down the mountain. I couldn't hear any dragons. I could barely see, for the shafts of light coming from up above were lessening. The tunnel was now pitch black, but I had no choice. I had to continue.

For nearly an hour I moved slowly with my hands extended, fearing that at any moment the tunnel might end or that I would come upon a sleeping dragon. I then saw what I had hoped for, light. A faint light was ahead. I slowly advanced, hoping to see an exit into the bright daylight, but it was only another shaft, the height of which I couldn't perceive. I was thankful though, for I could now continue without bumping my head and body about.

I then came upon a sight which perplexed me. It was a pile of weapons and armor. Swords, shields, and bows were heaped upon each other. They seemed to come from followers of the Great King. *Spoils of the dragon's victories,* I guessed. I hoped my bow wouldn't be added to it. I continued on and came to what seemed to be a room of some kind. I hesitated. It was small but wasn't made from natural rock. Someone, or something, had made it. As I slowly approached, I noticed it was a prison cell. It seemed too nasty and small to be a prison for humans. I knelt as quietly as I could and listened. I could hear breathing, though it was faint. I notched my arrow, fearful that if it was a dragon, it would awake. To my amazement, I heard a quiet whisper.

"Hello," the voice said. "Is anyone there?" It was the voice of a man.

"I am here," I whispered back.

I heard a dull chuckle. "Don't try to fool me," the voice said. "I am aware of your schemes."

"This is no trick," I said. "I am a girl. I am trying to escape the dragons."

There was silence, and then I saw a face poke around a corner from within the prison. It was the face of a man, older and with a long beard. His face was worn by torment and anguish that I couldn't imagine.

"You are no dragon," the man said. "Am I dreaming? I must be. Who are you?"

"My name is Elizabeth," I said, comforted to speak with another human in such a dark and desperate place. "Who are you? How long have you been here?"

"My name is Enoch," the man said, "and I have been here for no less than five years by my reckoning."

"Where do they keep your key?" I asked. "I can get you out."

"Look closely, my dear," he said kindly, "and you will notice no lock or hinge upon this grate, for it isn't a door but a window. When they put me in here, they did so for all eternity. But alas, seeing you and the thought of a brief conversation is more blessing and enjoyment than I could have hoped for. You have the appearance of a follower of the Great King."

"I am," I said, "and I take it that you are as well."

"Indeed," he replied.

"How did you come to be in this prison?"

"I was betrayed," he answered.

"Betrayed?" I said. "By whom?"

"That is a long story," he said, "though I suppose we have plenty of time for the telling. Suffice it to say that the enemy always has servants trying to infiltrate our ranks, and some of them are extremely convincing."

"You thought he was a follower of the Great King," I guessed, "and then he turned you in?"

Enoch smiled. "I thought *she* was a follower of the Great King," he said, "and then *she* turned me in."

"What happened to her?" I asked, and I instantly saw pain upon his aged and handsome face.

"They repaid her allegiance with their own deceit and malice," he said soberly. "They executed her on the spot, simply because it is what their sinful flesh desired at the moment. I never understand why people choose to make deals with liars. It is a foolish endeavor."

He took a deep breath and came back to the moment. "Well," he said with a grin, "that's my story. How is it that you came to be here this day?"

I conveyed to Enoch my story, including the dragon's egg, my narrow escape, and the meeting of the dragon and the three women. He listened with mixed emotion.

"You were fortunate to escape the dragon you hatched," he said. "Very few do. As you noticed, your arrow would barely penetrate its hide. That was because of the poison of deception that you were unknowingly consuming. You were thinking that dragons could be regarded as *'not that bad'* or even as *'good'*. But you know what the Scroll says, don't you?"

"It says, 'All dragons are evil. They are all abominations to the Great King.'"

"Amen," he said. "Tell me about your parents."

"I only have a father," I said. "His name is Samuel."

"Captain Samuel of Ravenhill?" he asked curiously.

"The same," I confirmed.

"But how is that?" he asked. "That is confusing to me, unless I have been in here for more years than I have known. Samuel is a dear friend of mine, from my younger years. His wife has been gone for years as well as his only daughter."

"His daughter?" I repeated. The man hesitated, unsure of what to make of this mystery.

"He adopted me," I explained, "when I was young, but I didn't know he had a daughter."

"Forgive me," Enoch said. "I don't want to betray Samuel's confidence."

"I understand," I said.

"Though," he continued, "it is likely that neither of us will again see the light of day, and I feel at liberty. So, listen now to the tale I tell you, and learn the heart of your father. Samuel had a beautiful daughter, much like yourself, long ago it now seems. Her name was Rebecca. She was his jewel, his treasure, for her mother had died bringing her into this world. He loved her, trained her, and raised her up to be a warrior for the Great King. Her aim with the bow was unmatched, as was her knowledge of the Scroll. She had such ambition and heart. She fell in love with a man named Paul. He was also a gift of the Great King, a gem amongst youth. They were soon betrothed.

"Then one fateful day, a group of us went dragon hunting. We ended up coming upon a legion of dragons. It was overwhelming. Paul was cut off from us and was beyond any of our capability to rescue. Rebecca fought through the legion, despite Paul's cries for her to turn back. She came to his side, and not even a moment later, the two of them were engulfed in flames and death took them. It was a good death, and it was indeed just like Rebecca to do so. Samuel honored her choice. He held his head up in thanksgiving. But still, with his wife and daughter gone, he was never the same."

Enoch took a deep breath. "My heart always hurts for Samuel when I think of Rebecca. And yet, it also rejoices. The strongest love that the Great King gives us is also the love that hurts the most. And now, in seeing you here, I see the mercy of the Great King. Despite your failures, I believe the Great King is going to raise you up, just as he did Rebecca. You will make your father proud in the end."

I closed my eyes, trying to hold back my tears, but it was in vain. To hear this story of the man I loved the most, to learn of a sister that I never met, and to have before me a path that would honor them both, it was a weight of blessed emotion.

"Thank you for telling me," I said. "I wish there was some way to get you out of this cage."

"The only thing that would cut through these bars is my sword," he replied. "And I haven't seen it at all these five years."

I gasped in hope and hurried back to the pile of weapons, and returned carrying with me as many swords as I could hold. Enoch grabbed his immediately, his strength seeming to instantly return to his body. Within a few seconds his bars were broken asunder, and he was free.

"What now?" I asked with renewed hope and comfort at the blessing of having a male warrior with me.

"We make our way to the East," he replied.

"You will help me get home?" I asked.

"Of course," he replied with a smile, "but first we have important business, unfinished business, to see to."

"What do you mean?" I asked nervously.

"You hatched a dragon," he said. "You fed it and grew it. Your honor commands you to hunt it and kill it."

"I don't think I can," I said, my eyes tearing up.

"What can a follower of the Great King accomplish?" he asked. "What does the Scroll say?"

"I can accomplish all things," I replied soberly.

"Exactly," he said. "You've come this far. You will conquer. Don't worry. I will train you."

"But the forest seems endless," I said. "How will I find the dragon?"

"I wouldn't worry about that," he said with a smile. "I'm sure it will find you."

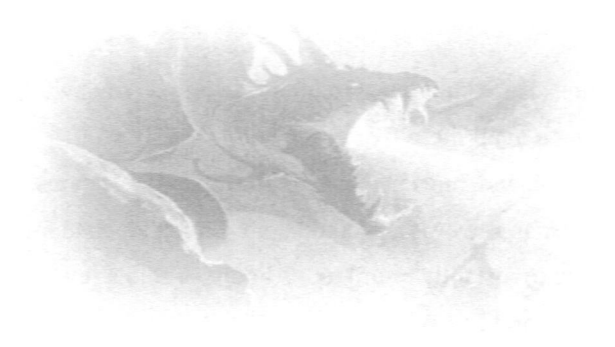

Chapter 25

Enoch led me further down the tunnel I had been traveling. "How do you know which way to go?" I asked quietly.

"Because this is the way she led me before I was ensnared. It was right here," he said, pointing to a bend in the tunnel. "The moment she betrayed me, the dragon congratulated her on her deception, told her that it was time for her reward, and devoured her whole right in front of me."

"That's awful," I said in horror.

"Yes, but not surprising, as you yourself have learned the hard way. Dragons can never be trusted. The only fate of those three women you spoke of, who are dealing with the dragons, is a sure death by the very claws of the ones they serve."

We then came to an exit, which seemed to be at the roots of the mountain. Enoch crouched low at the entrance. "There are many dragons about," he said after some time, "though none too near us." He then looked at me. "Do you know why your aim and power were lacking with the dragon?"

I thought for a moment, my guilt and shame still heavy upon my conscience. "Because I was afraid?"

"That's a big part of it, yes," he confirmed. "Fear is your biggest enemy. Doubt is also linked to fear. Listen carefully, Elizabeth. You fear and you doubt because you think that it is your effort alone that determines the outcome. There is another person aiming the bow and pulling the string within you: The Great King. As the Scroll says, *Take aim and shoot well, for it is the Great King who works in you both to aim and to destroy your foe*. If it was indeed all up to you to aim and destroy the foe, then fear and doubt would be expected. But you must not hunt alone. He is with you, and He fights for you. You must believe, Elizabeth. Then, no dragon will be able to stand against you."

We then went out into the thick forest. I followed Enoch's lead as we crept from tree to tree and sprinted across open meadows. For a man who was likely in his sixties, Enoch had great strength and speed, and it seemed to me that his time in the dungeons of the enemy had little to no effect on his skillfulness or resolve.

We then came to an open patch in the thick forest, no more than twenty yards across. Enoch stopped and looked about. He inhaled the air deeply, and took me by the hand to lead me into the middle of the opening. He did so with a calmness as if we were upon the plains outside of the forest.

"What are we doing?" I whispered nervously. "We can be seen."

"Do not fear," he answered. "Put an arrow to your bow string and close your eyes." I obeyed. The labor of my breathing was evidence of my trepidation.

I then heard his voice. It was more distant from me than I would have preferred. "Enoch," I said gently, my eyes still closed. "Please don't leave me."

"I will never leave you, child," he replied, "but I will train you. You must find your confidence in your Maker."

I stood there, my closed eyes enveloping me in utter darkness, in the middle of a forest filled with dragons. My body began to tremble.

167

"You think you are in danger," Enoch said plainly. "You think you are in darkness. You think you will soon be left alone. You must learn to see with more than your natural eyes, for they will lead you astray. You aren't in any danger. I tell you the truth, you are just as safe as if you were within your home, surrounded by your family, or asleep in your bed. For the Great King is just as much in control here as He is there. You think all is dark? I tell you the truth, there is a light shining about you that would make the sun seem like pitch darkness. Breathe, Elizabeth. Sense the presence of your Creator. Believe the words of the Scroll. Sense the safety. See the light."

As Enoch spoke, something happened. His words seemed to penetrate the deepest parts of my soul. I felt that if I had opened my eyes, the Great King would be standing before me, smiling at me. I pictured that I was surrounded by the host of the heavens and that light was streaming forth from my body, a light before which all dragons would flee in terror. I suddenly felt such a love as I had scarcely felt before, such a belonging. I felt a burden released. I felt truly free of fear.

Enoch's voice reflected an understanding that he likewise sensed my deliverance. "Keep your eyes closed," he said, "pull back your bow, and aim."

"What am I aiming at?" I asked.

"Darkness," he replied.

"But all is dark," I said curiously.

"You're looking again with the wrong eyes, child," he instructed. "All around you and in you and through you is only light all the time, but darkness draws nigh. You must pierce the darkness with an arrow of light."

I was overwhelmed, but I now knew where my true allegiance lay. I would be deceived no longer and prayed for clarity. *Great King, give me eyes to see and ears to hear. I can't do this without you.*

I slowly turned in a circle, my bow drawn, my eyes closed, within the dragon-filled forest. My eyes were shut, but my true eyes were opened. I dared to believe, regardless of what the world would have said, that the Great King was with me and that I was safe in His arms, come what may. I quickly stopped turning, unable to explain why. I released my arrow, and immediately heard it strike its mark. A loud dragon cry filled the air.

"Ha!" Enoch shouted in joy.

I opened my eyes, and coming through the trees in my direction was a red dragon, large and formidable. To say I wasn't at all afraid would be a falsehood, but to say that I was terrified would also be untrue. I was aware of the gravity of the situation, but something had changed. Whereas, before I would have been panic-stricken, I was now at peace within the storm. Enoch charged between me and my foe.

"Nock another arrow," he said loudly but with a calm voice. The dragon rose up when challenged by Enoch's sword. "Shoot again!" he commanded.

My arrow again hit its mark, sinking deep within the chest of the enemy. The dragon fell to the ground, breathed its last, and was no more. Enoch looked at me with an expression of immeasurable joy. Tears likewise came to my eyes and I ran into his arms.

"Well done," he said. "How do you feel?"

I stood back and looked at him and then at the dragon. Something had happened to me. What I had just experienced was a milestone in my life. It was a Rite of Passage. I had a confidence and peace that years of training had led me to, but that this one moment had fully brought to fruition.

"I feel free," I said.

"And that you are," he confirmed. "You are a daughter of light, a princess of Zion, and maiden of virtue. You entered this forest and girl. You will leave it a woman. But let us move on, for your true battle is yet to take place. Your pet dragon hunts you relentlessly. But now, it will be the hunted. Come."

With these words we sprinted on together, moving with stealth from tree to tree. I knew what markings to look for, as did Enoch from my description of the beast. Only two hours later we found what we were seeking. Next to a marsh, there in the mud, were the marks of the dragon I had hatched only two months before.

"These tracks are not yet an hour old," Enoch said coming to my side. "Let us hurry. Evening will soon be upon us." The tracks led us to a cluster of boulders, scattered upon the ground. There upon the highest boulder, near a large oak tree, was the dragon. Enoch quickly darted behind a tree. I understood his mind. This was something that I had to do. The dragon inhaled deeply and sensed my presence.

"Well," it said with a smile. "I thought some other dragon had the pleasure of devouring your flesh. I am so pleased to find out I was wrong, for here you are, all alone, and you've stumbled upon that which you have been trying to avoid."

"I didn't stumble upon you," I said calmly. "I was hunting you." A look of surprise and doubt flashed for a moment upon the dragon's face. "I learned a lesson with you that I will never have to learn again," I said. "For that I thank you."

I took a few steps closer to the enemy, my bow in my left hand and three arrows clenched in between the fingers of my right hand. The dragon seemed to sense something different in its opponent.

"Sweet friend," it said gently, slinking down off of the rock and coming nearer. "Why do we need to fight and speak in such a way. You named me, Beautiful, remember? You then shot an arrow at me, but you could barely pierce the thickness of my hide. You can't beat me. We should be friends."

Then, as quick as a flash, the dragon lunged forward with speed like that of a cheetah. I raised the arrows and fired each of them within the span of two seconds. The three arrows pierced through my opponent with such force that they sank into a large oak tree that was behind the beast, all stained in the blood of my foe, whose corpse lay lifeless on the ground.

"Your arrows went straight through him," Enoch observed, coming to my side, "and they still had the strength to pierce solid oak. The Great King has given you a contentment and faith that makes your arrows fly like few I've ever witnessed."

"His name be praised," I said in response, my eyes still fixed upon the carcass of my foe. I was pleased to discover that all the fond emotion that I had attached with that vile creature had disappeared. I saw it for what it was: pure evil, death, and abhorrence.

"Well done," Enoch said again. "You now know how to see. The Great King is with you."

"Thank you, Enoch," I said. "Without you and your training and skill, I would not have survived."

"Ha!" Enoch said. "I may be saying the same to you in a few minutes."

"What do you mean?" I said curiously.

"We both escaped from a stronghold of the enemy," he explained, "I a prisoner, and you a spy. Nothing makes a dragon's blood boil more than that. They still haven't found you, and I sense that they have learned of my absence."

"You mean they are still pursuing us?" I asked nervously.

"They will be upon us in only a few moments," he said calmly. "The ground is already beginning to tremble under the weight of their stampede."

Chapter 26

"What do we do?!" I cried aloud. "Should we run?"

"We can't outrun them," Enoch said, "not this deep within the forest."

"So what do we do?!" I repeated.

"The same thing we did before," he said. "Nothing has changed. Trust the Great King. Ready your weapon. Be confident in the one that is in you. He is sovereign. You have shown your honor and your true allegiance, Elizabeth. If you die today, you die free and an overcomer. Get ready. Here they come!"

I could now feel the ground shaking as Enoch had previously mentioned. I readied my bow, determined to kill as many as I could. I then saw at least a dozen red dragons sprinting to where we were. Just before they came upon us, Enoch ran forward and sank his sword within the ground with a shout. Instantly, a line of earth rose up before us twelve feet high, creating a barrier between us and the foe. His timing was so sudden that many of our enemies crashed into the earthen wall, some falling to the ground, others crying out in anger. Two dragons rose above the wall only to meet two of my arrows piercing their heads.

"Well done!" Enoch shouted above the carnage and roaring. He then stuck his sword in the ground again, just before me, this time elevating the earth underneath me to thirty feet, bringing me up above much of the tree line.

"Shoot them all!" he shouted as he engaged another dragon. I now had a complete view of all the dragons, including the black dragons now circling the air around us. I sent a steady stream of arrows in all directions, the tips of which hit their marks and sank deep within our foes. Upon that pinnacle, with dragons all about me, I was at complete peace. Despite all of the darkness which surrounded me, I felt as if I was an angel of light, and that each of my arrows were extensions of the power and judgment of the Great King. I felt renewed, reborn, resurrected. I was a woman who had fallen into the pit of her own folly, only to rise by the power and wisdom of the Great King.

Despite our skill, however, the enemy began to overwhelm us, for they were many. My arrows were also nearly spent. I called out for the aid of Enoch, but looking below I beheld him also overcome. I took out my last arrow and aimed it at a black dragon flying towards me. I had pierced this creature twice already, but hadn't taken it down. It inhaled deeply as to consume me with its fire.

I knew this was my final battle this side of heaven. I pulled back my arrow with all of my might and let it loose. It struck the giant dragon and wounded it, but it still wasn't enough to bring it down. I prepared myself for the fire that was about to come, but suddenly around two score arrows struck the creature all at once, knocking it out of the sky. I looked down to see the entire fellowship of my people pour into the warzone. I shouted out a cry of victory and began to descend the summit I had been upon. Leah came to my side and handed me a full quiver of arrows.

"Spare no arrows!" she shouted above the roar of battle. Back to back with both her and Ruth, I fought on. I then beheld Nathan engage a hell hound single-handedly and behead it. Soon all of our foes were either scattered or killed.

My father and I embraced.

"Oh, my dear daughter," he said, tears running down his cheeks. "Beyond all hope I find you alive and well."

"Not only alive, but strong," Enoch said from nearby. "Your daughter has crossed over from girl to woman."

"She has indeed!" Leah agreed with tears in her eyes. She looked upon me as one does a sister who carries all of her hopes and dreams.

"My dear Elizabeth," my father said with pride and affection in his voice.

My soul was so stirred within me in that moment. I knew that I should have been devoured by the dragon I hatched. I knew that I should have been vanquished by the many enemies who had pursued me. I knew that I didn't deserve the grace that had been given to me, and that I had lied to my father and so many others by deceiving them. I fell at my father's feet.

"Oh, my father!" I cried, tears falling to the green grass below. "Oh, my father! Forgive me! I have sinned against you and against heaven! I am not worthy to be called your daughter! I hatched a dragon egg in secret. I deceived you all, but I see my error! I repent! I embrace the Scroll. With all of my heart and soul I embrace the Scroll, and I love our Great King!"

All of the fellowship had now circled around me. My father gently lifted me up to my feet.   "Look into my eyes, my daughter," he said.

I obeyed his request, and as I did, I saw in those understanding eyes a love and acceptance that I knew could only be from heaven.

"You are my daughter," he said, "and these are your people. We see you as the Great King sees you: pure, undefiled, righteous, and good. You have repented. All is forgiven. All is well. It is as if it never happened." Other hands were upon me now, for the circle had tightened.

"Kneel," Samuel said gently. Then, taking my bow, he christened me. "The skill you have shown today is testimony of your words, that you have rejected the world and have embraced the Scroll. You are no longer a girl, but are now a woman, a woman who is of age and prepared for the hunt, for courtship, and for greater honor."

I stood to my feet, receiving my bow, and everyone cheered. Samuel then turned and embraced Enoch. "I never thought I'd see you this side of heaven," he said. "You look weary beyond imagination."

"I am more alive than ever," Enoch replied, "though I wager I will rest better tonight than I have in many moons."

"Let us leave this forest," Benjamin said. "We return now to Ravenhill, and there we will celebrate our brother Enoch and sister Elizabeth both returning to us as from the dead."

I embraced Leah and softly wept on her shoulder as we made our way back towards our village. "You were right," I said. "Everything you taught me, everything you are, all of it is right."

"It is the Scroll that is right," she said smiling. "It is up to you to follow it."

"I will," I said. "With my entire heart I will. I honestly can't believe that I ever left it. It all seemed so innocent as it happened."

"That is how deception always feels," Leah commented. "It is a slow fade from truth."

"It is indeed," I agreed. "This woman, Vashti, at first she said the Scroll was good, only a bit outdated; then she said it was wrong; and finally she said it was evil. I seemed to be convinced bit by bit, as her words were slowly chipping away at my resolve. But now that I see the light, I can't believe I ever denied it."

"It is a brilliant strategy of the enemy," Leah said. "They know that if they outright declare the Scroll to be false they will have no chance of gaining your allegiance. They begin, as you said, by planting a small seed of doubt in your mind; then, after they've poured water upon it for a while, they take it a step

175

further. Eventually, because you have already denied the infallibility of the Scroll, it is a small step to just outright reject it."

As our fellowship continued our exodus out of the woodland, my mind turned to Hannah. She wasn't with the company, and I wondered if she had been left behind to tend the young. "Where is Hannah?" I asked Leah. "How is she?"

Leah's face was grim. "I fear that the enemy's grip on her is remarkably strong," she said. "I fear that she is beyond our aid or hope." Her answer grieved me though it was not a surprise.

"But," I said, "there's always hope, isn't there?"

"Of course," she said. "It's never too late, but sometimes there's such a hold on someone that it seems impossible. All things are possible with the Great King, and if she does come back to the light it will only be by the miracle of His doing."

"Surely she can't be that much changed," I said, trying to convince myself that things were better than Leah had revealed. "I've only been gone a few days."

"The seed of deception was long ago planted in her heart," she testified, "as you yourself know. This in turn has long been watered with the poison of maidenism, and now that the sun of so-called *equality* has shined upon it, the fruit of darkness has burst forth. She has changed much, Elizabeth, though all the necessary pieces were there, waiting for the time to blossom. This is not a mere whim, but a foundational issue with Hannah."

"I must go to her," I said. "I must talk some sense into her."

"You will find her at the market," Leah said, "though you might find it hard to recognize her."

Chapter 27

I was soon at home and in bed. My father and I visited briefly before I fell asleep from utter exhaustion. The next morning I enjoyed a wonderful meal and glorious fellowship with my father, which I had not had for many months. I was so grateful for the mercy of the Great King and felt so unworthy to have received it. When the meal was finished, I went to search for Hannah.

As I walked through the market that morning, I viewed my surroundings in a way I never had done before. It was as if I saw an invisible battle raging over every person, over every soul. It was a territorial battle. The soul of every person was the prize, and the mind of every person was the battlefield. Instead of simply seeing them as people going about their daily lives, I observed them as people who were thinking in certain ways. How did they view the Scroll? Who was the Great King? What were the answers to the questions of life, purpose, and destiny? Each of them had answers to these, whether they knew it or not, and those answers shaped everything about them.

My eyes scanned everywhere for Hannah. She wasn't at our usual post. I then saw a girl that looked like Hannah, but who I initially disregarded. However, after a second, and then a third glance, I realized that it was Hannah. Her appearance had changed dramatically.

She hadn't yet noticed me, so I simply took in what I was seeing. Her hair had been cut. It did not look identical to that of a man, but neither was it like that of a woman. What was also shocking to me was her clothing. It lacked the propriety and modesty according to which we had been raised, and it revealed parts of her frame that were shameful. As I observed her interact with the few other people around her, I realized that it was not only her outer appearance that had changed, but her personality as well. She was no longer quiet and guarded with her words and thoughts but seemed to take pleasure in parading her heart to others. It reminded me of what Leah had told me once. *'We don't judge people by their outward appearance, but we do understand that the outer appearance is a reflection of the inner person. It shows us symptoms of what is happening in their minds.'* Hannah's inner person had been corrupted and conformed to the world, and now her outside was matching that reality.

The final blow, however, was when Troy approached her, wrapped his arms around her, kissed her, and then sat beside her with their hands interlocked. This boy, who for over a year had shown me interest and had confessed his love for me, who had only a few days earlier declared to me that I was the only girl for him, was now with another girl, my childhood friend.

Our eyes then met, and I made my way to her. I could tell she was likely as uncomfortable in our meeting as I was, though she tried to conceal it.

"Elizabeth," she said excitedly. "Where have you been? I heard that you ran away or something of the sort. It's good to see you."

"It is good to see you as well," I replied kindly. "I am fine."

"I am so glad to hear it," she said. "I must tell you that I myself am happier than ever before in my life."

At these words Troy smiled and kissed her on the cheek. I hesitated. I wasn't sure what to say. The few young ladies who were there with Hannah just sat smiling and listening to Hannah's words as if she was a leader amongst them.

"While I was away," I said softly. "I learned many things. I realized many things. I understood that ideas are powerful."

"Let me keep you from wasting your time," Hannah said, her countenance changing. "My mother and father have tried what you are trying, as have others. It is folly on their part. I have found my true calling."

"Which is what exactly?" I asked.

"To live my life the way I want to live it," she said, glancing at Troy with a smile.

"You do realize," I said unapologetically, "that this boy confessed his love for me only a few days ago?"

Hannah returned a sardonic smirk. "Well, I suppose he didn't find what he was looking for," she said harshly.

"I agree with you," I said calmly. "He was looking for someone to manipulate and use for his selfish and sinful purposes. I wasn't that girl."

"Oh, please," Hannah continued, aiming to justify herself. "Don't try to flatter yourself with your *holy and pure* convictions. What a waste of time. I have found my true purpose."

"Is it a purpose laid out in the Scroll?" I asked.

"Don't bring the Scroll into this," she said with a disdainful glance. "So much of your life is directed by just a few pieces of paper. Haven't you considered that maybe it isn't trustworthy? Haven't you considered that what we were taught was wrong?"

"I have," I said kindly and yet with serious expression, "and it has proven itself."

"For you perhaps," she replied. "What is true for you might not be true for me."

My eyebrows raised at this comment. "What did you just say, Hannah?" I asked gently.

"I said that what is true for you might not be true for me," she repeated with a hint of impatience in her voice.

"I don't think that's possible," I said, trying to be sensitive and gentle. "Either something is true, or it isn't. My heart is broken for you, that you would throw away simple rules of logic. The enemy has made you a captive."

"The enemy?" Hannah said, her expression now full of offense. "I am freer and happier than ever before. How could that be the work of the enemy? It is you, I'm afraid, that is still in shackles and chains. Vashti has helped me break free of such burdens. She has rescued my soul."

Her expression then turned from that of offense to compassion and sympathy. "Oh, Elizabeth," she said. "Don't you see how they've deceived you into giving up your full potential? You just do whatever you're told. You don't get to live for yourself. Please, listen to Vashti and allow her to show you the truth, just as she showed me. Ever since I fully embraced her message, I've felt such freedom. You can have the same thing."

Fortunately, because of all that I had seen in the past few days, along with my victory over the dragon, there was no part of my soul that was moved by Hannah's words. The previous week, by the grace of the Great King, I had been transformed from a woman nearly overcome by the enemy, to a woman empowered to overcome the enemy. I realized in that moment, more than ever before, that even though Hannah claimed to have found peace and happiness, she was emptier than she had ever been.

The few women who were around us suddenly stirred, and Hannah's face glowed with immeasurable joy. I turned to find Vashti approaching us. Her presence brought about much emotion, for I had seen her in the presence of the enemy, and yet, her beauty and charisma were staggering. Hannah and those around her embraced their leader who greeted them all with a sense of affection and loyalty.

"Elizabeth," she said smiling, "it's so good to see you."

She then put her arms around me and held me close. I should have been repulsed by her presence, but there was still something about her that made me envy her. I reasoned that it was her beauty. Even though I knew of her loyalty to evil and her wicked agenda, a small part of me still desired her attractiveness. This reality brought me great pain and frustration, but it couldn't be ignored.

"Doesn't Hannah look more beautiful than ever?!" she asked me, putting her hand on Hannah's shoulder.

"She is very beautiful," I said, unsure of how to respond.

"Hannah has become one of us now," Vashti said. "And look at her, happier and freer than ever before. It is your turn now, Elizabeth. I feel that with you by our side, we will truly be invincible. It is time for the females to rise up and take back what both men and society have robbed from them. You are a powerful woman, Elizabeth, and oh so beautiful. If you join us, not only will you have power and influence, but you will have a beauty that few women possess. Men will love you. Women will envy you. I must be honest, Elizabeth. I believe you have eluded us long enough. You said the other day you were with me, but I still see doubt in your eyes. You have wavered back and forth long enough. It's time for you, just like Hannah, to choose. And I believe your choice is obvious."

"It is indeed obvious," a familiar voice said. "She will never, ever join you." I turned around and looked behind me. It was Leah.

Chapter 28

Everything was quiet for a moment. Due to Vashti's reputation, about ten women were gathered around us, and more were coming nearer. I was face to face with Vashti. Leah simply stood there, still, quiet, and confident. She had defied the woman whom many in our village regarded as a modern prophetess, and yet, there was no fear in her eyes.

"Oh now, what is this?" Vashti said mockingly, looking Leah up and down. "A fully clothed woman," she continued, "sheltered, plain, and friendless. She is already burdened with a youngling at her side and very pregnant with another. I'm shocked to find you out of your home. I'm shocked that you've even been allowed by your husband to travel alone and speak your mind."

All the women present seemed to stand around Vashti in support, while Leah was all alone. I slowly shuffled to one side to avoid being directly between them.

"I am often outside of my home," Leah said gently, "though I love to be there. And this child by my side, as well as this life within my womb, aren't burdens, but they are joys and blessings. I pray that the Great King gives me many more of them. Despite what you think, I am always permitted to speak my mind, though I don't always take the opportunity."

"Ha!" Vashti replied scornfully. "You are obviously not allowed to dress the way you please. Look at you! How uncomfortable you must be."

"I am very comfortable," Leah replied. "What makes me uncomfortable is the prospect of dressing in such a way that displays my body to the world."

"You see what I mean?" Vashti said, turning to the women around her. "What foolishness and slavery!"

"It is actually wisdom and freedom," Leah replied calmly. "I've only been given one body, and I've only been given one heart, and I want to protect them both. To offer yourself solely to your husband is a joy and blessing that all can experience if they walk in the wisdom of the Scroll."

"Wisdom and freedom?" Vashti retorted, trying to find a way to win the verbal conflict. "There's nothing wrong with a girl showing off her body. It doesn't hurt anything."

"Actually, it very often does," Leah replied, seeming to enjoy the opportunity to proclaim the truths of the Scroll. "The body and the heart are linked. If a girl becomes accustomed to freely displaying her body, it makes her accustomed to displaying and passing around her heart. Such a practice will bring misery. My advice is that a woman should allow her clothing to be a frame for her face, not her body."

"Oh, what nonsense!" Vashti shouted. "You are a plain girl and therefore wouldn't understand. It is no wonder you resolved to be a homemaker."

Leah smiled ever so slightly. "Your insults are to no avail," she stated straightforwardly. "Say what you will. I know who I am, and I know to whom I belong. I have come here for Elizabeth."

"Are you her superior?" Vashti asked. "Can't she go where she wants to go? You aren't going to take her anywhere."

"You misunderstand me," Leah said. "I'm not going to take her *body* anywhere, but rather I am here to claim her mind and soul. You can't have them. You almost obtained them, but the Great King has claimed this girl as His own."

As the two women continued to speak to each other, a circle formed around them. The conversation was getting more heated, though mainly by Vashti. As I was watching them speak to each other, so much emotion was racing through my body. I loved Leah dearly, and trusted her, but there was still a small spark that Vashti was able to light in my heart that caused my head and soul to groan in frustration.

I suddenly felt a gentle grip on my forearm, and turning to my side, I beheld Ruth. "Keep watching them," she whispered in my ear.

I looked back upon Vashti and Leah, and something began to happen. A light began to shine around Leah while a darkness began to envelop Vashti. I had to keep myself calm. I didn't yet know what was happening. I then realized that Ruth was using her ability and was opening my eyes to the invisible realm. The light around Leah seemed to shine ever brighter, and as I looked upon her, I beheld the most beautiful creature I had ever laid my eyes upon. She was as an angel, wrapped in deeds of righteousness and shining as the sun. Her voice was as the sound of rushing waters while her hair was as dazzling as ocean crests crashing upon rocks, sending their spray into the air about them. Her eyes were as fine jewels that sparkle like the stars. I couldn't take my eyes off of her. The beauty that I once admired upon Vashti's face was nothing compared to this. There was no comparison, for the chasm between them was so large.

I then turned my gaze upon Vashti, and I nearly screamed out loud. Her appearance was like that of which I had never seen, much less imagined. She was the most repulsive, most hideous thing I had ever beheld. Her appearance was indeed worse than words can describe, and to do so would be to recount the darkest nightmare imaginable. Her figure didn't even resemble something that could be considered alive. I shuddered and quickly turned my gaze, for her appearance was so entirely reprehensible that I felt consciousness slipping from me.

"You see," Ruth whispered in my ear. "What is beauty? What is virtue? These can only be understood by those who are able to see true reality. Look upon Leah. That is beauty such as only obedience to the Scroll can give. This is how women of the Great King make themselves beautiful, by being women of submission, purpose, and life. The so-called *beauty* of this world, in comparison, is nothing to be admired. It is death. It is ugly and repulsive. The Great King is calling you to be beautiful, Elizabeth. He is calling you to be an angelic maiden of virtue, beauty, and wisdom. The path is at your feet. You must walk it."

The small seed of desire for Vashti's approval and for her beauty had completely vanished from my heart. Indeed, it was utterly destroyed. I felt a burden removed from me and a great joy replace it. Following the Scroll's wisdom and truth for womanhood was no longer something I merely agreed with, it was something I longed to embrace. That beautiful seed of truth had not only been sown in my heart, but it had now grown into something strong and immovable. Ruth removed her touch, and my sight was restored to an earthly vision. I still retained in my memory the images of Leah and Vashti, which never left my mind. Both pictures remained steadfast upon the forefront of my deepest thoughts.

The group of listeners had increased, and the two women were still in verbal conflict. "You will never win this argument," Vashti was saying. "My wisdom and knowledge are far superior."

"Your ego definitely is," Leah interjected, "but I am not trying to win an argument. I am trying to win people, including you, Vashti. You fail to understand, as all do whose eyes are blind, that you are deceived and that you are nurturing your own destruction. As for wisdom and knowledge, the Scroll is clear; you can have neither, unless you reverence the Creator of all things. He made us all male and female, and He alone therefore can assign and choose the life purpose connected to each gender."

Vashti scoffed. "You foolish Scroll-follower," she said. "Look at you. Your body is abused and worn out by the selfishness of a man who simply wants to use you for his own ends."

Leah seemed to marvel at Vashti's interpretation of her life. "Is that really what you think?" she asked. "You think that my body is abused? How? By giving birth to children?"

"Of course," Vashti confirmed, "and by simply being a servant and source of physical pleasure to your husband."

"I am indeed a source of physical pleasure to my husband, which yields just as much gladness and pleasure for myself," Leah testified with a sense of satisfaction. "My heart truly does hurt for you, and for all who think thus. For to serve and please my husband, and to bear and bring forth children into this world, is a satisfaction that is nigh difficult to measure, for it is overly abundant and remarkably beautiful. When you embrace the Scroll and its calling upon your life, you find true fulfillment. I am a rock to my husband, Nathan, and a crown upon his brow. I am a life bearer to my children, which again is a joy that is difficult to put into words. To picture my life without these things, without fulfilling and completing my husband, and without rearing children, seems to me unimaginable."

"Then you are to be pitied above all the vermin and vagabonds of this earth, you vile woman!" Vashti declared, her voice filled with rage and hatred. "Get out of here. You aren't worth one more second of my time. These women have heard enough of your heresy and foolish talk!"

"I will leave," Leah replied, "but I want you to know that I will pray for you, Vashti, and that I am taking Elizabeth with me."

"I don't want your filthy prayers," Vashti said, "and Elizabeth is staying right here. You can spoil your life on such nonsense, but there's still hope for this beautiful girl. She is not like you. She sees the truth and wants to live her life in the name of freedom."

"She…" Leah began.

"Silence!" Vashti demanded. "She can speak for herself and she can think for herself. She is no longer going to put up with your influence. Just as Hannah has come out from amongst your kind, so Elizabeth will follow, and in time she will lead us all to greater things than even I have accomplished." At this comment many around Vashti gasped with astonishment.

"Come," Vashti said gently, turning her eyes to me, and returning to a more proper and calm condition. "Come, sweet Elizabeth, and tell us all the good news. Tell us about the freedom that you are this day choosing for yourself and for all whom you will influence in the years to come."

I paused and thought for a moment. "Thank you, Vashti," I said. "I will gladly do so."

Chapter 29

I felt the power of the Great King come upon me, and looking upon Vashti, I no longer saw a woman to be admired or followed but one to be pitied, much like the searching women who surrounded her. A small crate was beside me, and I slowly stood upon it, elevating myself slightly above the gathering. Leah's gaze was fixed upon me, her expression revealing the hope and love which a sister has for another. There was a look of confidence in her eyes, knowing *who* I was as well as *whose* I was, but I could also tell there was a slight presence of anxiety, understanding the war which had raged within me. Vashti's gaze conversely reflected the selfish desire of pushing forward her own agenda.

"I have indeed chosen," I said, raising my voice for all to hear. "This day I have chosen a path, a path from which I will never wander. I have chosen a path that I am convinced, with every fiber of my being, to be the only path worth following. Vashti offers you all a life of supposed fulfillment. She offers you a sense of purpose and destiny, but I tell you the truth: these promises she offers are nothing more than lies and poison straight from the pits of the Great Dragon."

At this Vashti gasped out loud. "Follow her guidance if you want to," I continued. "You won't obtain true beauty, but only a counterfeit beauty which is skin deep and which in the end leads to death. Such a rejection of the Scroll will lead you all to the eternal fires of sulfur. As for myself, I will not go there, for I am a daughter of the Great King, within whom everlasting beauty resides. I honor and serve Him." As I spoke, I beheld tears of joy upon the cheeks of both Leah and Ruth.

"The Great King is my sovereign," I continued. "I am His. I am also the daughter of my earthly father, who I honor and obey. He is my overseer. And if I marry, my husband will be the head of my household and I will serve him and yield to him in all things. I will counsel him in all humility. I will build him up and complement him, and together we will be mighty. For just as the Scroll declares, so I declare that I was created for my husband." Again, Vashti let out a gasp of utter bewilderment.

"I will bear children, many children, if it's the will of my Creator," I continued, "and none of them will be given up to the Great Dragon as an offering while still in my womb."

"I've heard enough!" Vashti shouted. "Get down!"

"You have heard enough, perhaps," I said, "but they haven't. Hear me, all you ladies. Do you want fulfillment? Do you want beauty? True fulfillment and beauty are found only in obeying the Great King as set forth in the Scroll. He created you to be a woman with a purpose in mind. Embrace His purpose for you, and you will find true life and fulfillment. Women such as Vashti think they have power. They are mistaken. Their so-called power is counterfeit. Yield to the Great King, and you will find true beauty. It is the woman who is wrapped in modesty, gentleness, and submission who is truly gorgeous. It is the woman who doesn't run from femininity, but embraces it, that is truly a woman. The Great King wants this for each of you. It is not weakness but power. But you must reject this poison. You cannot embrace both at the same time. You must choose."

"Yes!" shouted Vashti, full of a rage, which none had yet seen from her. "You must choose! Who will choose me?! Who will choose me?!"

Many of those present applauded their approval. My heart sank because of their blindness, and yet, I knew that it was the Great King who opened eyes, and only the eyes which He willed to open. I then stepped down from the crate and embraced both Leah and Ruth.

"Well done," Leah said. "The Great King is with you. You have pleased him this day."

I turned to Hannah, who after hearing all that had been said, had a look of uncertainty upon her face. "Come back with us," I pleaded with her. "We truly love you, and we can help you find your true self. Walking down the path you are currently on will only lead to great sadness and destruction." Hannah looked down to the ground in thought and then glanced upon the face of Troy.

"Please Hannah," I said. "Will you come back with us?"

***

Hannah hesitated. I could see her mind racing, and it was clear that a battle was raging within her. At last she looked at me, and her appearance had a sudden resolve attached to it.

"No," she said defiantly. "I will not return with you. Not now. Not ever. I refuse to waste my life with the things you speak of. I will not be a door mat. My allegiance is with Vashti, and Troy is also with me."

"There!" Vashti said with a voice of aggression as she came to the side of Hannah. "At least one of you has wisdom." She then glared at Leah. "You are the one who caused this trouble. It is your narrowminded influence that has led Elizabeth astray."

"You are mistaken," Leah said calmly. "It is the power and love of the Great King that has led Elizabeth to the truth."

"You will pay for this," Vashti declared, her eyes full of fury and hate.

Leah replied with both gentleness and sincerity. "It is frustrating for you to know that your beauty isn't eternal," she said. "But know this: my words were spoken out of love for the Great King, love for Elizabeth, and also love for you Vashti. I will pray for you."

"Pray for me?" Vashti repeated with disgust. "You should rather pray for yourself!" She immediately nodded to three men, dressed in hooded cloaks, that I hadn't yet noticed. They surrounded us the three of us but were particularly focused upon Leah.

"Brothers," Vashti said with an air of authority in her voice, "these other ladies may leave, but this one, Leah, needs to come with us for a time. Her son can go, but she must stay. I am not yet finished with our conversation."

"You cannot take her," Ruth said with astonishment in her voice. "It isn't lawful. We will summon the magistrate if we must."

"You foolish girl," Vashti said. "Don't you realize? I own the magistrate. They are all mine. You had better step aside before I include you in my plans. Don't worry. Leah will return to you soon, but when she does, she will have more respect for the truth." The men then took Leah by her arms.

"Please release your grip, and do not touch me," Leah said, and the way she said it, with her soft and confident voice, made the men obliged to obey.

"Do my bidding!" Vashti said in a hushed fury. "Take custody of her now!" The men seemed to regain their former determination and took Leah by her arms.

"You are making a mistake," Leah said in a gentle yet sober voice.

"Surely," Vashti said mockingly. "Surely, a gentle Scroll-following woman such as yourself will not raise your hand and strike a man?"

"You are correct," Leah said as the men's grip tightened. "But he will." And she nodded behind them. Everyone's attention turned to find Nathan, standing as bold as a lion, with a look on his face that struck terror in me. It was fierce to behold. His eyes were fixed upon the three men.

"Unhand my wife now," he said, "and I will consider allowing you to leave here still able to walk." The three men hesitated, looking at each other uneasily, and remained unmoved. Nathan approached them slowly.

"Last chance," Nathan said. "Let her go, now."

"And if we don't?" the man nearest to Nathan asked.

What happened next occurred so quickly that it was difficult to take it all in. The next thing I knew, two of the men were on the ground upon their backs groaning in pain while the other one was cautiously walking backwards as to not let his eyes off Nathan. Leah was now free and behind her husband, safe and secure. Nathan then turned to his wife, and they together, along with Levi, made their way back home. They walked hand in hand, as calm as if they were strolling alone in the prairie on a cool spring morning. Ruth and I went with them.

From behind us we could hear the voice of Vashti. "You will regret this, Leah! You will regret this day!"

"Thank you," Leah said affectionately to her husband. "Thank you for coming to my rescue."

"Or course," he said. "I'm only thankful to the Great King that those men weren't armed and didn't push me to greater limits."

"But what of Hannah?" I asked. "Are we going to just leave her there?"

"She has made her choice," Leah replied. "We cannot force her. The narrow path is a road that one must walk down willingly."

"Agreed," Ruth said. "The road for Hannah is filled with much hurt and pain. I hope she will one day return, but it is doubtful."

"I did not hear all of the exchange that just took place," Nathan said, "but I did hear our sister Elizabeth declare the truth of the Scroll without doubt or fear." He turned to me and smiled.

At that moment I knew, more than ever before, that the Great King was so good and that His ways were true and right. I knew that I was on the side of true life, fulfillment, and victory.

I said farewell to my dear sisters as I entered my cottage. I sat down at the table with a sense of both freedom and exhaustion. The freedom was such a comfort. I knew that the battle would rage on, but I also knew that I had chosen my side in the contest. I was a follower of the Great King and the Scroll. The reality of no longer having to struggle with knowing which side to follow was such a relief and a joy.

The door of the cottage then opened, and Martha entered with a basket upon her arm. "I brought you some lunch," she said kindly.

"Oh, how kind," I said, extremely happy to be near to her. The old matron came and sat beside me, emptying the contents of her basket upon the table. "What a lovely feast," I observed, seeing the cheese, smoked sausage, and fruit.

"Ah yes," she said. "And I've also brought you another delicacy. Would you like to know how the story ends?"

"What story?" I replied.

"The story of the two lovers," she explained.

"The story is ending?" I marveled, saddened at the prospect of only one more insight into their lives while beaming with curiosity as to how the story would end.

"All stories must end," she said, "though in a way they live on in the lives of others who learn from them."

"Is it a happy ending?" I asked nervously.

"There's only one way to find out," she said, offering to me her hand. I took her hand, almost apprehensively, and closed my eyes. I soon saw the couple, there in the same setting that I had last seen them, speaking about the farm.

"My love," he said, taking her hands into his. "I know how much you love this farm. We have so many wonderful memories here, but I believe that a new land awaits us, out there somewhere. And I believe that until we take this leap of faith by selling this farm, we will not find the future blessing. Trust me. The Great King is with us. We just need to trust Him."

"But what if you're wrong?" she asked. "I don't at all think that it is a good idea to sell this land. What if we sell it and then never find something as nice?"

"I know it is a bit scary," the husband said gently and with a smile. "But again, you just have to trust me. You asked me to pray about this, and I have for many months now. The time has come. We need to move forward."

"No," the wife said, her tone grave and demanding. "I am not going to go along with something so foolish."

The look upon the husband's face nearly broke my heart. It was the look of a man so deflated, so dispirited. "Honey, please," he continued.

"No," she said firmly. "I will not hear any more talk like this. Until I hear and feel the same from the Great King, I am not going to take one step forward." The husband just sat there, his eyes glazed over with such a sense of despair that my eyes began to well up with tears.

The story then skipped forward what seemed a few years. The love that had been there seemed to be waning with time. They smiled less, and their conversations were fewer. The intimacy and joy which they shared at the inception of their marriage had vanished. As time went on, the husband suggested a few more steps forward concerning different matters in their lives, but with each suggestion was a dominance by the wife which eventually brought the man to a place of complete subjugation and numbness.

It was as if he lived his life with only fleeing moments of joy, sporadically popping up here and there, but his sense of daring and adventure which had initially been so attractive to his wife was now gone completely, and she resented him for it. It was as if she wanted that part of him back, but through her fear and desire for control, she had squelched it. And deep down she knew this, which only stirred more bitterness towards him and more self-loathing towards herself.

To say that my heart was crushed as I watched them progress into emotional and spiritual exile was an understatement. I was devastated. The story, which had begun with such beauty, romance, and life, was now ending with nothing of worth or admiration.

The husband had very little drive left in his life, except the desire to keep his wife from getting too upset, though it came at a cost, for he knew that in the end she had forfeited true happiness. He knew that she was only left with momentary reliefs which came from an empty sense of control. And he knew that in the end, these small *victories* as she considered them, only made her more and more empty. It was a horrible cycle that made me want to wake up from the nightmare. I continually tried to pull away from the story, though something inside of me compelled me to see it to the end.

More years came and went, their relationship reduced to that of mere acquaintances, neither taking pleasure in each other's company nor desiring it. The man had no expression of joy left in him, only emptiness. The woman, who at the beginning of the story was absolutely dazzling, was no longer attractive at all. Indeed, she had almost come to be repulsive. It was amazing to me how beauty could come and go from the same person. It was a deeper confirmation to me that beauty didn't stand alone, but that it was connected with our hearts and lives.

I continued to watch, the years going by faster and faster. The woman's brilliant red hair had now vanished into grey, and her smooth skin was wrinkled with age. More time elapsed, and for some reason, the woman was becoming familiar to me, as if I knew her. More years passed. She now resembled someone I thought I knew. Then, suddenly, it was clear. I fully recognized her, and my heart jumped with shock to such a degree that I yelled the woman's name.

"Martha!"

Chapter 30

I opened my eyes, full of tears, and looked upon Martha, frail and old, herself full of tears streaming down her cheeks. "It was you?" I asked with unbelief.

"It was," she said. "I was so in love. I was so beautiful. And he was so strong, so handsome, so brave. But through my fear, selfishness, and pride, I slowly drowned all the wonder of our love, and soon little was left except a longing for what had been and a frustration that it was gone."

"Martha, I'm so sorry," I said as I wept.

"Me too," she said softly, wiping the tears from her eyes. "And it brings me such pain to see it unfold in front of my eyes again, but I do it for your benefit, Elizabeth, that you may learn from my error. Do not give into fear or pride. Love, honor, and follow your man. In doing so, both of you will be set free."

We ate our meal together in silence, and I had to make an effort at times not to cry, for my heart was truly broken for this woman that I loved so dearly. My father then entered the cottage, and I stood to greet him.

"Sit down my beautiful daughter," he said with a smile, and after a brief pause continued. "I am so proud of you. You entered that forest a girl, and now you have returned a woman. And based on what I have heard from Nathan, Leah, and Ruth, you are a woman who is strong in the Great King and able to defend what you believe. You defeated Vashti today, though, I fear that more of her kind will be appearing. Ruth could see an evil in her that will bring destruction on our people if we do not make necessary changes. For as society walks away from the Great Scroll, such willfully evil people are produced. It cannot be helped. When light is taken away, darkness must fill the void. But you, my daughter, you are a ray of light in the hand of the Great King."

His words blessed my soul. Samuel had lost his first daughter, an event that would have produced in him a pain I couldn't imagine. But now, by the grace of the Great King, he had raised another daughter who had been tested, and through blood and fire, had overcome. Overwhelmed with emotion, I sank into his arms with tears of joy.

"Now," he said, "you both must ready yourselves, for there is a council this evening, not only for the men, but for all of the fellowship. We have some difficult decisions to make."

"What are we discussing?" I asked curiously.

"You for one," he said, "and Hannah for another. Our children are being tempted and tried in ways that are dangerous, and some are beginning to fall. This is unacceptable. We must consider radical measures if necessary. If we do not protect and preserve our lineage, then we have accomplished very little. This matter is at the heart of the Great King."

Later that evening I found myself sitting around a bonfire next to my father with the majority of the fellowship gathered, nearly fifty people.

"Hannah is lost to us," Benjamin said. "This makes the third lost sheep in as many years and is unacceptable. The schemes of our enemies are pressing down upon us more and more. We cannot lose our children like this. They are our future, our inheritance, our treasure."

"Not only that," Stephen added, "but the culture in Ravenhill has been growing more hostile towards our people. I fear that the mobs Nathan experienced in Anthropolis will soon be experienced here."

"I agree," Nathan said. "The interaction I had today in the marketplace confirms that the mobs of the enemy will increase. A follower of the Scroll can sense the darkness and tension."

Everyone remained silent with most eyes upon the ground, overcome at the gravity of the situation.

"The question we are here to answer," my father said, "is *what should we do?*"

"We must do what our brothers and sisters in Anthropolis did," Nathan declared. "We must seek a haven in the forest."

"But will the Great King do for us what He did for them?" my father asked.

"I don't know," Nathan replied, "and we won't know for sure unless we step out by faith."

"Agreed," Stephen said. "We must step out by faith. We must distance ourselves from this bad company that corrupts good morals."

"Into the forest?" another man repeated. "What do you mean? Dragons live there and could attack at any time. It will be dark and dangerous. Dragon breeders travel through the forest at times."

"That is true," my father agreed, "but how much are the souls of our children worth? I would rather risk death, hunger, and disease than risk the loss of their souls. Ruth had a glimpse of evil in the market that none of us can understand fully. These followers of the Great Dragon have their eyes set on our fellowship. They want to eliminate us. We must prepare."

"We should send a few families to scout an area," Benjamin said. "Some of you may not be able or ready to do this. Do not fear. This will not divide or separate this fellowship."

"Agreed," my father said. "It will be a process that we carefully move forward with. I will call upon four families, including my own, to go in the first wave."

"My family will go," Nathan said, and as he did, his wife put her hand upon his shoulder in support.

"My family as well," Stephen said. "I want my sons and daughters away from this village." The parents of Jonah likewise volunteered their family.

"Very well," my father said. "It is settled. Let us all continue to pray and prepare. There is a sense of urgency. The four families should leave within a fortnight, if that is acceptable with the heads of each family." All of the men involved nodded in agreement and the council was dismissed. I looked over my shoulder into the forest.

"Are we really going in there?" I asked my father. "I mean, in there to live?"

"We are going to try," he said. "I know this seems unimaginable, but I ask you to trust me, my daughter. I think you should know that there was a man who came to see me a few months ago. He came at night. You didn't see him."

"You mean the blind man?" I asked. "I did awaken for a portion of your conversation and fell back asleep."

"Yes," my father said. "That was the man. He told me late that evening that this would happen. He told me that for the sake of our offspring that we would have to be steppingstones for future generations."

"Who was he?"

"He was a friend of mine, an old friend. We trained and fought together many years ago, in the days of the Insurrection."

"The Insurrection?" I marveled. "You fought in that battle? But I assumed that Scroll followers would have no part in it."

My father smiled. "My sweet daughter, it was the Scroll followers who had the largest role to play in the Insurrection. They also laid the foundation for such a declaration and subsequent battle. Without the teaching of the Scroll, no such campaign would have been forged. It is also unfortunate that it bears the name,

Insurrection. A better title would be the Liberation. My father's eyes then seemed to drift back in time.

"Those were difficult days," he said in recollection. "They were evil days, for tyranny had taken hold in all of the land. But our cause was just, and the blessing of the Great King was with us."

"And your friend played a big part?" I asked curiously.

"More than just a big part," he replied. "It was he that forged our victory against the tyranny of the Collectivists. Without his leadership, we would have been utterly defeated, not only militarily, but also mentally."

"Will such a battle happen again?" I asked, "for it seems our lands are again diving into tyranny and evil."

"I don't think another liberation will take place," he admitted with a sad expression, "not unless something changes. You must understand, my dear, that the Liberation was only possible because the majority of the people of these lands revered the Great King. Only with a people who have civil morality can such a freedom take place. But now, in only two generations, the tides have turned. The reverence for the Great King is waning. And without it, no liberation of these lands will happen again. The good news, however, is that we can still follow the Great King and be His remnant people. These lands cannot thrive without His Kingdom, but His Kingdom can thrive without the devotion of these lands. We are free in Him. Nothing can stop us from being His people."

We were suddenly interrupted by Nathan. "Forgive me," he said, "but Jonah says he knows of a place that will be perfect. There's already a bit of a clearing there, and a spring as well."

"A spring?" my father repeated. "Well, that sounds wonderful. Reminds me of an oasis."

Ruth then entered the room with both excitement and eagerness upon her face. "Nathan!" she cried with both excitement and concern in her voice. "Hurry!"

"What is it?" Nathan asked his sister.

"Leah's water has broken, and the baby is coming quickly," she said.

Chapter 31

We sprinted to the small hut, and as we approached, we could hear Leah calling for her husband. As I came in the door, I felt my heart beating anxiously, for I had never seen a woman in labor before. I felt a rush of terror come over me, for memories of Leah's stillbirth entered my mind, and a part of me wanted to run out of the cabin.

Nathan quickly took Leah's hand as she lay in her bed. "Are you alright?" he asked with a thoughtful expression.

Leah took a few deep breaths with her eyes closed, and then she looked up at her true love. "I am well," she said, "I'm glad you are here. The baby is moving downward."

"Very good," he said. "You're doing wonderfully, my dear. You are going to bring a baby into this world. Relax and remember, the Great King is with you. You can do this."

Leah nodded, eyes closed, her breathing continuing in the same peaceful rhythm. She seemed to be in a world all her own, totally relaxing her body during what I guessed to be contractions. Her head was covered with sweat and her belly looked very large. I again felt anxiety to such a level that I wanted to rush from the room. I was afraid that something was going to go wrong, or that Leah was going to be hurt. I felt like the situation was out of control. Both Nathan and Ruth looked serious, yet calm, but I couldn't seem to find any sense of peace. Words from Vashti came back into my mind, as if echoing from the past: *Was it fair that Leah should be going through such pain? Was such treatment of her body worth it? Did Nathan truly love her?*

My mind was racing and I couldn't seem to slow it down. I was ashamed at the stress that was rising up in my soul, but I felt that I couldn't help it. I was fighting to believe what was most important: the Scroll, wifehood, motherhood, all of them were in the forefront of my thoughts.

Suddenly I realized that Leah's eyes were open and that they were fixed upon me. I opened my eyes wide in fear, holding back tears of both worry and shame. To my great surprise, I saw Leah smile.

"Don't be afraid my sister," she said, as if she was able to see within my very soul. "I am both well and happy. The pain is minimal when compared to the joy that is to follow. Look well upon what you will soon behold, for this is the greatest fulfillment of a woman." She then extended her hand to me, and I approached her and took hold of it. And with her embrace, all of my fear, doubt, and worry left me. I suddenly felt very safe, free, and joyful.

"To make another life," she said, "and to bring it into this world, is the greatest joy the Great King offers to His daughters. We are the life-givers, the nurturers, the foundation for the next generation. We are the true maidens of light."

She then looked at Nathan. "It is time my love," she said.

Nathan looked at me. "Get some hot cloths to help aid the pressure," he instructed me. "The baby will be here any minute."

I quickly did as he said. I then beheld something that took my breath away and brought tears of utter wonder and beauty to my eyes. Never before had I observed such blessing, such power, such tenderness. I witnessed a baby come into the world. Within only a moment it was all over. All labor and pain had ended, and Leah was holding her newborn son in her arms as Nathan kissed her head. She was smiling more than I had ever seen, and tears of happiness were flowing down her cheeks.

"He is so handsome," Ruth said, also weeping tears of joy. "Well done, my sister."

"Oh, he is perfect!" Leah exclaimed. "You see?" she said looking at me. "The Scroll is true. This is the greatest and most fulfilling privilege." Leah's firstborn son, Levi then entered the room. "Oh, my son," Leah said, pulling him up on her chest next to the baby. "Meet your baby brother."

"What is his name?" Ruth asked.

"His name is Adam," Leah answered. "And these two boys will be mighty men for the Great King. As best friends they will vanquish their foes. No dragon will be able to stand before them."

I left the cabin that evening with such a deep sense of purpose, peace, and clarity that I had never before experienced. It was as if the Great King, by His grace, was continuing, over and over, to show me the true purpose and pleasure of His daughters. Just when I thought that my abandonment of the ways of Vashti were finished, the Great King revealed another chink in my armor which I overcame. I felt that I was becoming more and more a true lady of the Scroll, and I realized how overwhelmingly blessed I was to be surrounded with women like Leah, Ruth, and Martha. And there, upon the open prairie, with the full moon shining upon my face, I fell to my knees to offer all my body, mind, and soul to the Great King.

"I am your daughter," I said, as I wept tears of joy. "Use me as You see fit. I yield myself fully to you. Help me to be Your faithful follower, and to obey You in all things. Please provide for me, in Your timing, a man who loves the Scroll. Help me to be a good helpmeet, to fulfill his vision, and to make him strong. And please give me the honor and joy to bring many children into this world. Give me strong sons who will fight for You. Give me noble daughters who will stand strong in Your word. I give myself fully, oh Great King, to You. Amen."

I was resolved. There was no going back. I had stood at the crossroads of ideas; I had looked to the north, south, east, and west; and I had found the only true path worth taking. The truth had set me free, and nothing would ever draw me back to the lies of the enemy. I felt that this experience with Leah and her newborn son was a final milestone in my transformation to freedom and resolve. It was like spring water and bright sunshine upon the fertile soul that the Great King had cultivated, and I, the seed, was now breaking forth. It was just as the Scroll said: *"Unless a seed falls to the ground and dies, it remains unchanged. But if it dies, it will grow into something no one could have ever imagined."* I was that seed. The Great King had allowed me to die. The lies, pride, and selfishness had finally begun to decay. It wasn't an easy process, but it was good. And now, the life of the Great King within me was bursting forth.

A week later, on my sixteenth birthday, our people traveled to the spot in the forest that Jonah had found. We fasted and prayed to the Great King, and He did for us just as He had done for our brothers in Anthropolis. He set up a spiritual border that wouldn't allow the enemy to enter. We named the location the Oasis, and within another week four of our families had lodgings built and gardens planted.

The following two months were wonderful, for my experience with Leah and her childbirth had put a stronger bond between us, especially in regard to her son, Adam. It was as if he was my nephew, and Leah my sister. Ruth and I also bonded closer through the event. Every day I would visit Adam and Leah and bring her food. The conversations we had were so precious and meaningful; they taught me how to speak like a true woman of the Scroll. However, my favorite daily routine was holding Adam and rocking him as Leah slept during the midday. I would watch him sleep, unable to take my gaze away from his face and tiny features, and I would dream of my own children whom I would one day bring into the world.

From these intimate times with Adam, as well as Levi, and through my conversations with Leah, I better understood my purpose as a woman. I was a maker of strong men. I would marry one man, and by the grace of the Great King, I would make him strong. I would bring sons into the world, and by the grace of the Great King, I would raise them to be strong. I would have daughters, whom I would raise up to do likewise. The force that my husband, my child and I would be, together for the Great King, would be strong and powerful. It was just as Leah would tell me: *When women make men strong, they find their greatest strength as women.*

I was realizing the difference between strong women in the eyes of the world versus strong women in the eyes of the Great King. According to the world, to be a strong woman is to be independent, in charge, and to be over men. It was to be your own master. In the Kingdom of the Great King, to be a strong woman is to be clothed with humility, gentleness, and discretion. Women of the world step on top of men and unknowingly cripple themselves. Women of the Great King assist their men, and together they change the world.

***

It had soon been ten weeks since Leah had given birth, and the Oasis was strong and secure. We would tend our flocks and gardens and train during the day, and we would often feast and fellowship together at night. There was a unity and love between us all, and I could tell that my father was happy with his decision to transition our people to the forest. It would be a slow transition, but it would, in the end, be an added protection, both physically and spiritually. This gave me great joy, to see him fulfilled in his leadership of not only the fellowship, but of me as well.

One evening, deep into the night, I was awakened by the sound of commotion. I could hear voices which seemed to be outside of my home. I quickly took hold of the candle next to my bed and lifted it high. My father was not in bed. I heard another loud noise; this time it sounded like a cry. I quickly threw a cloak about me and stepped outside. The waning moon was overhead, and I guessed it to be the middle of night. I could see torches, and it seemed that most of the fellowship was awake. I quickly made my way to the group. Another cry. This time I recognized the voice. It was Leah. She was crying uncontrollably.

"What's wrong?" I asked Nathan.

"He's gone," he replied frantically. "We looked everywhere and there are no signs of him. He's vanished into thin air!"

"Who's vanished?" I asked, terror coming to my voice.

"Adam!" he exclaimed.

Chapter 32

It is difficult to describe the feeling that was within my heart at that moment. As for Leah, I was unable to imagine her inner turmoil. I turned in a circle, looking upon the dark shadows of night, and called aloud for Adam in vain.

"Over here!" Jonah shouted. He was a stone's throw away from us and was crouched low to the ground with a torch in his hand. We all came to his side.

"What is it!?" Nathan asked, his voice full of panic.

"Tracks," he replied, "only a few hours old."

"Dragon tracks?" my father asked.

"No," he replied. "Human tracks. I guess it to be the tracks of a woman. They seem to be leading from Nathan's cottage into the forest."

"Vashti!" I said aloud. "She took him!" With these words, almost all of the women present instantly went for their bows and arrows and within less than a minute were assembled upon the edge of the forest.

"Jonah!" Leah called. "Find her now. Rescue my child!"

"I cannot run fast at night," he said, "especially while trying to follow her footsteps."

"Get torches!" Nathan called to those around him.

"And arm yourselves!" my father ordered. "We leave at once, all who are able and willing."

Within only a short moment most of our company from the Oasis was traveling within the forest with both weapons and torches. Jonah led our company, with Nathan and Leah close behind him. I was aside Ruth, and near to us were both my father and Benjamin. Stephen was also with us. In all, our company was nearly fifteen. A few volunteers had remained back at the Oasis with the children, many of whom had stayed fast asleep.

I could sense the anxiety of the fellowship, for to travel deep within the forest at night with torches blazing was a very dangerous idea. But we all knew that there was no other option. My heart pulsated with such anxiety and pain, and I could continually hear Ruth quietly weeping beside me.

We had been traveling for nearly an hour when Jonah broke the silence. "We are gaining on her," he said, "or whoever the person is." Suddenly I thought I heard one of the sounds that we all were hoping against. A low rumble was heard off to our left in the darkness, followed by a howl.

"We cannot delay our pursuit!" my father ordered. "Benjamin and Stephen, stay with me. The rest continue on with Jonah. We will catch up."

The three warriors stepped out of the line to the left. I then saw, by the light of their torches, a hell hound, its mouth opened wide, revealing its giant fangs. The three men raised swords and shields, while ordering us to continue, which we did, though it was difficult. A bright flame lit that area of the forest. Shouting was heard followed by the horrifying roar of the hound. Then all was quiet and soon the three men were back in the line.

"That encounter will likely draw more hounds or dragons to this area," Stephen said. "Be ready."

We continued on as fast as we could. Jonah led us, his vision fixed on the dimly lit forest set before him, his focus concentrated and uncompromising. He was a skillful scout, but this pushed his ability to its limit.

"The sun is rising," Benjamin observed. "We will soon be able to travel faster.

I looked up and noticed a faint, orange glow between the tree branches. We were now climbing some kind of a hill, and the trees were thinning.

"Look!" Nathan said. We all looked ahead, and I thought I saw a cloaked figure looking back at us and then spinning around and hurrying away. The person was about thirty yards ahead.

Due to our assent of the hill and the lessening of the trees, our visibility was improving. I could now see the figure, running from us up the hill, seeming to hold something like a basket in their arms. I could also see that the hill was about to come to a precipice.

"She's going to throw the baby from the cliff!" Ruth shouted, quickly dropping to a knee and drawing her bow.

"No!" my father commanded, grabbing her arm just as she released the arrow. The powerful dart flew forward and just missed the person's head by a fraction of an inch.

As we were coming upon the edge of the cliff, the person was standing still and seemed to be looking out over the landscape. The figure turned to face us. It was Vashti, and baby Adam could be heard cooing from within the basket.

"Don't come any closer!" she shouted, her faced filled with a wild excitement mixed with terror. "Any closer and the baby boy goes over the cliff."

"Vashti," Leah said gently. "Please. That baby is mine. He is innocent. Please give him back."

"Why should I?" Vashti said mockingly, delighted with the apparent power she possessed. "The most merciful thing a family does to one of its infants is to kill it. You should have killed this boy. Is he really to be raised in the forest in such a low estate? Is it right for him to be indoctrinated in such false notions and deceit?"

"Please," Leah repeated, her hand drawn outward in caution and concern. "Please don't hurt him. Take me instead."

"It is too late for that," Vashti replied.

"Please," Leah persisted. "I love him. Please give him back."

"You love him?" Vashti repeated. "Why? What has he done to merit your love? He is a burden. He has no ideas, or passions, or contributions to offer. He is just a little clump of body parts, and he is, unfortunately, made in your image, Leah. He is unfit to live."

"No," Leah replied. "He is made in the image of his Creator, just as you are. He has the right to live, and we have the right to raise him up as we see fit."

Vashti raised up her arm as to drop the basket over the cliff. Everyone gasped and little Adam began to whimper from within the basket. "I still don't understand," she said, seeming to marvel at the attitude of the group. "This child hasn't loved you. You don't even know its personality. Why do you care so much about its life?"

"For two reasons," Nathan replied, his powerful voice filing the valley. "First, because he is a creation of the Great King, just as my wife said. And second, he is our future. He is the future hope of our people."

"Your people?" Vashti questioned. "You mean, followers of the Great King?" Nathan nodded; Vashti smiled. "That isn't an adequate reason," she said as she looked down within the basket, her eyes fixed upon tiny Adam. She then returned her gaze to our fellowship, and her eyes were filled with hate and darkness.

"Wait," my father said boldly, yet with grace in his voice. "You know that murder is wrong. You can't kill an innocent baby."

"I can," she said, "and I will. And it won't just be the offspring of Scroll followers. It will be any other lifeform that is declared to be a burden or hindrance to society."

"And who decides who is valuable and who isn't?" my father asked.

"I do," she said, "along with those with me."

"The world won't let you kill their children," Nathan testified.

"Oh yes they will," she replied with an evil glare. "In the end, women will bring their babies to us, begging for us to take them. Just you wait and see. They will love us and sing our praises while we slowly kill off their ethnic heritage."

"Please," Leah said with desperation in her voice, "please have mercy."

"Mercy?" Vashti mocked. "You say you want mercy, and yet you have shown this baby no mercy. I will show you the best way." And with those words, she tossed the basket high into the air, far out over the cliff of the hillside, with nothing but hundreds of feet between it and the ground.

Chapter 33

In that moment time seemed to stop in my mind. Absolute despair is all I felt. Hopelessness, grief, and utter disbelief flooded my heart. Leah stretched out her arm and cried aloud, as did Nathan. At that same moment a shadow above us blotted out the sun and a large black dragon swooped down, as if on cue, and captured Adam's basket in its jaws and continued in flight deeper within the forest.

Vashti smirked at the anguish that each of us bore. "Look at you," she said with disgust upon her face. "You care so much about things that matter so little."

"Where is that dragon taking the child?" my father asked.

"That is not your concern," Vashti replied. "But I do want you to know that it will be a sacrifice offered for the Great Dragon. He loves the death of the innocent. That child was destined to belong to the Great Dragon, either now or later. If we wouldn't have captured him now, we would have in the years to come. All of your children will fall to us, either like Hannah or this baby. You will keep none of them, and your fellowship, therefore, will die with you."

"You are wrong!" Nathan said, lifting his voice in righteous anger. "That child belongs to the Great King, and He will rule with his Creator, either now or in eternity! You think you will conquer us, but you overlook this one simple fact: you wage a war whose outcome has already been determined. You fight a battle you cannot win!"

"You are the one who is wrong!" Vashti said. "The power of the Great Dragon is immeasurable. He has pledged to me power, beauty, and eternity. I will have everything while you will have nothing."

She then focused her gaze upon me. "I offered to you my love and fellowship," she said, "and you scorned and rejected me. Now you will suffer a life not worth living."

"You have been deceived," my father answered her. "The Great Dragon will turn on you in the end. You should repent while you have the chance."

I noticed Vashti look over our heads, and joining her gaze behind us I beheld a large black dragon diving upon us. Fire was pouring from its nostrils. "Dragon fire!" I shouted.

Everyone spun around in response to my alarm, and a wall of shields was put together just in time to spare us from being burnt alive. As we recovered from the sudden attack, we beheld the dragon continue on over the cliff with Vashti in its talons.

Leah immediately put her hand upon the shoulder of Jonah, who looked at my father for approval.

"Go," he said. "Follow that dragon and report back as soon as you are able." And instantly Jonah was gone in the direction of the black dragon.

"The situation has now changed," my father said to the group. "We were following a lone thief; now we are going into the very lair of the enemy. Not all should go. We cannot win an open battle, but we must rely on stealth and secrecy to win. Only a few should go. I know all of you would volunteer, but that simply will not do."

"Leah and I must clearly go," Nathan said.

"And what of your other son?" my father asked.

"Even in his young age, he would support our decision," Nathan testified. "He understands duty."

"I will go," Ruth said. "Adam is treasured to me above all other life. I must either see him safe or die trying."

"Very well," my father replied. "It will be the five of us: Jonah, Ruth, Leah, Nathan and me. All others will return at once to the Oasis."

As they spoke, my heart was on fire. I knew what I needed to do. I couldn't turn away.

"I will also go," I said desperately. "I must."

"Oh no," my father said, and all others agreed. "You must not do this, my daughter, though your heart bids you to. You must return to safety."

"My father," I said with tears flowing down my cheeks. "Oh, my father. If ever you loved me, hear me now. It was Leah and this child who fully removed the scales from my eyes. I must fight."

"But the mission is desperate," he replied, his eyes watering with emotion. "You may die and then you would never know what it is to live a full life, marry, or bear children."

"Father," I said as I wept. "I know about your beloved Rebecca. She was a warrior. She followed her heart, and she died. I know you are afraid for me, but you must allow me to likewise follow my heart."

My father was now weeping as well.

"But if I also lose you," he said, "then all that is in me will die, for the Great King has used you to rekindle my heart with purpose and love."

"But you know," I said, "that if I don't follow the leading of the Great King, then my life isn't worth living either. This is a risk we must both be willing to take. Don't worry about my future, or my marriage, or my children. Obedience and duty come before marriage and motherhood. My life is in the hands of the Great King. If I don't return from this adventure, then it is because of His good pleasure."

My father took a deep breath and looked up to the heavens and then back at me.

"So be it," he stated resolutely as he wiped the tears from his eyes. "Grip your bow tightly my daughter. For we are going into the serpent's nest."

Chapter 34

We prayed with our fellowship upon the mountain's edge, embraced one another, then went our separate ways; us deeper into the forest, and the others back to the Oasis.

"We will head in the general direction of the black dragon," my father said.

"Will Jonah be able to find us?" I asked.

"I'm sure of it," my father replied. "His skill is beyond his age."

Leah was holding back her tears.

"Take courage," my father said, addressing both Leah and Nathan. "It is just as my daughter declared. We are all in the hands of the Great King. Even now, your son is in His hands. We must trust Him."

For the rest of the day we traveled in silence. Our movements were quick and careful, and we were continually on guard against the enemy. An hour before sunset Jonah came upon us. He was out of breath and seemed utterly exhausted.

"So few," he said looking at us. "What happened?"

"The others are fine," Nathan said. "We have decided to pursue the enemy alone, in stealth and in secret. You have no obligation to join us, my friend. Each of us are committed to this task because of our love for this baby, as well as our love for one another. The choice is yours."

Jonah's eyes immediately turned to Ruth, and I saw a look of great affection welling up within them. "I will go with you," he said, "to the very end."

"What have you discovered?" my father asked.

"The child was taken to a mountain, nearly two days journey from here," he replied. "I wasn't able to find an easy way into the mountain. It has a main entrance, guarded by two formidable dragons. It seems to be a stronghold of the enemy."

"But is my son still living?" Leah asked in desperation.

"I'm sure he is," Jonah replied to our utter relief. "I was able to spy for a time upon the sentinels, and I heard them speak of the sacrifice that is to come by the new moon."

"New moon?" my father repeated. "That's the day after tomorrow. We must make haste."

We instantly set out, now being guided by Jonah, each step being as cautious and quiet as the one before. We risked no fires by evening and shared few words during the day. The question on my mind (and I guessed everyone else's) was, *how would we enter the mountain without raising an alarm?*

The following day the mountain came into sight, and we constantly beheld black dragons ascending and descending upon its peak. Not only that, but we could tell that the mountain was volcanic, for smoke was rising from its summit. On the following day, about noon, worn and weary, we reached the foot of the mountain.

"We don't have long," Nathan whispered. "The new moon will be here this evening. Jonah, where is the entrance?"

"It is around this bend," he replied. "But I have been praying that we would find another way."

"It is unlikely that there is," my father said. "Dragons usually leave no entrances within their strongholds smaller than their own bodies. If we had a week to search, maybe we could find a way, but we have only a few hours. They will make the sacrifice at midnight. The front door is our only option."

"Let us pause and pray," Ruth suggested, "if only for an hour if we can spare it. Perhaps the Great King will show us something."

"A noble and worthy suggestion," my father replied. "It is up to you Nathan."

"My sister is wise," the brave soldier replied. "We will find a safe place and pray." We found a small crevice and hugged in tight, hidden by brush only big enough for the six of us to huddle into.

"This will hide us from any dragons who may be on patrol," Jonah said. "Let us now petition our King."

We prayed silently, yet with an intensity that seemed to fill the small opening. We were desperate. Without the aid of the Great King, we knew our mission was hopeless. We suddenly heard a strange, unfamiliar sound. It was like many small hammers tapping on the ground. We waited patiently as the sound grew louder. We gripped our weapons, ready for any threat.

I then beheld them, only a few feet away from us moving upon the ground in a line, seemingly going around the mountain: scorpions. They were nearly four feet in length. I held my breath, fearful of creatures I had never seen before. In only a moment they all passed.

"Giant scorpions!" I exclaimed. "I've never heard of such creatures, and I counted over fifty of them!"

"Those were only babies," my father said soberly.

"Babies?" I repeated.

"Oh yes," he answered. "They get very large when they're full grown."

"I can't believe it," Nathan said, looking into his captain's eyes. "There's only one place where the giant scorpions dwell."

"Where's that?" I asked apprehensively.

"The lair of the Great Dragon," he replied.

"The Great Dragon?" Jonah exclaimed. "He is here?"

"It would seem so," my father said gravely. "He will be deep within the earth, but if an alarm is raised, he will be our greatest threat."

"That is even a better reason to avoid the front gate," Jonah reasoned.

"That's true," my father said.

"Then how do we get inside?" Ruth asked.

"The scorpions," Nathan replied. "That's the only way."

"What do you mean?" Leah asked.

"If the scorpions can get in," Nathan replied, "then so can we."

My father took a deep breath. "Nathan is right," he said. "It is our only hope. Hurry before we lose them." We quickly and cautiously exited our hiding place and went after the scorpions. We soon saw the last of them, turning toward the mountain and entering a small hole in the ground only three feet wide and two feet tall.

"Are we really going in there?" Ruth asked.

"We have no choice," Nathan said. "But none need go unless they feel led to. I will go first, and once I reach some kind of cavern inside, I will wait for the rest of you, and we will discuss our next move."

Within half a minute, all of us were within the small tunnel, crawling in pitch darkness. I could hear the *tap taps* of the scorpions ahead of us. My prayer was that they would only be moving away and not towards us. I soon felt someone grip my body. It was Leah, who had been ahead of me in the line. All was pitch black and quiet. I could tell that we were in an opening of some kind. My father was at the end of our procession and was soon with us. The tapping sounds had ceased, and yet it felt as if a thousand eyes were upon us. Nathan whispered so softly that we could barely hear him.

"I will risk a spark of light," he said. "Get your weapons ready." The silence was broken by the sound of striking flint, and a bright spark filled the small cavern.

I expected to see hundreds of scorpions all around us, but to my relief, the half second of illumination revealed us all alone within a tiny dwelling.

"Should we move along, spark by spark," Nathan asked quietly, "or should we light a torch?"

Even in the darkness I recognized the thoughtful breathing of my father. "I want to go in the dark," he said at last, "but if the enemy should come upon us, without any light we would be hopelessly slaughtered. We must risk the light, but let us keep it as concealed as possible in the rear of our company." And so, we moved forward, with a small torch held by Ruth at our rear. My father, Jonah, and Nathan led us.

I suddenly noticed something upon the cavern ceiling. I squinted my eyes and stared intensely to make out what it was. It was so still and camouflaged that none noticed it. As the tail suddenly moved, as if to strike, I realized it was a baby scorpion. I released my arrow and the creature was soon dead upon the ground.

"Well done," my father whispered. "We must be as silent as scorpions ourselves." We soon beheld a red glow coming from further up the passage. We put out our torch and crept ahead slowly.

"The heat in this place is unbearable," Leah said. "Can you feel it?"

"I do, indeed," Nathan replied, "and I believe that it is also the source of light."

"What do you mean?" Leah asked, but Nathan didn't need to answer, for we had come upon a fork in the passage. As we looked down the descending passage to the right, we beheld a river of lava. The mountain quaked slightly.

"This volcano seems unsettled," Ruth observed.

"And yet not in any danger of erupting," Samuel assured her. "I don't think dragons would have a stronghold that was in sudden danger of destruction."

The passage ascended upward and soon opened to a large cavern. It was thirty yards in diameter and nearly fifty yards in height, like a cylinder. The path we were on turned into a stone bridge that spanned the cavern, suspended within the middle. The chamber was well lit due to a lava river upon the edge of the cavern floor, some twenty yards below.

"Be careful," Samuel said, looking out upon the bridge. "It is fairly narrow."

"There is something below on the ground," Nathan said. "Do you see them moving?"

"Are they scorpions?" Ruth asked.

"They are dragons," Jonah said soberly. "Young red dragons. There are at least fifty of them." I then noticed a large passageway below, allowing the dragons to enter and exit the cavern.

"They don't seem to notice us," my father said. "The Great King be praised! Crawl across the bridge. Stay low and quiet. I feel we are getting close."

We crept across the narrow bridge. I dared not glance at the dragons below for fear of discovery, though I could hear them slinking about. We came to the other side and entered into another tunnel, this one branching into many directions. We followed the middle passageway and were soon upon another opening, much larger than the first. It seemed to be the center of the mountain.

There were many different passages that entered the large cavern, both above us and below us. Peeking out from the edge of our entrance, we took in our surroundings. The large floor of the mountain was about thirty yards below us and stretched far and wide, as if a small village could fit within it. A few rivers of lava crossed to and fro with many bridges of stone passing above them. Dragons and scorpions were everywhere, though most of them were young. Two huge scorpions were standing as guards upon both edges of the opening, and a formidable black dragon was walking about and seemed to be giving orders.

"Ruth," Samuel said softly. "What do you see?"

Ruth seemed to be looking beyond what we saw. She was looking deeper. "There is a darkness here that I have never beheld," she said with a serious expression. "It is deep in the earth and seems to be still."

"Anything else?" Leah asked desperately.

Ruth smiled. "Yes," she said. "There is a light. It is almost angelic. Do you not see it? There, in the middle of the chamber." We all looked intently.

"I see him," Leah said with quiet passion. Nathan gripped her arm as if to calm her. I joined their gaze and beheld tiny Adam lying peacefully upon a large flat stone with his basket beside him.

"We're only going to get one chance at this," Nathan said. "We must be strategic."

"But how?" my father said. "With all of us working as one, we could possibly get to the center and obtain the child, but how would we escape?"

"I will do it," Jonah said. "I am fast. I can get him."

"But your ability is for the forest and the plains," Nathan said. "It allows you to dodge trees and brush and rivers. This is stone, scorpion, dragon, and lava. You could easily stumble and fall to your own demise."

Jonah was intently studying the floor, as if planning his route of attack. "I will be fine," he said. "Just be ready. I will return to you here. And we will go out the same way we came in."

"But how will you get down there?" my father asked.

"Look here," Nathan said. "There is a ramp just to the side of this passage which goes to the ground level."

"And what happens if you fail?" my father asked. "What then?"

"That isn't an option," Jonah replied.

At that moment there was a great eruption of sound, for all of the dragons seemed to roar in unison, and a robed figure entered the great hall. "Our high priestess is here," the black dragon announced. The robed figure walked elegantly through the chamber.

"Greetings, my brethren!" she said as she removed her hood. I instantly recognized Vashti's voice and haughty spirit.

"Guards!" she continued. "Come and protect the sacrifice!" At this command the two giant scorpions made their way to the center of the chamber. Vashti removed a large dagger from her cloak. "It is time," she said.

Chapter 35

We stood in suspense and uncertainty of our next move. Vashti's arrogant voice broke the silence of our thoughts.

"Gadreel," she said aloud, addressing the black dragon. "I have fulfilled our master's wishes. I have robbed the soul of one of the children of a local fellowship. I have also brought a child sacrifice, an innocent child, the child of a Scroll-follower. herefore, I ask you, what of your promise? Is my reward ready?"

"Do not be too hasty to demand anything from me," Gadreel said, its voice causing the rock around us to vibrate. "You still have not delivered the main prize that our master desires."

"You mean the girl, Elizabeth?" Vashti replied with frustration in her voice. "I tried! She is untouchable!"

"You speak blasphemy!" Gadreel declared. "All of them can be reached. If you don't get them in the womb, then you get them as children. You use the theater, the Castle, the schoolhouse, and the market. You never end your pursuit."

"I will continue to pursue her soul," Vashti said begrudgingly, "but look at all I have done. Surely, I have earned my reward."

"We will see," Gadreel said musingly. "What you ask for is very great indeed." The dragon then spun in a circle, peering about, as if suddenly startled. We quickly ducked behind the stone wall of the outer passage. "Are any of your allies here with you?" it asked.

"My allies?" Vashti asked joining in the dragon's gaze. "Jezebel may come, but otherwise I don't think so."

"Hmm," the dragon remarked. "She must be here. I smell other humans."

"Well she isn't going to steal my glory," she said bitterly. "I retrieved this baby, and I'm going to be the one to sacrifice it. May we begin?"

The dragon looked about the cavern as in deep thought. "Very well," it said at last. "Call the faithful."

Vashti then let out a shout which was surprisingly loud. Scorpions and dragons began coming into the opening, assembling themselves in circles, like ripples in a pond. Fortunately, none came down our passageway.

"This isn't good," Nathan said amidst labored breathing. "You won't be able to make it through so many circles of beasts, Jonah."

"I didn't come this close just to witness my baby murdered," Leah said, also stricken with pain and anxiety.

"Even if it requires the sacrifice of us all," Ruth said soberly. "If only Jonah can get out with the child, and get him back to the Oasis, it will all be worth it."

"I will not allow you all to perish," Jonah said resolutely. "We must break up the circles and draw them all to one part of the cavern."

"A diversion," my father said, nodding his head in agreement. "That is the only way. We must be quick. It's now or never."

Vashti turned around slowly, seemingly overwhelmed with pleasure at the cloud of witnesses surrounding her. Hundreds of scorpions and dragons were gathered, and the dragon, Gadreel, was overshadowing her.

"The revolution begins!" she shouted for all to hear. "The weak, the oppressive, the intolerant, all of them will perish! Only those worthy will live upon the earth! And the Great Dragon will rule for all eternity! And I shall be his Queen! Bow down, all of you. Bow to your queen!" All present obeyed, including Gadreel. Vashti smiled with lustful delight. "And now," she said, turning her attention to tiny Adam, who was laid upon a stone altar beside his basket, "the blood of the innocent will be spilled as a sacrifice."

Suddenly there was a roar which pierced the ears of all. Everyone looked, along with Gadreel and all who were able, to the southern end of the gathering to behold a red dragon screaming in pain as a sword was pulled from its body by Nathan. Another cry instantly followed as arrows pierced the hides of several dragons only fifty yards away, at the edge of the circle. Leah and I were quickly emptying our quivers with such rapidity that dragons were continually crying out in pain and rage.

"Find them!" Vashti ordered. "Kill them all!"

Gadreel started striding toward us with a smile upon its face. I continued releasing arrows, though they were nearly spent. My eyes continually glanced at the middle of the circle for what mattered most. And then I saw him: Jonah. He was directly behind Vashti, who was intently looking towards us who were engaged in the battle. Jonah placed Adam in the basket and turned to run.

Gadreel must have seen the gleam of joy in our eyes, for he suddenly turned and gave a shout which seemed to nearly bring down the mountain. Vashti spun around and also screamed. "He has the baby!" she shouted. "Kill him!"

Scorpions and dragons were soon surrounding Jonah who was nearly to the far edge of the opening on the opposite side from us. He seemed overrun and trapped. "Quick!" Nathan said to Leah and me. "Back upon the outer trail! We must circle around to help him!"

The enemy had now abandoned us, and all of them were pursuing Jonah. As I ran around the outer trail, I kept my gaze fixed upon Jonah. We weren't going to get to him in time. My only hope was that he would find a sudden opening in the enemy lines to make a run for it. I could hear Leah running ahead of me, crying out as she ran. Jonah was now holding baby Adam in one hand and swinging his sword violently with the other. One of the giant scorpions had almost reached him, its stinger nearly thirty feet off of the ground. Suddenly I saw Ruth sprinting to Jonah, her bow and arrows clearing a path between the two of them.

"Hurry!" she shouted. "This way!"

They ran together for about fifty yards, shooting and slicing enemies as they ran, until they were nearly upon the edge of the chamber. The giant scorpion was now between them and the exit, and I could see my father upon the higher trail above calling out to them. The scorpion's giant pincher came down exactly upon Jonah with such speed that the gifted scout was unable to avoid its clutches. The scorpion lifted him high in the air; Jonah still held his sword in one hand and the basket in the other.

Vashti had been running all this time after them and had now arrived at the scorpion. "Grab the basket!" she commanded. "Quickly!" The scorpion used its other pincher to grab the basket out of Jonah's hand and handed it to Vashti, who shouted in vengeful gratification. Leah, Nathan, and I were nearly upon them. Leah was readying her bow and praying aloud to the Great King.

"There's nothing here!" Vashti shouted in anger, casting the empty basket upon the ground. Everyone's attention was turned to Ruth, who was now upon a boulder with the baby cradled in her arms, surrounded by foes on every side. The scorpion released Jonah, who fell to the floor seemingly void of life, and quickly advanced upon Ruth.

"Here!" my father shouted. He had come to a lower ledge and was now only fifteen feet above Ruth.

The scorpion was now upon her, and Gadreel was also drawing near. Without any further thought, Ruth tossed young Adam high into the air. The scorpion grabbed at him, and would have snatched the baby in mid-air, crushing his body.

But Nathan stretched forth his hand, and according to his ability, suddenly moved his son higher in the air, causing the scorpion to miss and allowing my father to catch him. Vashti cried out in anger and frustration. Ruth was now free of any burden, and quickly retrieving bow and arrow, began emptying her quiver upon the scorpion. The creature raised his stinger for a killing stroke, but suddenly jerked in pain, as Jonah sliced at the creature's hind legs.

Nathan, Leah, and I now arrived upon my father and Adam, who was soon in his mother's arms. "The Great King be praised!" she shouted.

We turned back to see both Ruth and Jonah within the scorpion's pinchers. The creature threw them with all its might into the adjacent stone wall of the cavern, knocking them to the ground in utter pain. Gadreel was instantly before them, inhaling a deep breath. "It is too late for them," my father said sadly. "Come! Or else none of us will escape here alive!"

Everyone fled with tears flowing down their cheeks, but I waited, only for a few seconds, to witness the end. And what I saw filled me with wonder. Jonah and Ruth were lying next to each other, their bodies broken and bruised. They were speaking, and I saw Jonah reach over and take Ruth's hand. I couldn't hear his words, but the reaction on Ruth's face, even amidst her pain and certain death, was beautiful. I had never experienced her expression, but I somehow recognized it. It was the look that a woman has when someone confesses his love for her. She replied with inaudible words, her face filled with joy and tears. And instantly the dragon fire took them.

"Elizabeth!" my father cried out. "Hurry!" I followed immediately.

"Where is the tunnel?" Nathan asked. "All of the passages look alike."

"It is here!" I said, stumbling upon it. No sooner did the words leave my mouth, then did a giant pincher come between me and my companions, striking the wall and bringing rock down between us.

"Run!" my father shouted. "Run and don't look back!" I quickly entered the narrow tunnel. A loud banging sound echoed behind me, likely another strike of the scorpion. The tunnel through which I ran caved in, cutting me off from my many enemies, but also from my father and loved ones. I knew there was no way to go back to them. My only hope was that they would find another way of escape.

There was a faint glow ahead, and I quickly ran towards it. I entered the small chamber we had crossed only an hour earlier. The bridge was still intact, spanning the opening of nearly thirty yards. Below, the ground was still covered with countless red dragons, who were all growling at me. But my attention wasn't upon them; it was upon the long serpent that was staring at me from the other side of the bridge; the same serpent who lured me from my house window all those years earlier; the same serpent who defeated me in my training years earlier. It looked down at the dragons and then up at me. "This time, Elizabeth, we will play for keeps."

Chapter 36

The serpent had grown since our last encounter and was nearly fifty feet in length, its body filling much of the chamber. I could hear the striking of the crumbled avalanche behind me, likely by the scorpion. The enemy was behind me, and my worst fear was before me.

"Remember last time?" the serpent said, stepping out upon the bridge. "Remember how you tried to run in fear?" The dragons below were constantly snapping and roaring like a pack of wild lions. "You couldn't beat me then," it said, "and you won't beat me now."

I was all alone. Ruth and Jonah were no more, and my other companions had likely shared their fate. The mountain quaked slightly, causing me to rebalance myself upon the bridge. The serpent took another step towards me.

"You're all alone," it said, as if it could read my mind. "You're all alone and your arrows are all spent." I quickly reached to the quiver upon my back. All gone. "Now you will die," it said.

I stood still, expecting to quake in fear at these words, but something had happened. I was standing before an enormous serpent, and yet, I wasn't afraid. I thought I was fooling myself, that I was only in shock, but I was unable to stir up any fear in my soul. I took a step toward my foe. I believed at that moment there was a great cloud of witnesses standing all around me, bold and strong. In front of all of them was the Great King Himself, ready to fight on my behalf. I took a breath, deeply and calmly, and a smile came to my face. "You are wrong," I said peacefully. "I am not alone. The Great King is with me."

"The Great King?" the serpent said mockingly. "I don't see Him anywhere. Where is He?"

"He is here," I said, pointing to my heart, "and He says that you are nothing but a lie. So, I tell you, that you are no more. You are nothing." The serpent suddenly had a look of fear, and it began to shrink.

"The Great King is with me," I said again, moving closer. "I am His daughter. I am fearfully and wonderfully made. His Scroll is perfect. Nothing can happen to me unless He so chooses." The serpent was clearly shrinking. It shouted at me and tried to swipe its front claws at me, but they didn't touch me.

"The Great King is the Most High Creator," I continued. "He made all things. He is Lord of heaven and earth. He is my Rock and my Fortress." The serpent then coughed fire balls at me, but I didn't even feel them.

"You are nothing," I said confidently. "The Great King is the way, the truth, and the life. You will now return to the abyss from whence you came." The serpent was now only a small snake, legless and powerless. I stomped its head, killing it, and flung it to the dragons below.

"Thank you," I said, my eyes closed and my hands lifted to the Great King. "I am free."

"Not yet," a voice said. It was Vashti.

***

She entered the chamber in front of me, where the serpent had been. Her face was bloody from battle, and the long knife was still in her hand. "If nothing else good comes from this day," she said solemnly, "at least you will perish." I held my bow in front of me.

"You should have brought a sword," she said mockingly, "but that wouldn't be feminine enough, would it?" We were now both out upon the narrow bridge.

"I don't want to fight you," I said. "My battle isn't with you but with the dragons."

"Then your battle is with me," she said. "You foolish girl. You could have had everything, but now you will die with nothing."

"Nothing could be further from the truth," I said. "If I die today, I will die with everything. I will inherit everything."

"You will inherit nothing!" she said as she moved closer. "You have forfeited everything. You could have been so beautiful, so powerful, so loved. But now you are ugly and alone."

"If you only had eyes to see with," I answered. "It is clear that you are blind, for I am radiant, and I have within me a power you cannot comprehend. I am loved by the Creator of the universe. You, however, have made Him your enemy. Nothing but eternal death awaits you if you don't repent. No matter what happens, I and my people have the victory."

"You think you've won?" she questioned with disgust in her voice. "You may have rescued the baby, but we will get all the rest. We will get them while still in the womb. We will get them in the academies. We will get them in the theaters. We will get them in the marketplace, just as we got Hannah. We will even get them in the Castles. We will get all of them."

"You will not get any of those whom the Great King has chosen for His own. He will have a remnant. He has claimed for His own a people from every clan and language. You fight a battle that you cannot win."

"I will win!" she shouted. "I will! In fifty years, there will not be any remains of your people!"

"In fifty years," I replied, "our posterity will be here. In a thousand years, our posterity will still be here."

"No, they won't!" she shouted.

"And for all eternity our people will be here," I declared, "but you will not be here. We will inherit the earth!"

"No!" she said, and she slashed her blade at me. I dodged. At that very moment the mountain rumbled, causing Vashti to lose her balance. She slipped off of the bridge and quickly grabbed hold of the side.

"Here!" I shouted. "Take my hand!" But it was too late. The rock broke off in her hand and she fell to the floor below. She seemed to still be conscious, but unable to move. At that moment I saw Gadreel enter from the large entrance below.

"Help me," she strained, barely able to speak.

"What happened?" the black dragon asked.

"Her back is broken," one of the red dragons replied.

"Then she is of no use to us anymore," Gadreel stated. "Do away with her."

"Gladly," the red dragons replied.

"No," she groaned. "No. You promised me!"

"You thought you were so beautiful," Gadreel mocked her. "It was never so."

"No!" Vashti shrieked, and looking up at me, our eyes met. At first, I thought I saw regret in her eyes, but as I looked again all I could see was utter hatred, a dark bitterness that was mixed with the emptiest and most pitied despair.

I turned and ran down the bridge, unable to bear the sight of her being devoured, though I could hear the sounds, her fading cry echoing through the cavern. Gadreel then noticed me. Dragon fire filled the chamber and followed me down the tunnel, singeing my hair. Another blast of fire followed it, and though the heat was unbearable, it did provide the light I needed to find the narrow scorpion tunnel through which we had entered the stronghold. I was soon upon my belly, crawling blindly down the hole, unable to see any light ahead or behind me. Soon the hole ended. I had exited the mountain, but the darkness was still very present.

'*The New Moon*,' I thought to myself. '*But where is the starlight?*' My question was soon answered by a bolt of lightning not far off and the loud thunder that followed.

I then heard shouting and quickly ran toward the sound. I came upon a sight that both confused and overjoyed me. I came upon what I guessed to be the main entrance of the mountain. It was a large opening, nearly fifty feet wide and just as high. Firelight was shining from within the giant corridor, illuminating the skirmish which raged upon its doorstep. My father, along with Nathan and Leah, were outside of the mountain, fighting off a force of nearly twenty red dragons. Nathan was limping, and my father had a leather strap around his head that was soaked in blood. What shocked me, however, was that they weren't alone. Enoch and Stephen were also there. I sprinted as fast as I could in their direction. Seeing me as I approached, Enoch tossed me a fresh quiver of arrows.

"Do your worst!" he shouted. Rain began to fall, and the lightning was near. Stephen then raised up his sword and struck the earth. All dragons fell upon their sides as if unable to keep their balance. I quickly released my arrows into their soft underbellies.

"We must close the door somehow!" my father shouted. "Too many are coming! We won't be able to stop them!"

"Nathan!" Enoch shouted. "Keep them from coming out!"

Nathan extended his hands toward the mountain entrance, where countless foes were emerging. They all seemed to be pushed back. Enoch then grabbed Stephen's sword in his left hand as he gripped his own sword in his right hand. Then leaping high in the air, he came down and sank both swords into the ground. Huge pillars of earth rose into the air, as if giant doors, closing the entrance. He then grabbed Nathan and Samuel's swords and sank them into the ground with a shout, and even more earthen pillars shot up, this time causing the mountain itself to begin to cave in.

Many black dragons from the peaks above began to descend. "Hurry!" Stephen shouted. "Follow me!"

We ran into the pitch darkness of the forest, the only light being the occasional lightning bolts that filled the sky. The thunder rattled around us to such a degree that we could barely hear the black dragons swooping about overhead. Thanks to the rain and thunder, they were unable to follow our scent or hear us. We moved slowly but steadily as the storm continued long into the night. It wasn't until the first gleams of daybreak, as the rain was a gentle sprinkle, that we stopped to rest. We were exhausted beyond description. We cast ourselves upon the earth and just breathed. I looked over at Leah, who was holding her content baby in her arms. I smiled and quickly fell asleep.

Chapter 37

When I awoke I felt a warmth upon my face. I was pleased to discover that it wasn't dragon's fire or molten lava but a simple campfire, and that my dearest friends were resting beside it.

"Here," Enoch said, handing me some roasted venison. "Eat." I quickly devoured the meat, my insides taking comfort in the nourishment. It was midday. The rain had subsided, and the bright sun was shining overhead.

"Only twenty minutes more of rest," Samuel said. "We must soon continue on. Even now the enemy might be upon our heels."

We all had many questions, and all accounts were given of what took place. After being separated from me, Nathan, Leah, and my father had continued to run around the perimeter of the large cavern and had taken another passage. After many twists and turns, Providence had allowed them to find a way out. Stephen and Enoch, after learning of our circumstance and mission, had decided to seek us out. They were instantly upon our trail and, by the expert tracking skills of Enoch, had arrived at the mountain only a few moments before my father and his companions exited the mountain. I relayed all that happened to me, beginning with my watching Jonah and Ruth and their exchange.

"From what you tell me, Elizabeth, it seems that he loved her and intended to pursue her," Leah said amidst tears.

"It is undoubtable," Nathan testified. "For only a fortnight ago, he confessed to me his love for my sister, asked permission to marry her, and was intending to ask her any day now."

"Why didn't you tell me?" Leah asked, startled at the news.

"I thought you would better appreciate the surprise," he replied.

"But my love," Leah said as she wept bitterly, "if I had known, I would have never allowed her to come with us. She could have been married in only a few weeks and become a mother in only a few months."

As Nathan replied, tears flowed down his cheeks, yet his voice remained as steady and manly as ever. "Do not fret my dear," he said gently. "I know my sister best of any. Even if she was already pledged to be married, she still would have come. Even if life was within her womb, she still would have done exactly what she did. She chose best. Even now, neither she nor Jonah are ashamed or regretful of their choice. They are in perfect bliss and peace."

My eyes filled with tears as I thought of Ruth. She was such a dear friend and woman. She had given the ultimate sacrifice. I knew that her reward in the Great King's presence would be great indeed.

"You brought most of the mountain down, Enoch," Stephen commented. "Do you think the Great Dragon, if he was there, was buried?"

"Only one person can defeat the Great Dragon," Enoch replied thoughtfully, "and that will not happen until the end of time as we know it. The Great Dragon may have been hindered for a time by the crumbling mountain, but it won't slow him down for very long. He is a strong and powerful foe."

We made our way back to the Oasis. The fellowship was waiting for us, all praying and fasting for our safe return. There was rejoicing for the safe return of Adam, but mourning for the loss of Ruth and Jonah. Captain Benjamin approached me soon after we arrived. "Elizabeth," he said gravely. "I have sad news. Martha has fallen ill." My heart was struck with pain.

"What happened? Is she going to be alright?"

"The fever came upon her two days ago," he replied. "I fear that she will not rise out of her bed again. She has little time left. She is now seeing Nathan and his family but has also asked that you go to her."

I quickly made my way to her small hut and, upon entering, found Nathan and his family circled around her. Words were being exchanged, and it seemed that they were saying their final farewells. Nathan, Leah, and their two sons then exited the dwelling. I quickly came to Martha's side and took her hand. It was cold, almost as if the life had already left it. Her breathing was labored.

"Martha," I said gently. "I'm so sorry you are not well. I'm sorry for Ruth."

"It was a good death," she said slowly. "Besides, I will be seeing her very shortly," she continued, her eyes barely open and a slight grin upon her face.

"Martha," I began.

"Don't speak," she said. "Just listen. You were as a granddaughter to me, a gift to me from the Great King in my last years. Now I have a gift for you. It will be my last. There's something I want to show you. Sit down." I obeyed. "Close your eyes."

I did so, and as she took my hand, the vision came. It was the story of Martha and her husband. It made my heart sink into despair and pain even more, for the once beautiful couple was still in misery. They were mere roommates. The husband had become so withered and miserable, tormented by the continual nagging and controlling nature of his wife, and she despised herself to such a degree that she considered ending her life prematurely. Life itself wasn't worth living.

Then something happened. I saw her walking through a scenic countryside all alone. The day was fair, and the birds were singing. Her soul was downcast, and bitterness was her only companion. She then came upon a young couple, sitting together upon a quilted blanket down by the river. She stood still and watched the couple. She breathed deeply every time they laughed. Her heart quivered every time they embraced. She saw a look upon the young woman's face that she had forgotten, and the man's smile and confidence reminded Martha of what her husband had once been.

First, envy and blame arose in her heart, but then it was cast aside by utter regret and sorrow. She stood there, as still as a tree, for a time unknown. Tears flowed down cheeks that hadn't felt them in years, and I watched with immeasurable emotion as the aged woman went from standing still to falling upon her knees. Her hands shot up in the air and she confessed her pride and selfishness to the Creator of all things. The couple then noticed her and came to her side with compassion. I watched with wonder as Martha simply kissed them with joy and encouraged them to continue on with their communion.

Then she hurried, as fast as she could to her home. Her husband was there, sitting in his chair, unmoved from how she had left him, his expression still the same. She fell to her knees and poured out her heart before him. The effect was like the first rays of spring upon the icicles still hanging from winter's chill. Or like a child who awakes from a night of sickness, only to find himself perfectly well.

The vision then moved forward to multiple days of joy and peace. The aged couple would walk in the prairie, holding hands and laughing. Her husband's face was just as it had been in the early years of their marriage, and hers was more beautiful than ever before. I saw her standing beside him, backing him up in decisions and honoring him with his vision for their family. He had gone from a man crippled and weak to a man strong and full of life.

Then I saw him upon his death bed, surrounded by family and friends. Joy was upon his face, and his last words were of the beauty of his wife and the gift of her friendship. He praised the Great King for giving him such a helpmeet, and he died in peace. And Martha, sad at the loss of her best friend, still had a glow of fulfillment upon her face as she walked away from his body. Tears rolled down my face as I opened my eyes.

"Oh Martha," I said, full of emotion.

"You see," she said smiling. "It is never too late."

"I'm so happy for you," I said, unable to stop my sobbing.

"And I for you," she said. "We are blessed beyond what we deserve." She then grimaced in pain and arched her back.

"Martha?" I said fearfully.

"It is alright," she said. "Listen to me. Listen to my final words."

"I am here," I said, rubbing her hand in mine. "I am listening."

"Never forget," she said. "Never forget who you are. You are a woman of light and a maiden of virtue, a daughter of the Great King. You follow Him with absolute resolve. Let nothing stop you. He must be your first love. Your husband will lack nothing, for you will be his greatest earthly treasure. Your children will be strong in the land and mighty. You will not lose any of them, for you will raise them all in the ways of the Scroll. Your strength will be your gentle and submissive spirit. Your power will be your unwavering faith in your role as a woman. Your beauty will be that of the stars that shine in the heavens. Your radiance with light the way for many to come.

"You have gone through the fire; you have been reduced to ashes; and you have come back strong and mighty. You are a phoenix, Elizabeth. You are an angel of fire. Remember, and let all women everywhere know that if they will repent and dare to believe the flawless words of the Scroll, the Great King can bring healing and change to any relationship or situation. Let them know that there is no greater fulfillment or life to be found than that of being a devoted, joyful wife and a loving mother. It is in your home that you change the world. You are a maker of strong men. You are a maker of virtuous women. The Great King is with you. Do not ever fear. There is never a reason to fear."

She then seemed to look beyond this world. "He will come," she said. "Your man will soon come. And together you will change the world." She then took a deep breath and was no more.

I put my head upon her chest and wept. My tears began as painful and desperate but soon turned joyful and happy, for this woman whom I loved so dearly had overcome and won. I exited the simple dwelling and looked up at the bright clouds floating high above. *'Now the battle is mine,'* I said to myself. *'Now I must fight and overcome.'* Deep in my soul I knew that I would fight and that I would indeed overcome. The Great King was my victory, and He had called me to be a maiden of light.

And now I speak to you, my dear sisters of Zion. The battle line has been drawn before your feet. You must choose. Will you fight for the Great King, or will you join the ranks of His enemies? The world will mock you. Let them. People won't understand you. Pray for them. You must be confident in what you know to be true. Walk in purity. Set yourself apart from the darkness of this world. Surround yourself only with other daughters of Zion who hold true to the Scroll.

If the Great King chooses to provide that amazing man with whom you will become one, follow him and love him and serve him with all of your heart. He will be blessed to have you. You will be a crown on his head. Don't be poison in his veins, but rather be the strength and passion of his heart. If the Great King gives you children, cherish them and train them in the ways of the Scroll. Raise your sons to be bold lions, and raise your daughters to be gentle warriors. Your offspring will change the world.

You will overcome, in all things, if you hold true to the Scroll and to the Great King. Do not give in to the empty temptations of this world. All that the world loves, all that it holds dear, will soon be reduced to ashes. And yet, you will shine forever in the universe. I love you with all of my heart, and I long to see you within the eternal halls of the Great King. May His name be praised forever and ever. Amen!

Epilogue

"I can't believe that it's been two years since Martha, Ruth, and Jonah died," I said, standing next to Leah at their tombstones.

"Neither can I," she replied. "I miss them dearly, though, I take comfort in the fact that I will see them again."

"As do I," I agreed. "I also rejoice that they found good deaths. I hope a good death finds me."

"I'm sure it will," Leah said with a smile, "for the Great King is with you." We returned to her cottage, where Nathan was instructing Levi on the porch. He was questioning his son in the doctrine of our people.

"Who made you?" Nathan asked.

"The Great King," Levi answered.

"Why did He make you?" Nathan asked as he smiled and rubbed the head of his son.

"For His own glory."

"How do you glorify the Great King?"

"I glorify the Great King by loving Him and obeying what He commands."

"And how do you know how to love him and obey him?"

"The Scroll is the only rule by which I can know how to love and obey the Great King."

Nathan then took his son, Levi, by the hand. "Listen to me, my son. The people of the world, and many from the Castle, have adopted a different culture than that of the Scroll. They seek a perfect life, free from trial, hardship, or ailment. Don't misunderstand me, it isn't that things such as comfort and ease are wrong, but they aren't our top priority."

"If a life free from hardship isn't our priority, what is?" Levi asked, his young voice a pleasing sound to my ears.

"Our main priority is to endure amidst any hardships that find us," Nathan answered soberly. "Such a life glorifies the Great King. We must embrace the strenuous life, as we press forward in hope of things to come. This life, when compared to eternity, is nothing. It isn't wrong to pray for blessing and comfort, but such things are not always the King's will. Yet endurance always is. We are pilgrims, my son. And we must never lose sight of our eternal homeland."

Leah and I smiled as the interaction between the father and son continued. Adam was also there, toddling about in the bright green grass. I then noticed my father in the periphery of my vision. He entered the Oasis and immediately sought me out. His expression was one of anxiety and excitement mixed together.

"Come with me," he said in a soft voice. "Quickly." I followed him into the forest, traveling down paths not normally followed.

"What is it, father?" I asked. "Why are we going this way?"

"He is here," he said, seemingly to himself. "He is actually here in Ravenhill."

"Who is here?" I asked with much curiosity, for I could tell that my father's soul was stirring with emotion.

"The question is," he continued without noticing me, "is his heart with us or with the enemy?" At these words a large measure of concern and fear came upon his face.

"Whose heart, Father?" I asked with increased passion as we continued along through the thicket. "Who is here in Ravenhill?"

We were now coming to the edge of the tree line which looked upon the village. "Look there," he said, pointing to a group of men who were constructing a small cottage. I looked and beheld many men, but almost immediately one of them captured my complete attention: his handsome features, his wonderful smile, his lifegiving laugh. I gasped.

"There is another phoenix," my father said. "Your childhood friend has risen from the ashes."

"Caleb," I said softly, my heart trembling within my soul.

Books and Video series by

Jared Dodd

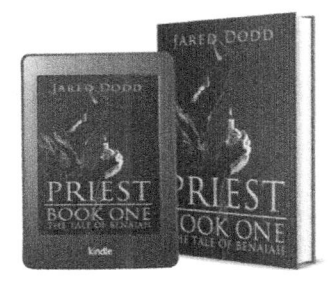

Find out more at jareddodd.com

Made in the USA
Columbia, SC
23 December 2021

52657334R00137